Serious Things

Serious Things

Gregory Norminton

SCEPTRE

First published in Great Britain in 2008 by Sceptre
An imprint of Hodder & Stoughton
An Hachette Livre UK company

1

A CIP catalogue record for this title is available from the British Library

ISBN 978 0 340 83467 1

Typeset in Sabon by Hewer Text UK Ltd, Edinburgh
Printed and bound by Clays Ltd

FSC
Mixed Sources
Product group from well-managed
forests and other controlled sources

Cert no. SGS - COC - 2061
www.fsc.org
© 1996 Forest Stewardship Council

Hodder & Stoughton policy is to use papers that are natural, renewable
and recyclable products and made from wood grown in sustainable forests.
The logging and manufacturing processes are expected to conform
to the environmental regulations of the country of origin.

Hodder & Stoughton Ltd
A division of Hodder Headline
338 Euston Road
London NW1 3BH

www.hodder.co.uk

To Emma

You don't have to be small to be inconspicuous. Largeness is also good for hiding: you can bury your childhood in it. As for strangers, they see only an affliction. They will shuffle on their hams to avoid it on a bus, they will look away as from some moral weakness and shrink, in the commuter crush of an Underground train, lest they touch any part of the gross anatomy. Old people lament the uniform that time imposes, how greyness confines them to a bland and ignorable collective. The same applies to the overweight. We disappear as individuals. Too common a sight, the proof of some national failure, we must be anonymous.

I was not always shaped like this; nor am I happy about my size. Just once, however, being fat could have served me. On this occasion (a heart's earthquake that not even the closest observer might have registered) I would have welcomed the disguise. But the ghost of the old Bruno Jackson was recognised and, with the rising of that familiar voice in greeting, I was summoned back instantly to a world of pain.

The invitation had come from an old university friend, Fay Corcoran, to celebrate her engagement at the flat she shared with her rich, glib partner in Maida Vale. It was a baking summer's evening and a group of kids was kicking a football to death outside, giving the white stucco avenue with its weary rowans an atmosphere of the township. Having left the Department in a hurry and braved the lurching oven of the number 16 bus, I was, despite a rinse in the immaculate sanctuary of Fay's bathroom, far from my poor best when Anthony Blunden discovered me, glass in hand, loitering by the bookshelves in the stifling living room.

'My God, would you believe it? *Bruno*. It must be thirteen years.'

Something clicked off in my brain, like falling asleep at the wheel, and when seconds later my wits returned I found my eyes darting for shelter. There was a reek of aftershave. He had a neat shaving cut on his chin. A pale Indian woman, watching me with plum-dark eyes, stood beside him as if at any moment to tug on his sleeve.

'You do remember me?'

The question was provoking: even to *imagine* that I might have forgotten. Anthony, however, grinned as if nothing out of the ordinary had ever passed between us. 'How,' he asked, 'do you know Hugo?'

'Fay. Uh, it's Fay I know.'

'Same here. She and Dipali were friends at school, like us. *Hey* . . .' This was almost a yelp. Anthony reached beside him for the Indian woman's arm and steered her between us. 'Bruno, this is Dipali, my good wife.' The determined, possibly oblivious, anachronism of his phrasing was familiar. Dipali Blunden raised heavy, greased eyelids. There was reticence in her glance but also a hint of sexuality, which, in my case, she offered out of pure courtesy. 'Would you believe,' said her husband, 'that Bruno was my closest friend at Kingsley?'

I sensed his eyes follow Dipali's hand as it slipped into mine. Her palm was unpleasantly dry; the tendons had a shifting vagueness. 'You're not,' she asked with a smile, 'in finance like everybody else?'

'On the contrary,' I said. A crease of perplexity bridged her dark, tamed eyebrows. 'I work at the Department for Transport.'

Anthony Blunden, whose physical presence I was still trying to inure myself to, pressed forward. 'Are you still painting? That used to be your thing, didn't it? You were pretty good, if I remember, always loitering in the art department.' He stood too close and I trembled to meet his eyes: those hazel eyes that used to turn green above the green jumper he wore at school. When I looked, however, champagne had given them a woozy sheen. I recognised a frantic hilarity that in our shared youth I might have mistaken for genius.

'I studied economics at university,' I said to Dipali; but she was looking at her husband, one arm bent and poised, like a painter standing back from a canvas. 'That's how I came to be friends with Fay. She was always going to be entrepreneurial but I opted for government.'

Anthony said, 'Spin doctor, are you?'

'Don't be ridiculous.'

'Ah, right, you must be some kind of special adviser.'

'I'm a civil servant. I work on road toll pricing policy.'

Anthony took half a step back, or else he swayed momentarily. Without sequence, he reached out to pat my belly. 'You've filled out a bit, haven't you? Not,' he added, stroking his notional paunch, 'that I'm one to brag.'

He was touching my arm now: a taller, broader Anthony. His blond, tousled hair was as rich as ever, especially compared to my receding scrub, and his face was shadowed with a russet beard which had only begun to assert itself when last I'd seen him. The ripe but faintly buttoned-down mouth – inherited from generations of weather-watching farmers – opened to reveal sharp incisors, the one savage flaw in a face otherwise perfectly suited to bluff civility.

'Proctor. Remember Proctor? This bully,' he explained to his wife, 'gave Bruno grief for years and one day we got our own back. I knew him a little at Oxford. Would you believe he's gone and had a sex change? For real: he came up to me, *she* came up to me, on the Tube about a month ago. All smiles: this roly-poly woman. I wondered if some moment of madness had caught up with me from my youth. But no: bloody Proctor. As I see you now.'

Dipali Blunden, standing her ground against the burbling mill of partygoers, pursed her small, aubergine-glossed lips. 'You never told me that story.'

'Didn't I? Well, the name wouldn't have meant anything to you. Bruno understands.' As if for support, Anthony pressed his wrist on my shoulder and began to reminisce, with little input from me, about stupid members of staff and malodorous contemporaries, omitting the only name that really mattered.

Disregarded, Dipali allowed her smile to fail. I watched her, this small feminine bundle, turn her back on her husband's remembrances and burrow into the crowd around Fay Corcoran.

'You remember,' Anthony said, 'that poor woman Miss Hartnoll? And the carpet shocks. God, what a bunch.'

'A bunch of *what*?' Fay's fiancé, Hugo, had invited himself into our corner.

Anthony answered without hesitation: 'Criminals.'

'Speaking of which,' said Hugo; and within seconds I had ceased to exist. Hugo Wilcox and Anthony Blunden – two handsome, braying, self-assured public school men – began to discuss high finance: the thrusting success of this firm or that, the fading potency on the One Hundred Index of some company in which both, corporate finance lawyers though from rival firms, had a stake.

Breathless, I made my escape to the bedroom.

Over a shambles of suit jackets and laptop cases, I hesitated briefly. Would Fay be offended by my sudden departure? Most likely she wouldn't even notice. Paying a quick visit to the bathroom, I used toilet paper to soak up my sweat and washed my trembling hands. There was only a three-metre dash between the bathroom and the front door but mine was thwarted by the Blundens, both of whom, reunited by necessity, were waiting to take my place.

'Oof,' said Anthony, as if we had collided. I felt blood rush to my already heated face. 'Where did you wander off to?'

'Uh, I've got to go.'

Anthony looked to his wife, then at me. 'You must at least leave us your number.'

I considered giving a false one. Anthony was patting his trouser pockets but Dipali, reaching into her small sequinned purse, brought out a pink-sheathed mobile phone and issued it to her husband. I could smell cigarettes and alcohol on his breath. His long thumb with the ivory crescent of its feminine nail podged the keypad.

Cornered, I felt like the Dutch boy with his finger in a dam.

'Go ahead,' said Anthony.

The courage to lie failed me, though I shared with this man a deceit vaster and more terrible than anything his wife could imagine. (Or could she? Had he told her everything and their marriage been founded on his confession, her forgiveness?) I recited my home phone number. Really, I protested, I had to leave. Anthony threatened me with a hug but relented, seeing my eyes.

The door latch yielded to my grip. I performed a half-turn beneath the lintel, cast my eyes over the Blundens' waists and stumbled, as it must have sounded, down the carpeted stairs. Breaking out of the house to the evening heat and a sough of endless traffic, I searched for a drain in the pavement and retched unproductively over it.

Then & Now

Then

They were serving tea on the lawn of Hereward House. It was meant to seem a cosy affair of white linen under apple boughs, with parents chatting and younger siblings chasing each other among the laurel bushes. I stood beside my mother, dumb with the pain of our impending separation, and watched as girls from the village disguised as maids passed with cucumber and egg sandwiches. Teachers were in attendance with their perfumed wives. I looked at the soft foliage of the Downs.

'Ah, Mrs Jackson. Philip Sedley: we spoke on the phone. And this is Bruno . . .' The housemaster of the Hereward, though quite young, was prematurely balding. He strained to keep his wife's arm as she tugged at their border collie. 'We no longer get so many boys from abroad. Army cutbacks, you know. And when we lose Hong Kong . . .' He looked at me and spoke as one board member might to another. 'I hope you like it here, Bruno. We'll make a temperate fellow of you yet.'

My mother simpered, I nodded, and the Sedleys drifted on to more substantial fare.

The boys with whom I was to share my life stood sullen as prizefighters between their parents, enduring for a moment longer the partings in their hair and the fastidious rectitude of their ties. Under the smiles of adults, we sized each other up.

I would learn my fellow inmates' names soon enough, and get to know their qualities. Only Laurence Nevins wore his nature in his face. While most of us were still children he was already pustular, a warning of transformations to come, with beard fluff begging to be trimmed above a minefield of acne and eye-whites the colour of curdled milk. Aside from Nevins, it was impossible in that garden to foretell who would be friend and who would be foe. There was plump, genial-looking Robbie Thwaite. There was Hugo Barclay, set to board even though his parents' farm was only a short car journey from the school, and Dan Chapman, a sportsman bound almost genetically to become, after I had left Kingsley in secret disgrace, the Head of House. Dull-witted but affable boys like John Toplady and Nigel Clare had yet to reveal their qualities. I did not know that Charlie Stoddard was rich and stupid, the future brawn to Nevins's cunning, or that in his weary eyes was the mark of our common doom: wanker's lethargy.

Over by the tennis courts, another reception was under way. Its parents and boys, teacups and orange squash, were divided from ours by a vegetable patch and soft-fruit frames. My mother was nodding and blinking at a brash couple who were 'strongly in favour' of Mrs Thatcher's poll tax, and to keep down the bile of fear in my throat I scanned the distant party.

Did my eyes fasten at once on Anthony? Among a dozen uniformed boys he stood out on account of his height and the straightness of his bearing. A large and garrulous family surrounded him. There were two pretty sisters, both parents, an avuncular-looking gentleman with hair that curled in a ducktail behind his ears, and two grandmothers rummaging in their purses for a farewell donation. The boy seemed unembarrassed by all this attention, while I shrank each time my mother touched my shoulder. It was his good fortune which struck me hardest; I think I half hated my parents at the time for sending me away. This other boy, with his adoring clan, would doubtless go home on weekend exeats. I pictured him strolling on a wide English lawn or yelling at the top of his voice as he rode a BMX bike. A gust of laughter swept through the family and the father tousled his son's head. Anthony's eyes coasted on the merriment, then brushed my gaze across the length of the garden.

I looked away, gnawing fruitcake to conceal my fluster, and realised with alarm that the sandwich trays had emptied and the tables were being cleared around us. Boys and their parents were making their way, in stately calm, around the side of Hereward House. The welcoming party was coming to an end and an air of desperation came over my mother.

'You've got that letter paper Auntie Nariza bought you. I'll write to you every week. Mr Sedley says you're welcome to use the telephone in his part of the house – at weekends – to receive our call. Don't forget to keep your laundry bag closed, it's only considerate . . .'

The instructions and assurances continued as the garden emptied. We were shepherded by Mrs Sedley and her collie to the front of the house, where bluffly and with seeming ease other parents took leave of their sons. The boys waved bravely. Cars started up on the gravel drive. Mr Houghton, the under-tutor, had promised my mother a lift to the airport, and he waited for her in his Peugeot – this gross, redheaded suitor – while she clutched me under the chestnut trees. I wanted her gone; I felt sick with apprehension, as on that time we waited to cross the storm-shaken Malacca Straits. My mother planted a kiss on my cheek. I could smell her powdery, rose-tinted perfume and the under-odour of perspiration.

'Be brave for me, Bruno,' she said, and waved over my head at the Sedleys waiting with their adopted brood under the red-brick porch. All the boys were watching us. I placed a shameful, surreptitious fist in my mother's belly to push her towards the car. Then I was running, hand on my cap, my face burning for want of quenching tears, to Hereward House and my new life.

Like much of Kingsley College, the Hereward has undergone, in the years since I was there, a thorough refurbishment. Doubtless it's a comfortable place now, more like a timeshare hotel than an old-fashioned boarding school. In my time it was still archaic. Even now I can feel the coarseness of its nylon carpets under my feet; I see the oily sheen of an exit light on the linoleum floor of a long corridor and wrinkle my nose at remembered odours, the accretion of Deep Heat and sweat, deodorant and semen, baked beans and cauliflower.

This was not what the brochure had promised. Hereward House projected a handsome Victorian exterior but the interior, for the boys at least, was distinctly shabby. The dining hall was a refectory of peeling paint and honours boards, one wall lined with the sorts of books you expect to find in a seaside boarding house, with long tables of scarred oak under a rattling window of ecclesial size which sucked in the summer heat and exhaled the winter chill. In the stark, neon-lit kitchen, industrial toasters guarded their latent tick and hum.

We followed a prefect who had come back early to be our guide. 'Each of you,' he said, plainly delighting in his task, 'will be assigned a college father. He will prepare you for the fag test. In return you will be his fag. You will make toast for him. You will do as he tells you. One day *you* will be college fathers so don't let me hear anybody complaining.'

We traipsed down a dark corridor that belonged to the Lower Sixth; then to a TV room and snooker tables and the chilling prospect of a windowless washroom. The prefect, Ackroyd, led us up a flight of stairs to Main Corridor: a Third World hotel of wooden partitions, each resident guaranteed only partial privacy. 'Don't get excited,' Ackroyd said, 'you lot have to share.'

Our stairwell was painted red and red was its sticky polythene floor, so that we felt like corpuscles in some inner organ or artery. Hereward House tucked us away – the scummy new boys – under the attic. There was a grim atrium lined with lockers for boots and sports gear, and three dormitories with narrow, military-style beds. We took shuffling turns to peer at the plywood cubicles of our washroom.

'You'll share this washroom with the prefects,' said Ackroyd. 'Same rules apply as for toast. If we catch any of you wanking, it'll be Sunday detention.'

The prefects, Ackroyd explained, lived in the apartments on the west wing of our floor, with the turret room reserved, as a special privilege, for the Head of House.

'That's convenient,' whispered Hugo Barclay, who revealed that he had a brother in the Third Set and relished the authority this gave him. 'The prefects will have someone to warm the loo seats in winter.'

We were settled into our dormitories. To avoid squabbles, Ackroyd had been given a list and informed us of arrangements. I was relieved to be put in with Barclay (he had an assurance I lacked) but dismayed to see Laurence Nevins fling his horrible body on the bed next to mine. 'Bagsy this cupboard,' he said. 'You can have the one by the door. What's your name again? Not your Christian name.' I told him. 'Jacksy?'

'Jack*son*.'

'Pruno Jacksy?'

Hugo Barclay looked out of his window at the green of the Downs. A sycamore rustled behind the flimsy drawn-back curtains. I wondered what had become of the boys from that other garden party. Barclay explained that once or twice a year our tribe was obliged to show hospitality to others. Having a garden of our own made Hereward boys 'soft': suburban geeks to the urban hipsters of the Main School dorms.

Ackroyd returned, having settled the others next door. 'Dinner's in college,' he said. 'We get breakfast in house. Sedley wants you to bring your luggage upstairs. Room inspections at nine – it'll be Houghton, he's big on tidiness. Noggins, isn't it? Nevins then. You'll have to get that hair cut. Don't huff, I don't make the rules.' Ackroyd inspected the three of us: Nevins recumbent, Hugo leaning at the window, myself standing as if to attention. 'Posters,' he said, and thumped one of the plasterboards on the wall. 'Put up what you like. Only rule: no tits, no muff.' He walked to the door. I made much, in my anguish, of a softening in his features. 'You'll get used to it. It's quieter up here. If you want my advice, I'd stay where it's safest. Oh, and for God's sake don't sit on the radiators. No one likes the smell of scorched flesh.'

We brought up our luggage. It was an early test of community, since none of us could lug up his case unaided. I worked with Barclay and John Toplady: the latter a thickset, earnest redhead who spoke at length and without the least encouragement about his father's several cars. Toplady was not too bright but physical strength gave him the security to be kind. We settled our things – clothes folded or compressed into chunky drawers, tuck boxes shoved under our beds – then headed into college for tea: me, Toplady, Barclay and Robbie Thwaite, who had to waddle out of his slowness to keep up.

Kingsley College started life as a country house, the gift of a grateful nation to Admiral William Montague in recognition of various naval victories against the French. In keeping with his stolid and somewhat unimaginative character, Montague's house is bulky, a martial oblong of ruddy brick surfacing from the swell of the Downs. For a century it served its original purpose but the state forgot its gratitude to the admiral's descendants and, at the end of the nineteenth century, a rich industrialist of Christian

Stoic persuasions bought the estate and founded a school devoted to the manly virtues of sport, science and colonial service. Red-brick annexes gathered about the original house. Sheep pasture was disciplined, hillocks were levelled for rugby and cricket, hedgerows were grubbed up and replaced with avenues of small-leaved lime. In early years the college must have seemed a grand addition to England's public schools. By the time I attended, however, there was a creeping shabbiness about the whole complex. The brick proved to be frangible, sandstone cornices were leprous and plaques bearing Latin inscriptions were dis-appearing under a palimpsest of penknife graffiti. Still, the bulk of Main College kept its forbidding grandeur, so that our hearts sank as we approached it.

A plump, scowling porter directed us to the dining hall: a 1920s annexe as big as a warehouse or film studio. We negotiated the maze of the serving counters; then sat in a defensive square in a corner of the cavernous hall, eating and watching as a hundred new boys milled about the cutlery trays. Did we imagine it, or were they more at home than us: boisterously shoving, enmities and alliances already beginning?

Hugo Barclay surveyed the rumpus. 'My brother says when term starts we'll be wolfing it down. Senior boys like to have the place to themselves. If they catch a First Setter lingering, he'll be for it.'

My friends, as I hoped they would become, began to explain themselves, describing their fathers' jobs and what preparatory schools they had attended. I, undeclared expatri-ate, half listened, my attention distracted by the paintings on the walls with their old, imperial themes: the crushing of the Indian Mutiny, the death of Wolfe in Quebec, nawabs and nabobs in ceremonial splendour receiving the Emperor, for-gotten naval battles going up in smoke and tattered main-sails.

'How about you, Jackson?' John Toplady peered at me over his pudding bowl. 'Where are you from?'

'Malaysia. My father's a sort of teacher. That's why they've sent me here.'

'You don't look very tanned,' said Robbie Thwaite. 'Are you Malaysian?'

'Um – British.'

'That's all right, then,' said Toplady.

After dinner we returned to the Hereward and watched TV for an hour before being sent up to our dorms. I moved quickly into my pyjamas. Lawrence Nevins tried to wedge his shirt between his thighs as he hopped into boxer shorts but I glimpsed his stumpy cock. Mr Houghton was late for inspection. I imagined this had something to do with my mother, and sucked wretchedly on images of a delayed flight, or some disaster that had caught up with them on the road.

When Mr Houghton finally appeared, I was relieved to see him and at the same time furiously jealous. He had been with her last. What had they said to each other on the way to the airport? Mr Houghton was too preoccupied with trying to remember our names and inspecting our narrow dwellings to reassure me that she had got off safely. I watched his angular, uneven face for news but none was offered. 'Jolly good,' he said when inspection was finished. Nevins had already put up magazine cutouts of supermodels and film stars; Mr Houghton noted the replete bras and pouting lips without comment. 'Lights out in ten minutes, boys. Reveille at seven thirty. Tomorrow it'll be Ackroyd who bangs the gong but once the others are back the duties will fall to you. I think, ah, you're being given the guided tour tomorrow. Are we settling in all right?' He did not wait for an answer but nodded and bade us goodnight.

'Tosser,' whispered Nevins when he had gone.

In the dark I felt giddy with homesickness. Nevins and Barclay tried to freak each other out with talk of the fag test: how difficult it would be and how humiliating. 'Jockstraps only,' said Barclay, 'in front of a porn mag. If you get a hard-on you have to sing a song.' There were, I ascertained from their mutterings, both a formal fag test to look forward to and a secret one: the prefects' induction ceremony. It was tradition, Barclay said. Everyone went through it. I waited until their talk had stopped and the deep breathing began before surrendering to silent tears.

The next day Ackroyd took us on a tour of the grounds, pointing out the buildings and their uses. The sun blazed in a sky slashed with aircraft contrails; but while Robbie Thwaite sweated and others grew sullen, the heat gave me no trouble. In the warm light of day the grounds of the college seemed luminous and every tree and every bird in its branches was new to me. Our group poked about the chemistry block and I watched the haze dissolve on a prospect of the weald. Outside the school tuck shop (where in flight from misery later that term I would discover the consolations of carbohydrate) I crouched on the gravel path to rescue an overturned beetle. Thinking nothing of its size but admiring its jaws, I turned it over with a leaf. Nevins and Stoddard were sent back to look for me and would almost certainly have stamped on it had they seen what I was doing. I nudged the beetle to safety and ran to join them.

We progressed from modern languages to the old gym, now converted to a theatre, where in the 1970s a sixth-former was reputedly found hanging from the rafters. Then we strode across dry grass and through an oak wood to the edge of the playing fields. 'I hope you boys are good at rugger. Hereward colts have slipped badly since I was in your year. You're going to have to raise standards.'

On our way back to the house, Lawrence Nevins and Charlie Stoddard cemented their alliance by treading on my heels. When my shoe came off I howled in protest and received a rebuke from Ackroyd. Stoddard booted my shoe into the bushes and without saying another word I hopped wretchedly after it.

The afternoon was taken up with briefings of an almost military briskness, Mr Sedley receiving us in his study and handing out photocopies full of information about our coming year at Kingsley. On the strength of my Common Entrance results I was in the top sets for English and French and maths. Sunlight yawned across the carpet. Thirstily I edged forward to bathe my face in it. The blood in my eyelids glowed; I could see the filaments of veins. Then a mass of cloud returned me to shadow. I opened my eyes on strangers, the colours of the room faded, and when at last we filed out of the study, Hereward House seemed nothing but a maze of dark corridors, a burrow of antique wood and dented plaster.

We went out to supper grumbling like veterans at the prospect of evening chapel, and Robbie Thwaite coined his first, apt, pun. 'Give us this day our daily dread.' There was plenty to pray for. Tomorrow morning the rest of college was coming back from holiday.

Hereward House trembled with the new arrivals. They took possession of the building, their competing music blaring from personal stereos. Mr Houghton gathered our timorous band together and set us to work collecting empty luggage boxes from the rooms of our elders: taller, louder boys who regarded us with studied contempt. We gawped at the partition walls with their soft-porn friezes. From his room at the far end of Main Corridor, a portly joker with Walkman headphones about his neck watched our efforts. 'Aah,' he sighed, 'aren't they *adorable*? Do they miss their mummies? Do they need tucking up in bed at night?' Nigel Clare and I carried the joker's case down to the cellar. His name was stencilled on the wood: A. G. PROCTOR.

'You want to watch out for Proctor,' said Hugo Barclay as we passed him on the stairs. 'The guy's a bastard.'

There was much for us to learn: house slang, who to trust and who to avoid, the whole complex politics of the place. Bullies like Andy Proctor could be nasty – and there was a generalised fear of showing kindness – but the most persistent trouble came from our immediate superiors in the Second Set. These boys, jubilant to have outgrown the lowest rank, raided our dormitories and stole our food. Robbie Thwaite came back one afternoon from games to find his bed painstakingly dismantled, spring from spring. I could hear him sobbing after lights-out as he struggled without aid to reassemble it. There was nothing to be done: Kingsley College had a long-established hierarchy of abuse, each year heaping it on its successor, with First Setters at the very bottom, 'squeezed like lemons' as Robbie put it. In our free time we cowered in our rooms at the top of the house, the sloping ceilings and low windows over parkland a grim parody of the Victorian nursery. For every willed act of generosity (Barclay sharing his tuck, Nigel Clare helping Stoddard with his algebra) there was more casual cruelty. I don't mean physical abuse, which was rare, so much as a carping, sour intolerance. Nervous loyalty to the friendships left over from preparatory school doomed me, the expatriate, to isolation. The telephone calls from my parents, for which I waited under the stairs in the Sedleys' musty hall, only amplified the pain of our separation and left me afterwards plunged in deep sorrow, trudging back to the heartless clamour of the dormitory.

I lived for bedtime, when I could wallow in self-pity under my blankets, indulging in the delicious pain – like pressing on a hangnail – of picturing my bedroom back home and my parents going about their business in the damp, embracing heat. The English night was intolerably quiet: only the sighs of passing cars and the breathing of my neighbours instead of cicadas and the bright percussion of frogs. I hated getting up in the mornings: roused by the gong or, worse, having to process with it myself down the corridors, striking it with a furry mallet and rousing abuse from my groaning housemates. The physical weight of school life wore me down. I felt it as we moved through the guts of the dining hall, in the humiliating exposure of our pubescent bodies in the shower block and the hot breaths of our opponents as we roared into a rugby scrum. I had been pressed into the pack on account of my bulk, though fearing injury and mud I tended to run in subtle crab fashion away from the ball while giving an impression of hearty engagement. My cowardice was recognised and Ackroyd scolded me in the communal filth of the showers.

On the day of the fag test, we sat, after Saturday lessons, in the Hereward dining hall. The official part of the test (concerning masters and traditions, the names and nicknames in college geography, and such historical curiosities as the resting place of Admiral Montague's horse's bollocks) gave me little trouble. Then as now, I was an assiduous learner. In the evening, however, we sat like doomed convicts in our dormitory, waiting for our summons to the Head of House's turret. In my room, Hugo Barclay went first and came back after ten minutes, grinning excessively. He sat down on his bed and opened a paperback.

'What's it like?' Nevins asked.

'That's for you to find out.'

'Is it painful?'

Barclay shrugged, his eyes hooded. 'I mustn't give the game away.'

Nevins was summoned next. Embarrassed and relieved laughter seeped through the partitions as others in my year returned from their ordeals. The waiting was a calculated pain in itself (no wonder Dan Chapman was called up first: the prefects were bestowing status) and I looked for reassurance from Hugo Barclay. He had lain down, his back to the room. 'What is it they make us do exactly?' There was no reply and I wondered if he was pretending to sleep. 'Barclay?'

'*Hssh.*'

Outside all was black: I could see my reflection ghostlike in the windowpane. There were adult voices in the stairwell. Nevins hurried into the room, his face an ugly red. The annexe lights flashed on and I recognised Mr Sedley's voice but not the anger in it. Mr Houghton was with him. He came into our room, rubbing his large, raw hands together as if they were frozen. 'Evening, boys,' he said. 'Now I want you to know that no blame is attached to any of you over this. There's no, ah, shame involved. What happened this evening . . . what Mr Sedley interrupted . . . is no longer tolerated, that's all.'

Someone, presumably the new headmaster, had decreed against induction ceremonies. Traditionalists in the Common Room may have objected but housemasters complied, bursting in on pupils in the middle of their ancient rites. I alone had escaped the humiliating test and could persuade nobody to tell me what it had involved. It was a secret that I was not entitled to share. I had been spared and everyone knew it: the scolded prefects, handsome Noyes, the Head of House, and every sardonic face at breakfast the next morning.

The first weeks and months of my life in England would have been unbearable – I would have envied the dead – had it not been for the kindness of two boys. The first of these, surprisingly given the debacle of the fag test, was William Noyes. At the time I thought they must have plucked our names from a hat, or drawn straws. How else could the lowest member of the Hereward end up with the Head of House for college father?

I reported as it were for duty to his apartment in the cold

turret. Noyes spared me such humiliating tasks as loo-seat warming (Hugo Barclay had exaggerated nothing) and sorting out his dirty laundry. There was no need for me to brave the break-time scrum in the kitchen; for Noyes had inherited, as one of the perks of his station, a toaster more antique than a gramophone, a malevolent object that snapped the bread from my fingers, sucked it fumingly as though mulling over some ancient grievance, then spat out brittle slates that were perfectly to Noyes's liking. I was allowed a piece or two glazed with his mother's marmalade: sweet, sticky ooze the colour of amber which I savoured as I cast my eyes over his music collection.

William Noyes was a scholar and a sportsman. Perhaps he has never topped the triumph of his school days. There was nothing conventional about him, so that it was difficult for a foreigner to understand how he got away with it; for while his fellows loafed and loped about in heavy blokeishness, Noyes was ambiguous. He never wore his shirt outside his trousers or shortened his tie. He sported the quaintest items in the Kingsley uniform: the Edwardian skullcap, the prefect's embroidered waistcoat, even enamel cufflinks in the college red and green. His purpose in life was to charm. He made conquests, male and female, with his contained swagger and was soon to secure himself a place at Cambridge. I too was won over, sprawling in his window-seat while he talked about politics (Mrs Thatcher, he said, was heading for a fall) and literature (had I read the obscene poems of someone called Rochester?). He allowed me to play games on his home computer and my admiration for him grew as he let me into his confidence. He did not, he said, get on with Mr Sedley. Strictly between the two of us (and I assured him of my discretion), he suspected that our housemaster regretted his appointment. 'I make it a point of principle to uphold tradition. Half the masters at Kingsley are closet lefties. It's us boys who have to do the conserving. We've been through it: we know the value of the old ways.' He leaned forward, crimping his black hair with his fingers. 'Don't you agree, Bruno?'

'Yes,' I said, 'absolutely.'

Noyes stood up and brushed the crumbs from his waistcoat. He was very slender. His hands were large, rope-veined, the only inelegant thing about him. 'Run along now,' he would say, and then, looking at himself in the mirror, he would add, as if to console me: 'I shall want my bath at seven o'clock.'

'I won't forget, Noyes.'

Nor have I. His kindness may have been ostentatious and I no more to him than a pet, a perversion licensed by, and demonstrative of, his authority; yet the time I spent in his company was one of my few pleasures during that first year in Hereward House. Beyond the refuge of his turret I felt crushed by strangers, witnesses to my every mood, the overcrowding such that I used to fake constipation for the shuffling solitude of a toilet cubicle.

Compared with the dormitory's dark confinement, the world of the classrooms was sunlit. I liked the green shade of chestnut trees through windows smeared with pollen; I liked the smell of wood polish on the broad teak counters of the chemistry labs and the tranquil expansion of water pipes in the Latin block, with its atmosphere redolent of mouldy primers. I felt safe in the company of schoolmasters: they weren't capricious like my peers. Some boys boasted of their contempt for them, but I approved of the diffident or garrulous men who muttered and yawped through our classes.

Samuel Bridge – *Mr* Bridge – was not yet among them.

The second boy to treat me decently, after William Noyes, was in my English set. Under the RSC production posters that attempted to brighten up the grey bunker of the department, I learned the identity of the favoured son whom I had glimpsed in the Hereward garden.

Anthony Blunden was in Eversley House: one of the more prestigious of the dormitories. From what I saw of him in lessons, he seemed entirely at home with himself, so that whatever squalor or indignity attached to our first-year status could make no inroads on his self-esteem. That first morning he seemed not to recognise me as I crept, hotly flushing, to a plastic chair beside the draughty window. Ancient Mr Hegarty (a Second World War veteran who had forgotten to remove the prop of his martial moustache) talked us through the year's programme. He got us to read from *Dr Jekyll and Mr Hyde*, putting on a dubious Scottish accent for his frequent interventions. Anthony, when the task of sight-reading fell to him, read with ostentatious proficiency, improving on Hegarty's accent until the old man suspected sarcasm and passed the narration to his neighbour.

Over the next few weeks, I longed to approach Anthony Blunden. He warmed up the cold classroom with his brashness and wit. I couldn't tell whether other boys in our class liked or disliked him. Perhaps they didn't yet have the confidence to make up their minds. Anthony was excused his loudness, his over-eagerness to offer sometimes jarring opinions to Mr Hegarty, on account of his looks and a self-assurance that few dared believe could be unfounded. My status, on the other hand, was well known. Most boys were reluctant to sit next to me. One of them, a mop-topped blond whose name I've forgotten, made the effort to snigger whenever I read aloud. I was actorly: I tried to invest the words with meaning but my dramatic intonations received only mockery from my peers and bristling irritation from Mr Hegarty.

Anthony played no part in my humiliation. He was above such games. In the run-up to half-term exeat (which I would spend alone in college, knocking about the abandoned corridors like the first man to board the *Mary Celeste*), he introduced himself to me by pushing me against the wall.

I should explain that I was running late, having sat too long at Noyes's computer, and entered the classroom to find my peers in demure and suspicious silence waiting for the master. I was conscious of the tug of their eyes as I approached my chair. I put my books on the table. Somebody said something designed to distract me – whereupon Anthony kicked out his chair and barged into my shoulder.

My head jerked and my breath escaped in a startled blurt. The plasterboard shoved me back. Surprised silence from our classmates gave way to pantomime jeering. 'Spoilsport,' said the blond. Anthony presented him with a lordly middle finger and, seeing the hurt and bafflement on my face, pointed to the drawing pin that was sitting, sharp end up, in the centre of my chair.

'A little prick for a bigger one,' he said. 'Wouldn't that have been clever?'

Mr Hegarty appeared in the doorway and raked his throat. Anthony picked up his fallen chair and righted it, while I swept the tack to the floor. I sat, in an ecstasy of embarrassment, longing for my blush to fade. 'Splendid,' said Mr Hegarty. 'A spelling test to get the juices flowing.'

I had difficulty keeping my focus that morning. After the test we made a hash of some poems by Tennyson. Hegarty was irritable, throwing pearls before swine. Anthony did not return my gaze. I had to scamper to catch up with him afterwards. He walked fast – striding to lunch without company, his textbooks tucked under his arm.

'Thanks for that,' I said, a little breathless.

Anthony smiled at my collar and quickened his pace.

'Why did you do it?'

'Because it was stupid,' he said.

'You didn't have to.'

'Would you have noticed the drawing pin? I don't think so, Jackson. You're not very sharp, are you?'

I snuffled obligingly at the pun. Despite his earlier solidarity, Anthony seemed to want to keep his distance. I peeled away tactfully and pretended to head for the lockers by the toilets. I didn't want to jeopardise what had been gained. Though he did not consent to friendship, the tall and beautiful English boy had acknowledged my existence.

Now

My supervisor sat only two rooms from mine; you could hop to her office without losing breath; yet it was by email that she rebuked me. Had I any problems at home, she wondered, or difficulties healthwise? She hoped I was not still conflicted about the road-building programme. It was my job to calculate the costs-to-profit ratio for the satellite toll system, and, being a half-decent manager, Julia had noticed my lapses of concentration during the ministerial briefing. I broke into a sweat and the scalp seemed to recede on the frame of my skull as I read her email. I wrote back complaining of post-viral tiredness; a beloved cousin (who doesn't exist) had recently been diagnosed with cancer. When Julia passed my cubicle in the afternoon, she offered me a sympathetic smile.

Before the screensaver's vacuous drift, I reflected on the true cause of my distraction. The meeting at Fay Corcoran's had shaken me more than I could have imagined. I was afraid to go to sleep at night and, after a month's dieting, began to overeat, coming back to my flat with bagels and cream cheese and chocolate digestives, all of which I pushed into my face while watching mindless television. Beyond the confines of my flat I was a mass of nerves. The bubble of insulation that Londoners build about themselves had burst. I walked to work with hunched shoulders, as if at any moment a car might lash into me. Buses seemed intent on creeping up and sneezing in my ear; I was so incapable of ignoring the rip of aircraft that I found myself scurrying for the air-conditioned numbness of the Department offices. Once inside, I brooded over cups of coffee and guzzled bottled water so frozen that it made my teeth ache.

I could reveal none of my distress to my father. Every second Sunday I went to see him. My mother had pioneered our heavy lunches, with their fruity Australian wines designed to knock us out over coffee. Now, five years after her death, it was unimaginable to either of us that the tradition might lapse, though we rarely enjoyed upholding it.

That first visit after seeing Anthony again, I must have betrayed my nerves, scattering the blankets of the Sunday supplements with more than the usual restlessness. Dad was on the sofa pretending to read, but I could sense the flicker of his gaze. If only once he'd managed to vent his frustration (I mean truly vent, with explicit words, instead of his usual quips and euphemisms) perhaps we might have prevented the freeze in our relationship. But the disputes that used to quicken us were long ago extinguished. There is an air of exhaustion between us, of passionate combatants locked long ago in stalemate. I keep most of myself from my father: he no longer takes the trouble of hiding the worst.

'On the bus the other day,' he said, 'two lads behind me, I assumed they were black, they *sounded* black. *Lack diss, lack dat* – horrible noises. The bus stopped outside Tesco, I saw them get off. They were white as my backside in winter.'

Bent over the review section, I seemed to be half listening. To my father, whose every pronouncement once held weight for a staff of twenty, this was intolerable. He picked me up on it with a suppressed tremble of rage in his voice.

'What do you want me to say?' I said.

'Don't you think it's a shame that the English language is descending into street slang? If all the young start speaking that way it will be the end of cockney.'

'What do you care?'

'If I wanted to be in Trench Town I'd buy myself a bullet-proof jacket and go and live there.'

'That's kind of racist.'

'How is it racist not to recognise one's own country?'

'You haven't been in your own country for most of your adult life.'

My father looked at his speckled hand and picked scurf from a knuckle. 'I suppose that's the trouble, isn't it? Not really belonging anywhere.'

I did not like to think of Dad as being lost but sometimes he seemed it. Cultural diversity that he so valued in Kuala Lumpur was in England an irritant to him. The old country had no right to change so bewilderingly in his absence.

My father worked for thirty-eight years for the British Council: an institution starved in his eyes, besieged and emasculated, by successive governments back home. When he railed against the suppression of anything that didn't have a benefit immediately intelligible to the 'reptilian eyes' of civil servants, I flinched to feel myself included in the ranks of the enemy. Port and idleness had reinforced his favourite complaint: 'The bloody lack of self-confidence, Bruno. It's our national disease.' I myself was a sufferer, he seemed to imply: a fact all the more baffling to him given his own combative nature. When he was in charge in KL, Dad would say, securing a meniscus in his sherry glass, he used to be something of a rebel, ever ready to defend his staff from the pusillanimous interference of his superiors. Now in retirement, a Chelsea pensioner as he put it (though really he lives on the edge of

Fulham), he distracted himself with local causes, churning out letters against bus lanes, intrusive speed cameras or the over-zealous pruning of trees by the council. It grieved him beyond measure that I had taken refuge in the Department for Trans-port: a behemoth that embodied, in his opinion, 'intrusive and short-termist government'.

But I mustn't give the impression that we never laughed, Dad and me, or that our time together was always a chore. When I was a child, before the name of Kingsley had ever been men-tioned, my father was playful. I remember his stooped and cawing impressions of tropical birds when we visited the bird park near our home, and his bounding after the tennis ball when we played cricket in the garden, a red palm serving as our wicket and Mum imagining scorpions in every bush. Dad was still capable of enthusiasm in those days. I was the keeper of his boyish flame: when it faltered in me, it failed in him.

Even so, we retain interests in common. We are both keen chess players (me cautious and disciplined, Dad a reckless gambler), so that an external witness, deaf to the competitive whirring of our brains, might read in our bowed heads above the chequered board a scene of domestic peace. Much may be owed to genetics, for we share a sense of humour, we read similar books, and whenever our conversations get mired in weary topics or threaten to stray into forbidden territory, we can always bond over his selection of antique TV dramas. In these ways we tolerate each other's love.

'Anyway, when did you turn into a guardian of political correctness?' Dad put the question lightly, as though it were benign. 'Don't tell me you've surrendered to the *bien-pensants*.' We were laying the table at this point, Dad persisting in the tradition of using the Jackson silver. I decided not to give him the satisfaction of a reply. 'It must be the influence of all those departmental memos.'

'Oh, Dad, you can't put those out. They're tarnished.'

He shrugged in the manner of a shabby clown and polished the dessert spoons on his sleeve. I went to fetch the roast.

'Where are Mum's oven gloves?' I asked a few minutes later.

Dad chewed meditatively, gazing at the tablecloth. 'I replaced them, I think.'

'Why?'

'I suppose because they were worn.'

'They were fine last week.'

'There was a hole in them, Bruno.'

'You must have made it! They were perfectly good oven gloves!'

My father's reply, so simple, shocked me. 'I can't live in a museum, you know.'

The strain of the past week added to my usual intolerance to make me petulant. I berated him for his carelessness with household things. How many of Mum's belongings had he scorched or thrown away? Dad knew what I was getting at, resented it and eventually, in a stentorian voice I rarely want to hear, told me to leave the subject be.

He apologised for shouting; I apologised for making him shout.

Improbable as it may seem, I can actually date the first time I heard my father raise his voice in anger. It was on the telephone when, half the world between us, I told him of my wish to leave Kingsley College. I remember his bafflement – the awful, furry silence on the line that preceded his outburst. He has never understood my decision to leave, and I could not, for reasons that must become clear, possibly have explained it to him.

'It was the move that did for you,' he said that time they came to dinner in Manchester. I was in my first year as an economics student in the wrong institution, having failed to follow my parents to the Oxford college where they had met and fallen in love. Mum made light of my choice, as she put it, but Dad could not hide his disappointment. The narrative loop was unclosed: the apotheosis of a marriage now threatened by the diagnosis of a small tumour in my mother's breast was not to happen.

'Those damn sixth-form colleges: it's all computer games and modish teaching. Kingsley had a reputation for making scholars. I read your reports: you were on track.'

'Christopher . . .' I remember Mum's hand catching his on the tablecloth. She turned to me with unaffected curiosity. 'Tell us about the friends you've made. What societies have you joined?'

This was an invitation to talk about chess. I took it, as did Dad, with as much grace as I could muster. The brave face does not come easily to us, unless it's fortified with sarcasm. Even after I graduated with a First (thus achieving some redemption in his eyes), Dad could not disguise his bewilderment at the replacement of his jovial, opinionated boy with such a cautious adult. We were dealing at the time with Mum's illness: the sudden appetite of her recurring cancer. He must have seen her terrified and weeping but with me she was always cheerful. Mum was raised – in long-extinct colonial fashion – never to distress or embarrass others. Even in illness she found it necessary (I hope it helped) to act as a bridge between her two men. What we could not speak openly, she translated for us in private. She was our confidante and interpreter. It was to her that I answered Dad's veiled questions, telling her in the garden, under the roaring bellies of aircraft, that there would probably never be any girlfriends.

I wonder (and then really dare not imagine) how she broke it to him. *Did* she break it to him? Certainly all references to sex, even *Carry On* innuendo, have been censored from Dad's conversation since. Would he have been consoled to know that I was functionally celibate: my regular friends all female, straight or already spoken for? There was Deepak, of course: beautiful Deepak, met at the NFT, so softly spoken, so elegantly contained in his physical spareness, who came to London to study mathematics and was looking for kindness among the natives. Sweetly, soothingly, out of loneliness perhaps, he called me his friend. He would have been appalled to know the things I did to him in the darkness of my nights.

After lunch and a second go at the papers, after the washing up and a spot of gardening with Radio 3 to block out the noise from Heathrow, we sat indoors, drinking tea. He told me about the latest injustice, the coming folly of this or that development. We sat among my mother's things, the whole house reflecting her tastes, and I couldn't speak about the turmoil inside me. We found ourselves breathing an atmosphere even less comfortable than usual, and all the toxins were mine, brought back from Fay Corcoran's party.

I explained some of these things to Jenny when we met for supper. We often went out on Monday nights, the idea being to console ourselves for the start of another working week. Jenny watched, smiling, as I mimicked my father. She knows him well enough and he seems to approve of her, dreams of her perhaps for a daughter-in-law, liking the brisk humour and old-fashioned Englishness that disguise a lot of torments.

'I swear he's inventing a personality for his old age: a comfortable shell to retreat into.' Hearing his dispatches from the New King's Road, I said, was like seeing into the future. How many years would I spend listening, with clenched toes, to the satire of a bright-eyed, suspicious, watchful old man?

'He's not that old,' said Jenny. 'Besides, you're always young so long as you're paying attention.'

'There is that, the eavesdropping old ferret.' I wiped my brow and complained about the heat. Being slight and disinclined in warm weather to weigh herself down with too many clothes, Jenny didn't sympathise. What she fears is the cold – especially at night, in her cold bed at night. 'What *is* it with London these days?' I said. 'It's like a bloody oven.'

'Better than shivering in the shade.'

'It didn't used to affect me. I grew up in this sort of humidity. But I suppose I'm acclimatised to a different planet.' Nowadays, with so much extra Bruno to cart around, my life is an endless battle with perspiration. The move from warm interior to cool exterior, in the winter, and vice versa in the summer – the repetitive variations in ambient temperature all year round – leave me glazed with sweat. My father, who has at least the advantage of having been born in this country, suffers the same difficulty and together, like disparate oldies glad to find a common gripe, we marvel at our fellow Londoners insulated like boilers in their winter coats, sitting on a heated train without the shadow of a bead of moisture on their faces.

'You seem a bit tetchy this evening, Bruno. If you don't mind my saying. A bit on edge.'

'I'm sorry.'

'There's no need to apologise. Is everything OK?'

Jenny's concern for me is genuine and I return it. We met at Manchester in the offices of a short-lived poetry press. I liked her immediately for her dry humour, her shrewd and shrewish looks. Since then I've put on the weight that she has lost and she has pursued a once shared ambition to be, somehow or other, a professional poet. The occasional sale of a poem to a tiny magazine is not, of course, sufficient to keep her in spangles and sequins, so she works six days a week in a perennially near-bankrupt bookshop off the Charing Cross Road. She is always

34

short of money; but it's not her finances I worry about. Despite her outward pluck, Jenny Gould suffers from a wretched promiscuity: each picked-up customer or performance poet (the uglier the better) serving as a penance for some undiagnosed and probably inherited sinfulness. Why Catholics can't just lapse is beyond me: they have to make a Passion out of it.

'You've been preoccupied all evening,' she said. 'You haven't even noticed the waiter.' I looked back in token gesture over my shoulder. 'There's something you're not telling me. Has the Monk of Whitehall found romance?'

'Chance would be a fine thing.'

'You're not still pining for that Indian guy?'

I shook my head, snapping a breadstick and pushing the crumbs about the table. I wanted to talk but needed to be careful. 'I, uh . . . I have met someone actually. From the past.'

'Oh yeah?'

'Not like that. He's married. I mean he's not . . . We were friends at school.'

'I didn't think you had any friends at school.'

'That's the sob story I usually give. In actual fact I had one. A very close friend. He . . . wasn't good for me.'

Jenny heard the unfamiliar note in my voice and sat up. There was a soft, inquisitive intake of breath such as usually heralds a shrewd deduction. 'Was he the reason you left in the sixth form?'

'Partly – not really – oh God, I don't know. Anyway, I met him at Fay's.' Jenny doesn't like Fay Corcoran. Coming from the same world, she knows too well its superficial mildness, its secret permafrost. She has rid herself (without adopting an estuary twang) of the drawling entitlement of those public school vowels. 'Don't look at me in that tone of voice,' I said, 'she's a darling really.'

'Tell me what happened.'

'Well, he – this friend – came bounding up to me as if nothing had ever happened. It was like we'd simply been in different rooms for the past twelve years and now we were bumping into each other again. It was . . . very strange.'

'Why wasn't he good for you?'

The question brought me up sharp. Before Jenny's interrogative gaze, a whole armada of reflexes closed the port of revelation. 'Let's just say we parted on bitter terms. I hadn't seen or spoken to him in all these years. And then all of a sudden there he is in my face. The stupid thing is: I gave him my phone number.'

'Is that bad?'

'Well . . .'

Jenny moistened her lips with a wine-stained tongue. She was intrigued, piqued, and sat forward, her bony hands straying unguardedly over the table so that I glimpsed, without wishing to, the unhealed scratches on her wrist. 'Would you *like* to hear from him again?'

I regretted having broached the topic and called the waiter over.

'Bruno, please . . .'

'No, no, it's my pleasure.'

The token gesture made, Jenny sat back to digest her meal. I reclaimed my credit card, having offered the waiter an undeservedly generous tip. A civil servant needs bohemian friends if he wants to feel flush.

There was Fay's party – the old mess churned up – and then everything in life seemed to resettle. I regained some of that bland composure to which my system long ago became accustomed. The old dream of sheer mountains, gills of black rock, a disappearing thread of pale blond hair, abated, to be replaced by the usual jumble of prosaic experience.

Things even got better in the wider world: abused Nature turned down her thermostat, the roadside veld drank her meagre rain, and I was getting ready for an evening stroll in Vauxhall Park when the telephone rang.

I kicked off my loafers and picked up.

'Hello?' Electronic air buzzed on the line. 'Hello, who is this?' Whoever was calling seemed to sit up. 'Look, are you sure you have the right number? This is Bruno Jack—'

'Sorry, just reading something on my screen.'

'What?'

'Apologies, really I should know better. Bruno, it's Anthony.' Now it was my turn to be silent. 'Hello?'

'What do you want?'

'Anthony Blunden.'

'Yes. Why are you calling?'

'Oh. Well, you gave me your number. I must say it *was* a surprise. Fay's such a social butterfly, you never know who she'll turn up. Hugo, though, is a top bloke, really, we're ever so pleased.' Anthony took an audible breath before changing tack. 'You know, you were awfully cagey. Dipali picked up on it immediately: she didn't want to say anything, of course, she's too polite, but she found your behaviour a bit odd. Are you still there?'

'Yes.'

'I told her not to take it personally but she was left wondering, Bruno. She asked me all sorts of questions. I mean, you ran away. It was . . . noticeable.'

'Suspicious, you mean?'

'Look, I don't want to be rude but is everything all right?'

'What?'

He began tampering with some object on his desk. I could hear a small plastic noise. 'What did you think of Dipali? She's wonderful, isn't she? Best thing that ever happened to me. How about you? Is there, uh . . . a significant other?'

'What do you want?'

The plastic fiddling stopped. I could almost hear him squirm. 'We thought maybe . . .'

'*We?*'

'Bruno, she's on to something. Sorry to speak so frankly: it always was my trouble. The point is I don't like leaving things as we left them. As you left them. I had to talk to her, Bruno. I had to tell her things about our friendship . . .'

On to something? He said she was on to something? Then his wife didn't know?

'The point is: do you want to come to dinner?'

'No.'

'What?'

'I don't think that would work.'

'If you've got any special dietary needs . . .'

'Don't be fucking ridiculous.' Pause. 'Sorry. I'm sorry, I shouldn't have said . . .'

'Not at all.'

'It's just . . . the surprise, you know.'

'We'll have a drink beforehand, just the two of us.'

'I don't want to.'

'Listen—'

'You don't have to worry. I'm not about to break silence, not after all this time.'

Anthony hesitated. 'Dipali will be disappointed.'

'Give her my apologies.'

'What should I say?'

'I don't know. Tell her that I'm going abroad.'

'Are you?'

'Of course not.' I was staring almost passionately at the notepad beside the phone. Eventually I said, 'Can I ask why?'

'Why what?'

'Do you want to see me?'

'Why do I want to? Well, because . . . I suppose I'm curious to see what's become of you.'

My patience failed. 'Nothing. Nothing has become of me,' I said, and hung up.

Then

For the Christmas holidays I flew home to Kuala Lumpur. The strangeness of that return still presses on me. The house stood as before; in the garden where my father and I resumed our games of French cricket, the shaggy oil palms with bromeliads in their scales pursued their vegetable lives. Because I had changed and it had not, my bedroom seemed to belong in a museum and I sensed, like a revenant visiting the scenes of a former life, that you can never go home again.

As soon as I had settled in, I hooked up with Irshad, my neighbour, who, knowing nothing of my new status as a social outcast, accompanied me to the cinema and on walks about the Lake Gardens. Irshad was uncommonly interested in crawling things. He had bottled trapdoor spiders that we studied in their brine, tilting the specimens to give them a semblance of life. His father, a wealthy Petronas man, had set up for him a heated glass tank containing scorpions which we teased with probing pencils. I liked Irshad: he was playful and generous with the spoils of his father's success. Nor was he my only friend. From my old prep school there remained Sudeep, a confusing and exciting flirt, and cricketing ace Gurmit Lal, who knew all there was to know about Formula One and whose younger sister Nadzirah smiled at me too much and couldn't disguise her fascination with my

European hair. But my greatest friend was Sebastian, the only child of Dutch engineers, with whom I would stroll, gorging on dim sum and sugar cane juice, among the street *kedais*: two European kids who could make jaws drop when they answered back in coarse Malay.

Christmas was a joyous affair, with my mother's dear friend, Aunt Nariza, visiting from Kota Bharu and Sebastian's parents calling on us on Boxing Day with games and presents. I managed to put out of mind my impending return to England. It seemed remote in the midst of festivities: an unfortunate interlude rather than the beginning of a new life. I never mentioned to my parents how unhappy I was there. I was learning already to be secretive.

The holidays evaporated too quickly: a reality I tried to escape in the company of my friends or lolling about the garden reading *The Lord of the Rings*. The day before my flight, I was a teenage horror, surly and incommunicative. Then, after a sweating night, I was swept up in action: my parents and friends and kindly Mr Phang our chauffeur waving me through the portals at the airport.

Thirteen hours later, from the car of bumptious Mr Houghton, I stepped on to the drive of Hereward House to begin another stretch of schooling.

My strongest impressions of those months so insultingly known as 'Spring Term' are of dark afternoons and interminable nights, of burning toes as one stepped from cold tiles into the shower, and fingers so frozen that acid seemed to have taken the place of blood. Roused by the gong, I tickled in darkness the cold mouths of my slippers. Breakfast was a gore-fest of greasy sausage and congealed beans, presided over by the chewing zombies of the upper sets. Every day was hard work. I hated the press of wet clay on my knees after games of rugby; I struggled to waken under the sky's closed lid. Of course, things were to improve as the term progressed and I acclimatised, but the compensations of late winter – those bright days when birds dust off their song and crocuses hatch under naked boughs – seemed remote in January. The British winter, I was discovering, lacks the cold sparkle of snow: it is an endurance test yearly undergone by sixty million people. Bland assurances that the upswing had begun and the hours of darkness were shrinking did little to relieve the gloom of being locked indoors scarcely after lunch and spending hours cramped under electric light.

If my first days back in England were unremittingly grim, my mood improved when lessons resumed and I was infected with the involuntary excitement of seeing familiar faces: a hope against all reason that absence from a place might have changed it for the better. I took comfort in work, especially maths, and spent restful hours sketching parsnips or winter bulbs on the long benches of the art room. In English, Anthony Blunden refrained from shuffling away from me when I sat next to him. The other boys paid no attention when – swallowing a pang like heartburn – I asked him about his holidays. 'Oh, you know,' he said, and raised his shoulders in a yawn.

'Did it snow?'

'When?'

'While I was away.'

'I expect so.'

'I was in Malaysia. It's where my parents live.'

'We went to Barbados.' He said nothing more. I wanted him to lean in and listen to *my* story: to feel myself sink into his confidence. But Anthony was in the cloister of his own imagination and I, excluded, could only follow the sure sweep of his jaw, the feminine curve of his lips and the oily seams of his eyelids.

Throughout Mr Hegarty's lesson (we were 'having a look' at Ted Hughes) I found myself distracted by my neighbour. I could feel the heat emanating from his thigh where it almost touched mine. His breathing was heavy and regular, until Hegarty broke the stupor of his monologue and set us a spelling test. Anthony sprawled over his notebook, his forehead close to the green wool of his arm as if at any moment he might fall asleep on it. Once, as we all struggled with 'eccentric' and Mr Hegarty had paced to the far side of the classroom, I felt a thrill of elicit pleasure as Anthony's eyes flickered to my page . . . I flaunted it at him.

'Jackson!' said Mr Hegarty. 'This is not teamwork. And Mr Blunden, keep your eyes to yourself.'

It was the first time I'd ever been scolded. I blushed for the rest of the lesson, feeling or imagining that I felt a blast of accusation from those coveted eyes beside me. Afterwards I tried to catch up with Anthony but the faster I scampered, the more he strode out of reach, pointedly seeking the sanctuary of our different class-rooms.

His reproach did not last long. Anthony, who showed a real enthusiasm for words, for the gloss and power they offer, seemed to recognise in me a kindred spirit and, though he never sought me out, he was scrupulously blasé when I made the effort to sit next to him. We spoke sometimes when Hegarty was late, or had to excuse himself, poor man, in the middle of a lesson. I learned about Anthony's dog, a Jack Russell called Bacon, and about his mother, who did something or other in landscape gardening. Anthony made fun of smelly old Hegarty; our headmaster was a clown, he said. I tried to enlist his moral solidarity against the bullies in our class but Anthony wouldn't give me the satisfaction. Though he never joined in their taunting, he remained careful not to befriend me openly, knowing what a taint such association brings.

I faced similar problems in Hereward House. Privately (that is, walking back from the playing fields or brushing our teeth before lights-out), Robbie Thwaite and John Toplady were my friends, while boys of higher status like Hugo Barclay and Dan Chapman never tried to 'confiscate' my food or deface the posters I had put up, in a kind of provocation, depicting the fauna of my country: the lurid and malodorous rafflesia flower, a Bruegelesque troupe of proboscis monkeys, a pygmy elephant from Borneo. Even though it was a minority that took delight in tormenting me (and looking back, I feel not so much pity as exasperation with myself for letting it happen), the majority never shuffled to my defence.

I did myself no favours. For all my intelligence, I failed to understand what it was that distinguished the popular boy from the unpopular, the ignored from the tormented. Bullies are rarely intelligent but they have a kind of feral instinct, a nose for meekness or pliability which gives them all their strength. Perhaps it's merely the cunning of being the first to lay down the rules, framing, as it were, the terms of engagement. Lawrence Nevins had plenty of cunning. I had no idea what he would become but firmly expected him to make a loud commercial success of his twenties. Louts like Charlie Stoddard dwindle to domestic tyrants; people like Nevins rule the world. As for the others, they developed strategies to keep out of trouble. And then there were the seraphic few who seemed to live above the fray.

I thought Anthony was one of these. So at the time did he. It frustrated me that I was always on the edge of his confidence; that despite our evident likeness (we alone felt the tug and heft of words) he kept aloof, did not see me as his acolyte, the dark unlovely foil to his beauty. Unrequited, I watched him read *The Lord of the Flies* and imagined as nobody else could the lineaments of Golding's schoolboy hero.

Easter! It was the Easter holidays and I was not flying home but it hardly mattered because my parents were coming. On leave for a month, they drove to college a day after all the other boys had left. I received them like the inheritor of a country seat, Mr and Mrs Sedley standing behind me like loyal retainers. My father was all bluff charm and over coffee he worked his magic on Mrs Sedley while Mr Sedley burbled on about chalk downs and sheep farming. Mum's fingers fidgeted in her lap. I sat on the ribbed and bloated settee while the adults chatted, and gazed out of the window at a garden made suddenly familiar and benign by the presence of those I loved. When the Sedleys suggested a stroll in the grounds, every step we took together seemed to exorcise the place.

We made our getaway in a hired car: west to London and my Uncle Roger's house on Putney Common.

For the next few weeks I felt, through velvet-backed chairs and comfortable sofas, the throbbing pulse of the capital. Buses trailed litter and life behind them. We browsed about the common, where I discovered daffodils and gorse flowers and the song of temperate birds, so frail and tender after their Malaysian counterparts. My parents tried to get me to talk about school but I gave only vague answers, wanting to forget about Kingsley. For a rare time in my life, I mastered the profound art of Being in the Moment. There were books to read, after all, and journeys of discovery to be made. Sometimes, with Uncle Roger (when he could get away from his White City office), we headed into town and ticked off the sights. We visited Greenwich and the Tower of London and explored the grand cathedral of the Natural History Museum, where under the fibreglass belly of a whale I let my mother take my hand.

My parents waited two weeks to tell me about Mum's health scare. Those were the words they used, their tone modulating from jovial to serious as we ate our picnic on the banks of the River Cherwell. We had gone to Oxford for the day, my parents wanting to show me the college where they had studied and fallen so precociously in love. The honeyed stone, the wrought-iron gates so politely shut on the non-elect, the ivied quads—

45

'What do you mean?' I struggled to keep my voice from quavering. 'What's the matter? Is it *serious*?'

Mum folded her legs elegantly beneath her on the rug. 'Everything's fine. Honestly, Bruno, it was a false alarm. But you know that Grandma had it . . .'

'*You* don't have it, do you?'

'No.' The timbre of her voice was strong. I turned it about in my mind for falseness. 'We just thought you ought to know. We're not a family that keeps secrets.'

So I knew: there was nothing to worry about. Dad ruffled my hair and challenged me to take charge of the punt. We drifted under a thorn bush and crouched, hooting with laughter, while Dad attempted to lever us away from the bank.

There was a further trauma that holiday. My voice broke. It had been warping for a time – a rare, audacious call on the playing field beginning in a high treble and ending in a low, humiliating croak. I had been afraid of the change, expecting it to hurt, but in the end it was like a soft internal release, the passing of an ineluctable threshold. One night we watched *A Fish Called Wanda* – my parents and Uncle Roger and me – and I blushed at the sex scenes and bleated goodnight, and when I got up the next day a stranger had taken up residence in my throat. Dad was in town already and Uncle Roger at work, but Mum greeted me over the cereal bowls. I replied and she concealed her sadness. 'Goodness, Bruno,' she said; nothing more. I felt embarrassed (what else is a broken voice but the announcement of a sexual self?) and at the same time proud. I expected to revert to my own voice occasionally but my piping days were over.

That night or the one after, I masturbated in my bedroom only feet from my snoring parents and hobbled in shock to the bathroom when, with a spasm close to pain and immeasurably desolate, I produced a spot of milky fluid.

Uncle Roger's house, then, was the place where my childhood

ended. Caught up in puberty, I wanted to pull back, to regress to lost and irrecoverable certainties. Despite the no-secrets ideal of the Jackson family, I could not speak about my transformation, though it was obvious to all, and I must have been insufferable for the last few days of my parents' leave. They took me to London Zoo and I stared sullenly at a caged and pacing tiger. It paid me no attention. Despite my best intentions, I could not shake off my frustration and grief at what was coming.

The day came with its wrench of separation. We'll be together soon! Time passes quickly!

'England is a joy now,' my father told me. 'I wish I could stay with you for the hawthorn and the cricket and the warm beer. Enjoy it, Bruno. As Kipling once said' (but Dad paraphrased) 'this is the best foreign country you'll ever visit.'

'And if I press here?'

'Oww. Oww, *ahh*!' Anthony Blunden raised his knees towards his belly and Sister's hand. She did not remove her fingers but prodded a little harder.

'Do you feel sick at all?'

Anthony appeared to consider the question. The sister looked at the cricket master, who was still in his whites and smelled of grass. She removed her hand and Anthony flinched.

'Appendix?' wondered the cricket master. 'He was complaining before we started.'

'I so wanted to bat,' said Anthony, almost pleadingly.

The sister peremptorily pressed him down on the bed. 'He doesn't have other symptoms,' she said.

'I do feel a bit sick, actually.'

'You haven't got a fever.'

'I feel awful, sir. Really.'

I looked at the sister. A scowl was brewing on her face. But the cricket master, Mr Dilks, had scoffed at claims of sickness before, until a pupil collapsed in a frothing fit and his parents threatened to sue him over a lost sliver of tongue. Anthony had chosen his target wisely. 'Maybe,' said Mr Dilks, 'we should keep him in for observation. I'll phone the Eversley.'

The sister let him have his way. She was a plain, grey woman who smelled of flour and plastic bands. I imagined she lived alone with ill-tempered cats. Maybe she loved Mr Dilks and couldn't show it? When their footsteps had faded in the corridor, Anthony let his legs slide on the mattress. He looked at me where I lay, snivelling and cloth-headed, by the sanatorium window. 'You'd better not give that to me,' he said.

'What do you have, Blunden?'

'Allergy. There's a chemistry test tomorrow.' He grinned. There was a softness in the corners of his lips that suggested kindness.

'You mean—?'

'Don't act surprised. Are you really feeling ill?'

'Yes, actually.'

Anthony contemplated me more carefully. 'Yeah, you do look pretty rough. In Summer Term, too. And I suppose you *like* chemistry.'

'I don't understand a word of it.'

Anthony looked at the closed door and lifted himself to a sitting position. On my bed I tried to do the same, though my head was clogged and spinning. 'I'm better with words,' he said. 'You know: poetry and stuff.' He seemed to want my agreement.

'I know,' I said. 'Me too.'

'You're Hegarty's pet. He thinks you're William Shakespeare.'

I watched him looking around the sickroom. There were no other boys about, though only that morning a sixth-former had come in heaving up his breakfast. I'd heard Dr Praed in consultation with Sister. They'd agreed it was alcohol poisoning.

'I'm thirsty,' I said. Anthony got to his feet and wandered to the medicine cabinet. He gave it a speculative tug. 'Do you suppose they'll keep you in overnight?' Anthony looked at me and shrugged. 'Blunden?'

'What?'

'Could you get me a glass of water?'

He went to the sink and the sister came in. My heart leapt but Anthony dissembled quickly. 'It's Jackson,' he croaked.

'What is?'

'He asked—'

'I wanted a glass of water,' I said.

The sister looked at me, her thin lips compressed. She crossed the room and took the glass from Anthony's grip. 'You're not to get out of bed, do you hear? Not until Dr Praed has seen you and then you'll get into pyjamas. Bruno, don't start exploiting people's good nature.'

'I wasn't.'

'Don't argue. Drink.' While I sipped from the glass, Anthony returned, wincing with imagined pain, to his bed. He smirked conspiratorially behind the sister's back.

When she had gone again, I was keen to resume our conversation but couldn't think of anything to say. For a minute or more we lay on our beds, breathing in silence. Actually I snivelled. 'Please tell me you're not going to do that all night,' said Anthony.

I reached under my pillow for a tangle of tissues. I blew my nose as discreetly as possible and checked myself from inspecting the contents. 'It's a lot worse in Malaysia,' I said.

'What is?'

'Having a cold. I mean, it's hot there and humid.' Anthony made a high, bugling sound of his yawn. He stretched out like a cat. 'Have you been, Blunden?'

'What?'

'To Malaysia.'

'Why would I want to go to Malaysia?'

'I don't know.'

'You're *here* now, aren't you.' It was a statement, flat and without malice. I turned to the wall to conceal my red face. 'I can't stand bloody cricket. Silly mid fuck off and deep shit.'

'Fine leg.'

'And Dilks is a plonker. Have you noticed how he always chooses the same boys to bowl? I bet he fancies them. Well, he doesn't fancy me, thank God. Or you, I imagine.'

I tried not to think about Mr Dilks. It wasn't true, was it? 'But he's married,' I said.

'Rugby's better, of course. So long as you're not in the pack. What do you play?'

'Hooker.'

'And a fag.'

'I don't like it much.'

'Being a fag?'

'I much prefer . . .' What did I prefer? The solitariness of swimming, or knocking about the tennis court with Gurmit Lal. When I wasn't press-ganged into a team, I had nobody to let down but myself. 'I'm not really a team player.'

'You're an individualist.' I gulped at these words and couldn't help smiling. 'Watch out,' said Anthony, though he was the only one faking: 'Here comes Prat.'

The door opened and Dr Praed came in, followed by the sister and Anthony's housemaster. They gathered about Anthony's bed and the sister pulled the curtain. I remember feeling mild panic. They would suss him out and I'd be deprived of my chance at making friends. I heard the doctor mutter and occasional yelps from the patient.

'You poor old chap,' said Anthony's housemaster, a sonorous Welsh baritone.

'I'll be all right, sir. I'm sure it's nothing.'

'That's just what I think,' said Sister, but this met with more muttering and a friendly cluck of Dr Praed's tongue. He drew back the curtains and I could see the conclave.

'We'll keep you in tonight, just in case. Sometimes these things can blow up and it's better to be on the safe side.'

Anthony lay writhing, his hands pressed against his belly. I watched his housemaster pat him on the arm. 'Chin up, lad. You'll be all right.'

The bluff, middle-aged men withdrew, leaving Anthony to be chivvied into sanatorium pyjamas. I was careful to look away as he undressed.

'I'll have my eye on you,' said the sister, and the note of warning was not lost on either of us. But there was nothing she could do: there were skilful shirkers and there were clumsy shirkers. When the sister had gone (having administered my Sudafed and a Lemsip), we breathed in the air of Anthony's success. 'That . . .' I said.

'Shush.' Anthony listened for the sister listening.

'She's gone,' I whispered. He was not so certain but eventually he relaxed and looked at me, smirking.

For one night we were together in the comfort and quiet of the sanatorium. The sister came in a couple more times to press Anthony's forehead and peek at his tongue. 'You'll be up on your feet tomorrow,' she said.

'The pain's awful, Sister. I feel every spasm.'

She tucked up his feet vengefully. It was still light outside and the sanatorium curtains glowed greenly. I could hear pupils tramping back from dinner and the groundsman's tractor over by the woods. I shut my eyes to savour the moment.

'Jackson.'

'What?'

'Are you awake?' I heard Anthony swing from his bed and pad across the floor. He breathed close to me. 'You were snoring.'

'I wasn't.' I opened my eyes to see him at the foot of my bed, peering under a corner of curtain. It was almost dark outside. 'Was I disturbing you?'

'It's too dark to read and I'm not sleepy.'

'Neither am I,' I lied. My head trembled and thrummed. I tried to hawk up phlegm from my throat. 'It's nice to have company,' I said.

'There's a nurse on duty, isn't there?'

'Mrs Graves.'

Anthony let the curtain drop. 'Can't sneak out for a fag, then.'

'I wouldn't advise it.' I thought about this for a minute. 'Have you got a cigarette?'

'Have you?'

I'd never tried, hating the smell. 'In my dorm,' I said.

Anthony seemed to take me at my word. He crept tactfully about the room, picking things up and trying the doors of locked cabinets. I tried to make him out in the gloom but a sneezing fit cannoned me back on my pillow.

'Have you pulled a sickie before, Blunden?'

'Anthony,' he said.

I swallowed an excess of saliva. 'I'm Bruno.'

'How about you?'

'Oh no,' I lied. 'This cold's real.'

'Sometimes one simply *must* get away. The people in this place!' He seemed to be putting on another's voice: it was camp and arch and superior. He flung himself theatrically into bed. 'Not that I don't enjoy life at the Eversley. You're in the Hereward, aren't you? The pansies' palace.'

'It isn't.'

'The fairy farm. Queer Castle.'

'Sod off.'

Anthony laughed openly and then, by the sound of it, gnawed his pillow to keep from betraying himself. Both of us waited for

Mrs Graves to come charging in but nothing happened. 'That's the first time I've heard you swear,' Anthony whispered when his confidence had returned. 'Shall I go and find some soap?'

We bantered for perhaps an hour. Anthony told me more about his life outside. His father was a High Court judge – with a string of points on his driving licence. 'Dad knows the law: that's how he knows where to bend it.' Mrs Blunden was the daughter of a long-dead Tory minister and had been a model back in the sixties. It had proved, according to Anthony, a good genetic mix: except for his sister Gemma. 'She inherited Mum's brains and Dad's looks. But then somebody had to.'

'I saw you,' I said, fighting the urge to sleep.

'When?'

'In the Hereward garden, at the beginning of the year.' Anthony could never have guessed how gilded his family seemed to me. I imagined clever laughter over Sunday roast, and picnics under willow trees on the bank of a river. 'Who was that man with the curly hair on his neck?'

'Uncle Thomas? He's my mum's brother.'

'What does he do?'

'God knows. Something to do with defence. Helicopters, I think, or aircraft.' Anthony talked on, describing his prep school, where he had picked up most of the prizes and then given them to his friends. It had nothing to do with talent, he assured me. 'I was just the brightest of a really stupid lot.'

'I miss my old school,' I said, candid from wooziness. 'It's in Kuala Lumpur. All my friends are there. I have a lot of friends, though that may surprise you.'

Anthony was silent. I raised myself on my elbows and tried by squinting to make him out against the far wall. 'I believe you,' he said eventually. 'Kingsley's a tough place.'

'Do you think so?'

A door slammed in the corridor and I heard Anthony shake the covers over his head. Footsteps sounded on the lino outside and the door handle turned. 'Now, boys, this isn't good enough. If you can't sleep with company, I'll have to separate you.'

'Sorry, Mrs Graves,' I said.

'It's my fault,' said Anthony. 'I'm keeping him awake.'

'Feeling better, are you?'

'It's the pain. I can't sleep.' But he retracted sufficiently when Mrs Graves threatened to wake up Dr Praed. He would be all right: it was probably just colic.

When I woke in the morning, Anthony was gone: sent packing to his chemistry test by a reassured housemaster. I tried not to be disappointed. I had, at last, a reason to get better.

Anthony did not reject me when I recovered. He sat next to me in English and called us, with private smugness, the Brains Trust. I was allowed into the private club that was Eversley House, where the music was raw and unfamiliar and the denizens grew their hair beyond the permissible length. He introduced me to a couple of his dorm mates but they showed little interest and I was more than happy to reciprocate. I invited Anthony, in turn, to the Hereward, but he always declined, liking things on his own terms and reluctant to be shown off as a trophy.

He showed me his room, which he shared with two surly cricketers. In disorderly piles about his desk were books I'd never heard of: adult-looking hardbacks by American novelists with German-sounding names. A little bronze Buddha meditated among postcards from San Francisco, Lake Geneva and Manhattan. 'Mum travels,' Anthony said. He showed me a collection of Roman coins stowed in a walnut display case inside his tuck box. 'I like the mad ones best. This is Caligula, who slept with his sister. And this is Nero, who fiddled while Rome burned. In fact he probably started it so he could rebuild everything. They were both murdered in the end.'

I held the coins almost reverently in my palm. To think they had been handled two thousand years ago: exchanged over onions in the marketplace, or disbursed to legionaries when they had completed their service. 'How did you get these?' I asked, as if they were treasure.

'It's called numismatics. There are shops. It's dead easy.'

Dead easy to a Blunden, perhaps. To me, so much of Anthony's life seemed remote and sophisticated; or else he was better than I was at displaying what he knew.

'Do you know the bomb shelter?' he said one morning between lessons. 'It's over by the armoury. There used to be loads of them during the war. You can still get in, though it's a bit of a shithole. Do you want to check it out?'

After lunch, in that charmed hiatus between work and sport, we made our way through dry beech woods to the grass-covered, lozenge-shaped mound of the bomb shelter. It was grim: a dank, mouldering space, with corrugation above us barely discernible by the daylight from the half-open metal door. There were wooden benches, grimy with age, on which generations of boys had carved stylised cocks and their initials. 'Who else comes here?' I wondered.

'No one that I know of.'

'It's forbidden, isn't it?'

'I should imagine. Does that bother you?'

Oddly enough, it didn't; I was being corrupted and it felt wonderful. 'If they really wanted to keep us out,' I said, 'they'd have blocked up the entrance, wouldn't they?'

We sat there imagining rats and spiders. The floor was gritty and my feet made a rasping noise when I fidgeted. I could make out the line of Anthony's cheek and his eyes regarding me from the opposite bench. 'This can be our place,' he said when he realised that I in turn was watching him. 'Where we can escape hoi polloi. You don't say "the". "Hoi" means "the".'

There was a spark and a flame and he sucked on a cigarette.

We made the bomb shelter our sanctuary. Once or twice we had to turn back when a senior boy emerged with a junior in tow; but on the whole we were undisturbed. We talked about our lives there – or rather, Anthony talked and I urged him on – and read erotic passages from novels pilfered from our dorm libraries: books with broken spines that opened conveniently at the choice pages. At Anthony's entreaty, I overcame my aversion to cigarettes and acquired the addiction it has taken me sixteen years to overcome. Anthony provided the smokes but I was the one who brought the chewing gum.

Our friendship, though intense, was not consistent. Alone with him I enjoyed Anthony's attention, but I dwindled in significance as soon as others were present. In the hothouse of the Eversley I glimpsed a different Anthony from the college gadabout. He seemed less at ease; he put on airs of self-assurance, like others with a reputation to uphold, and flirted brazenly with the prefects. I felt a dark pulse of jealousy whenever I witnessed his fawning and failed to recognise the suspicion with which most prefects received it. There was mockery in his smile that no amount of words could conceal. That air of confidence which meant, in the wider world of the school, that few boys liked him yet none dared call his bluff had already made him enemies in the intimacy of his dormitory.

So the last term of my first year came to a close and I discovered England's garden in summer: not the tired Downs of September but the new greens of June, when you can actually hear the leaves of sweet chestnuts crackling with sap. With my friends in house (Robbie Thwaite, who knew his birds, and amiable Toplady) and most especially with Anthony, I strolled about the sunny grounds and lazed under trees reading Tolkien and Terry Pratchett. Between the demands of lessons and meals, the playing fields and evening prep, Anthony and I would sneak off to our bomb shelter with our cigarettes and erotic prose. 'Shelter' is the apposite word: it was what I sought in him. Anthony would have aestheticised our friendship as a meeting of minds but I recognised it for what it was: a lifeline. I would listen to his stories from home: about his mum, who 'lunched', about his dad, who sent criminals down like some bewigged wrestler. I chose to believe in his glamorous family, in the old-fashioned assurance of its eccentricity. Anthony, in return, got the audience he craved. He made the effort to listen to my own stories (such as they were) and envied my boating forays into the Borneo jungle when I was eleven. Gradually I came to feel secure enough to manifest my enthusiasms. I lent him my fantasy novels and convinced him to play chess with me until it became clear that I would always win. It didn't matter that his enthusiasm for the game cooled each time I opened the magnetic travel set. In Anthony's eyes I had particular skills; I had seen places few other boys had seen. I was his secret sharer and his follower, with a place and purpose in our little world.

He made me see why I so hated life at Kingsley. At home, beneath the Malaysian sun, I had been confident of my legitimacy. The glances of my parents, of their staff and friends, reflected a warm light of approval. But at Kingsley I was transformed into an outcast: a thing of darkness, skulking and afraid, to be cuffed by boys who had never seen me *as I knew myself to be*, and held up for mockery as an example of weakness. I couldn't recognise the Bruno Jackson that others pretended to see. For months I had tried to get back to myself, hoping that some action or word might redeem me. But there was nothing I could do. The identity created for me by my enemies was the very proof of their power. No wonder I clung to Anthony Blunden when he looked beneath the cowl of my shame and addressed me as an equal. The reflection from his gaze, though infinitely weaker than the affection of my parents, gave me light enough to feel human again. My spirit clambered from darkness through the gap offered, no matter how small, by his friendship.

Now

I woke up laughing. It was a chuckle at first that bubbled into a laugh of bitter recognition. People in the office must have heard it.

I had ducked behind my hands only for a minute to escape the interrogation of the computer screen, but tiredness had tugged me under and my brain, hyperactive when the rest of me slumbered, filled with recollections of Anthony. I hate hanging up on people, turning away from arguments and leaving the tendons of anger exposed; at the same time I fly from what's awkward. I had been wrong to speak so rudely to him. The fault was all mine. Then I recognised the antiquity of these feelings: how effortlessly he used to make me feel guilty in his company. I got up to make myself another cup of coffee.

Maggie Goss was already at the machine, stirring white stuff into her dubious brew. 'As long as it's got caffeine in it,' she said, 'who cares what it tastes like? Have you seen the memo?'

'What memo?'

'There's going to be a demonstration against road widening in Cornwall.'

'The usual handful, I suppose?'

'I'm going to buy my lunch early just in case they get their act together.'

'They never get their act together.'

Maggie watched me taste the scalding coffee. 'I don't know how you can drink that neat.'

'Mind you,' I said, 'it's going to make a mess of Bodmin Moor.'

'If people will insist on driving.' We started on our separate ways but Maggie tacked back. 'What were you laughing about earlier?'

'I wasn't.'

'I heard a little bark.'

'I was coughing.'

'You could always share the joke.'

'I'd rather not. It was on me.'

In the end Maggie need not have troubled herself. There was half an hour of drum-thumping outside, a brief ululation of protest amplified through loudspeakers, then nothing but the usual rumble of traffic. I sat at my desk thinking about another demonstration, far from the centre of London, in which I had taken part years ago. This in turn brought Anthony to mind. A worm of curiosity had hatched inside me. It was always possible to call (I had written down his number from my phone) and this thought tormented me. I shut down as early as possible, gave my friend Jenny a call, and went to meet her at her bookshop.

Jenny looked tired and dishevelled. She had a load of stock-taking to do before she could leave. 'The old sod works you too hard,' I whispered, peering over Arts and Crafts at her employer. He was a taciturn, sad-eyed Scot with wiry grey hair and bifocals. Jenny had slept with him a couple of times to get herself out of his system. Now he depended on her for the shop's survival. 'Can't it wait till tomorrow?'

'No it can't. Bruno, *please*.'

I browsed for a time in the basement among dusty sci-fi and rotting Penguins, then went outside for a breath of air and strolled down Charing Cross Road to St Martin-in-the-Fields. A sexy black guy was chatting up some tourist on the steps, bringing his face close to hers as he pointed in her *A–Z*. The girl, who looked Spanish or possibly Greek, blushed from the roots of her hair all the way down to her throat.

I headed north up St Martin's Lane and stood outside the doors of the Coliseum, measuring my frustration. I was unhappy at work; the blowsy end of summer left me irritable; I longed for a degrading fuck. I wandered gloomily back to the bookshop and considered engaging its owner in a conversation about adultery, just to see the look on his face. I hated myself in this mood and decided that the demonstration was to blame: not because it had taken place but because so few people had attended.

'Is Jenny around?' I asked the Scot when I got back. Before lifting his head he folded a strip of lace on the page of the book he was reading.

'Downstairs,' he said.

'It's sunny outside.'

'Is it?'

'It's warm.'

'Glad to hear it.'

I made the stairs rumble as I went down to the basement. No wonder Jenny loves the sun: she gets none of it where she works. 'Nearly done,' she said, 'then I need a bloody drink.'

We strode arm in arm out of the bookshop.

'Does your boss think I'm your boyfriend by any chance?'

'Don't be silly.'

'It's not such a grotesque idea.'

The wine bar was packed and we perched – precariously in my case – on metal stools by the zinc, sipping our daiquiris. Jenny didn't want to talk about herself. How was my dad? she wondered. 'Cheering up,' I said with a noticeable lack of enthusiasm. 'I mean, last time I saw him I got this feeling . . . He just seems brighter.'

'That's good, isn't it? You're always complaining about him being a grumpy old so-and-so.'

'I know. I should be happy but I don't . . . I don't trust it somehow.'

'Do you think there's someone . . .?'

'No.'

'Are you sure?'

'He'd tell me.'

'Maybe he just hasn't got round to it.'

'He'd *tell* me, Jenny.'

She changed the subject. From politics we ambled to poetry, Jenny's latest readings in various North London pubs having been attended by small but devoted audiences. 'There's this new Irish guy, I think he's fabulous. Really good poet. Dead sexy.'

'I think you ought to go out with a GP.'

'What for?'

'OK, a lawyer, but for God's sake not another poet. They're ruthless, Jenny. They only want you for their verses.'

'As long as it's consenting.'

I did not buy her lascivious grin. Or was it that I hate to think of those I love having impulses I would gladly live without? 'Love between poets,' I said, 'is like cannibalism.'

Jenny tilted back her head for the last drop. 'Why, do you know any lawyers?'

'Dozens.'

'But you think they're all wankers.'

'Yup.'

Over dinner at Carluccio's, Jenny did not enquire into my romantic life, though ordinarily we love half drunkenly to whisper our secret desires. She ordered her usual cappuccino and picked with her spoon at my dessert. As I tried unsuccessfully to fend her off with my fork, Jenny threw me with a question.

'What's happened about that bloke from your past?'

I relinquished a sizeable scoop of cheesecake. 'Which bloke?'

'You know: that bad influence from your school days. Alasdair?'

'Anthony.'

'Any developments?'

'None.'

'He hasn't called you, then?'

'There'd have been nothing to say if he had.'

As we left, Jenny leaning against me in the warm air, I felt her hand fasten about my wrist. 'Sorry if I upset you. I didn't mean to.'

'I don't know what you're talking about.'

'Neither do I,' she said. 'Come on, walk me to my bus.'

I paid no attention to the time when I got home but stood under the hall light in a gross sweat, staring at the telephone number I had scribbled on my notepad. Was I really going to call? It would be madness: better to erase the number, better to throw the notepad into the bin or set fire to it. But then what had I to lose? The damage to my equilibrium had already been done. Can a wound reopened heal again? I felt the itch – like that beneath a scab – of an old obsession. To make sense of Anthony now might be to make sense of him thirteen years ago; and also of what happened in the Lakes. I glimpsed my fierce expression in the full-length mirror, picked up the telephone and watched my finger dance between the keys.

I took a deep breath as the network digested the numbers. A telephone buzzed in an unknown room on the other side of London. There was a beep and then Anthony's voice informing me that he was out of the office at the moment, could I leave a message? 'Alternatively you can try my mobile . . .' I wrote the number down feverishly, ran to the sink and drank like a goat from the tap. Gasping, with drops of water on my shirt, I returned to the telephone and dialled.

It was Dipali Blunden who answered. Her voice was thick with sleep, so that I lost my stride and mumbled like some graceless teenager: 'Is Anthony there?'

'Who's this?'

'Uh, we met at Fay Corcoran's party.'

'Hello?'

I glanced at my watch and realised that it was past midnight. 'Look, I know it's late . . .' There was silence on the line. Probably it was taken up by a yawn but in my drunkenness it sounded hostile and I decided to brazen it out. 'Can I speak to Anthony, please?'

'Is this work? Can't it wait until tomorrow?' I heard the distress of bedclothes and someone whispering away from the phone. Dipali failed or wilfully omitted to cover the mouthpiece with her hand: 'Why can't you turn the fucking thing off like I ask?'

There followed sounds of fumbling as the mobile changed hands.

'Hello?'

It was Anthony's voice. I bit the air and then dissolved into contrition. 'God, I'm so sorry. I had no idea of the time, will you apologise to your wife for me?'

'Is this Bruno?' There was more assertion than interrogation in his voice. I imagined him sitting up in bed with Dipali irritably cocooned beside him. 'Is everything all right? What's the matter?'

'Nothing. Look, I should let you sleep.'

'Hang on, I'm going to the bathroom . . .' The resonance altered and I could hear the rasp of an extractor fan. 'It's the middle of the night, Bruno. Don't you spin doctors ever sleep?'

'I was out and I lost track of time. I'm *so* sorry for waking you.'

'Not at all,' he replied amiably, 'though you had me worried for a minute.'

'I think we should meet.'

He was silent.

'Hello?'

'Yeah. *Sure.*' I looked down and saw that my left knee was trembling. 'Are you still there?'

'Sorry,' I said, 'yes.'

'Bruno, that would be great. I mean, it's what I was hoping you'd say last time I called, only you were so emphatic. Now listen, you must come over. Dipali's an excellent cook, if you don't mind me as a sort of sous-chef.'

'Maybe you could text me a time and the name of the street?' Intrepidly, I gave him my mobile number.

'How about Thursday?'

'OK,' I said with a wince.

'Oh no, hang on, I can't do Thursday. Dipali's got her yoga.'

'Look, if it's a problem . . .'

'Friday. I'm sure we're not doing anything. You're not vegetarian or anything, are you?'

'Ah, no.'

'Come here, then, and we'll cook for you.'

'All right,' I said.

'Good, Bruno. Friday it is.'

Then

Our French teacher was new to Kingsley and, by the sound of it, to English public school. She was Welsh, from the Valleys: a shrill, hipless, flat-chested woman with blushing ears that protruded from lank brown hair. From the instant she entered our classroom the boys had singled her out for special attention. 'Madame, madame,' they would chorus sarcastically.

'Made*moiselle*,' Miss Hartnoll corrected. 'What are you doing at the window?'

'Bishop saw a wild boar, madame.'

'Never mind that now: go and sit down.'

'How do you say "wild boar" in French, madame?'

'*Sanglier.*'

'How do you spell it?'

'Bishop, will you please *sit down*?'

'I've got piles, madame. It really hurts.'

In retreat Miss Hartnoll attempted to begin the lesson. 'Everybody open your textbooks at Chapter Three . . .'

'I don't think you're taking this seriously, madame. They've got really vicious teeth. They could kill a First Setter easily.'

'Bishop, if you don't sit down this minute I will send you out of the classroom.'

'Miss Hartnoll, can *I* be sent out of the classroom? I'm bursting for the loo.'

And so it went on: the ingenious tormenting of Miss Hartnoll. There were few women teachers among the staff at Kingsley, and most of them were married to masters. Miss Hartnoll had no such protection. The bullies in the class gauged her weakness and set about exploiting it. They slipped pornographic pictures into her copy of *Candide* and rubbed her writing off the whiteboard when she 'popped out' to fetch a book. Returning to find the affront, Miss Hartnoll would have no alternative but to ignore it, knowing as we did that she was incapable of effecting punishment.

'Miss Hartnoll?'

'Yes, Duncan.'

'What is "unless" again?'

'*A moins que.*' A dozen requests followed for her to repeat it. 'Look, it's not difficult. *A moins que, a moins que.*'

The class was close to eruption.

'Am a wanker,' said Duncan.

'That's right,' said Miss Hartnoll. The class erupted. 'Though you might try saying it with more of a French accent.'

Innocence could not save Miss Hartnoll. Having been accustomed in our first year to cowering, it was now too great a temptation to pass up the chance to bully a teacher.

'Settle down, settle down, *please* . . .' I came to hate the sound of that high-pitched, despairing voice. As the weeks passed, its owner lost weight before our eyes. The more she pleaded for cooperation, the bolder her antagonists became. There was the usual combination of insolence, open chatter and ostentatious sleeping. Nick Bishop went farther, asking Miss Hartnoll to translate gynaecological terms that he pretended to have stumbled across in some extracurricular reading. 'I'm not going to answer that,' she replied with a shiver.

Sometimes, when the light caught her from the window, it was possible to make out a faint cirrus of down furring her cheeks. Other boys noticed and Duncan Fine went so far as to ask her the French for 'bearded lady'. That it could be a symptom of starvation occurred to none of us.

'Static shocks,' Duncan announced one morning after break when Miss Hartnoll was still in the staffroom. 'Look . . .' He rubbed his feet on the blue nylon carpet, raised a finger and connected the tip of it to his neighbour's neck. The other boy jerked and let out a yelp of pain.

'You try,' said Duncan, and to his credit, I suppose, he submitted to the same treatment.

When Miss Hartnoll arrived, burdened beneath a pile of exercise books, she was greeted by ominous quiet. Everyone sat up in expectation. Miss Hartnoll looked at us askance and then began to hand back our homework. '*Ow*,' she shrilled as Nick Bishop reached out and touched her knuckles.

'Sorry, madame,' said Nick, retracting his finger.

Miss Hartnoll wavered and moved on. I heard the furtive scuffle of boys charging up. When two more shocks had been delivered, a silent mirthless frenzy began.

'Stop it,' cried Miss Hartnoll, snatching back her hand. Twelve pairs of eyes fixed her with intent. The only sound was of shoes rubbing against the carpet. 'Stop it *now*! That hurts!' But her orders went unheeded and, before she reached me with the exercise books, Miss Hartnoll dropped the lot and rushed out of the classroom.

Triumph gave way to apprehension as we waited to see what would happen. Surely the Head of Languages would be summoned or, worse, the Deputy Master; but fifteen or twenty minutes passed unsupervised and, when lesson time was up, we simply left the building.

The next day we were spared French but on Friday it was Monsieur Geissmann who awaited us in Miss Hartnoll's place. He was cunning and sardonic: a heavyweight. 'Up here, Fine,' he said to a cowering Duncan, 'where I can see you.'

Monsieur Geissmann did not have to raise his voice: we sat obediently listening to him (I for one had trouble concentrating), and when someone asked about Miss Hartnoll, he gave little away. 'She's off sick for the time being.'

As Michaelmas Term dragged on, Miss Hartnoll's absence continued and rumours began to spread that she had been hospitalised after taking an overdose of sleeping pills. Others claimed that she had drowned herself, or cut her wrists, while a charitable few liked to believe that she had run off with a lover. Whatever the truth, Monsieur Geissmann would never be drawn on Miss Hartnoll's fate.

When I told Anthony what had happened, he insisted that I had no reason to feel guilty. Inaction was not the same as action, he implied, and I chose to believe him because it was easier that way. From the way he spoke it was obvious that my friend had spent his holidays reading, for his vocabulary was full of archaisms. The boys who persecuted Miss Hartnoll were 'beasts', their manners 'simply ghastly'. His parents, he said, had spent the whole of their Cretan holidays 'in a frightful tiff' and he was 'quite sure they'll divorce if they know what's good for them'. He liked to speak in this antiquated fashion and I, though with limited success, tried to copy him. The perception it gave us of a shared superiority reinforced our friendship. We were already thinking in terms of 'them' and 'us'.

Seeing Anthony again at the start of term had been the high point of my return. He offered me some chocolate biscuits. He showed me a Roman coin his father had bought him, and wondered at my lack of a tan as a way of drawing attention to his own.

'We hung out on the beach,' he said. 'There were these gorgeous girls, I mean they were old, they must have been at least twenty. One of them stayed in the room next to mine. I could hear her moving about at night. She really fancied me.'

We left the Eversley and walked through late summer heat towards the tuck shop. I was excited to tell him what I had done, and attempted to describe a trip to the rainforests of Taman Negara National Park. Anthony was more interested in talking about his own holiday.

'It was baking,' he said. 'All the skin on my back flaked off, it was absolutely gross . . .'

'There were these insects,' I countered, 'with long what looked like trunks and these red spots on the end, like a clown's nose. And the noise the jungle made after dark . . .'

'It sounds absolutely frightful.'

I laughed at his affected language and he looked at me with what I interpreted as mock affront.

For our GCSEs the forms had been altered to reflect our abilities, and I was delighted to find myself with Anthony in two more subjects. One of our new teachers was Mr Plater, a strict and cantankerous Latinist who still used the wet V of the old school: 'Ah-way atque wah-lay', and 'Wainy weeny weechy'. Anthony sat next to me and attempted, with subtle grunts and groans, to make me snigger.

'Stop it – stop it,' I whispered, grinning.

'Anything you wish to share with the class, Jackson?'

This was Mr Wimbush, our jingoistic history master.

'No, sir.'

'Perhaps you'd care to remind us what we were talking about.'

'The Maginot line, sir.'

'What?'

'The Maginot line, sir, to stop the Germans advancing into France.'

Mr Wimbush looked at me with slow, decided malice. 'All that proves, Jackson, is that like most devious worms you can listen and chatter at the same time.'

'Yes, sir.'

Mr Wimbush was not a happy man. He was unmarried; had opted out of or was deemed unfit for housemastering duties; and his greatest achievement (at least the most obvious) appeared to be his russet, sergeant major's moustache. Mr Wimbush smelled musty, like the home of an elderly dog lover, and his breath when he leaned over us was excremental. Perhaps his one quality, as far as boys were concerned, was the ease with which he could be diverted from his lesson. Anthony knew this better than most and it was perhaps to take the heat off me that he asked Mr Wimbush his opinions of the looming war.

'Tricky one, Blunden, very tricky. The British know a thing or two about desert warfare – and we practically invented the states in the Gulf. In fact it was Winston Churchill who first authorised the gassing of Iraqi Arabs. A fractious bunch they were then, too. Regrettably, God, in His inscrutable wisdom, put all that oil beneath their feet.'

'Is Saddam Hussein as bad as Hitler, sir?'

'In numbers of dead, Mr Coulter, not in the slightest. Hitler was a singularly nasty phenomenon. But the measure of tyranny depends on where you stand when the bomb falls . . . or the boot.'

'Do you think we'll *boot* him out, sir?' This engendered a ripple of insincere laughter.

'We are dealing with the invasion and brutal occupation of a sovereign kingdom. We, do not forget, also inhabit a kingdom and such things cannot be allowed to stand. Even as we speak, a vast international army is gathering to see that right prevails. It won't be pleasant but it shouldn't be too difficult either. Arab nations are very poor fighters. Just look at what Israel has achieved against them.'

We decided quite early, Anthony and me, that we didn't like Mr Wimbush, while Mr Plater bored us as much as his subject. We were slower, however, in making up our minds about our new English teacher, who had just arrived at Kingsley from some inner city comprehensive.

Mr Bridge was young, from a wholly different era to his predecessor, and this gave him novelty value.

'The works we're going to be studying,' he said in our first lesson, 'are in my opinion wonderful. And I'm not just saying that as a teacher, I'm saying it as a *reader*.' Our set had not changed since Mr Hegarty had taught us, so Mr Bridge inherited an established collection of pouts and slouches. By his nonchalant demeanour he left us in no doubt that he had seen worse. 'Reading a story is like getting to live an extra life. It means freedom to move in space and time. And yet look . . . it's just an object, pretty flat, a bit of paper in a binding. Do you think this book's precious?'

'Me, sir?'

'Why not you? Is it precious, this book?'

'Uh – yes, sir.'

'Really? It's just a book. Good fuel, I suppose, if you're freezing and have nothing else to burn. But precious, like a human life, or the planet we live on? No – you see, what matters are the *words* the book contains. And the words are only important insofar as they enter your head and change things there. Now I'll make a bet with you. If you give these novels and plays and poems *space in your minds*, I guarantee that our lessons will not even feel like work.' I, too, caught the sneer on a couple of faces. Mr Bridge took off his jacket and fitted it about the shoulders of his chair. 'On the other hand,' he said, 'if you just want to piss about, that's entirely up to you. But it would be your loss.'

Mr Bridge did not square up to us as Mr Wimbush might have done, nor curry favour by selecting victims against whom everyone might unite. He never harangued us or attempted to bore us into submission. When his blood was up he spoke in metaphor and some boys never got used to it.

'*You* are the ones who make literature,' he once said. 'Just add the spark of your imagination to the dry powder of the words.'

Doubtless he seemed ridiculous to some, and even I thought him theatrical. He used to roll up his sleeves, like a mechanic about to delve into the parts of an engine, and set his watch on the table before beginning a lesson. It was like a ritual: the divestment of mundane affairs before snapping the spine of whatever edition he was using and plunging into its innards. Mr Bridge was not a snob like Mr Hegarty. He never interrupted a clumsy reader or tried to improve his style. He let our yawping, public school vowels ride roughshod over *Beowulf* and the poems of Ted Hughes, contributing only to clarify an image or explain the meaning of a difficult word. I liked him and the way he did things. Anthony pretended to be more sceptical, calling him 'a trendy lefty'; but he gave himself away in lessons, punching the air with a volunteering arm and showing off his precocious reading.

It was typical of Anthony not to credit those who inspired him. Getting on at school meant, for most boys, attempting to fuse with the powerful, but Anthony was unusual. He wanted to seem extraordinary. His affectations of speech and precocious general knowledge gave him an air of superiority that infuriated those he secretly craved to impress. Just occasionally he would be caught out – and his humiliation only strengthened my desire to be his friend.

One lunchtime, for instance, when overcrowding had stranded several boys at our table, Anthony began to boast of his sexual achievements: 'I touched this girl's tits at a party. She took off her top and we must have snogged for about an hour.'

'What was her name?' This was a boy called Julian, one of the sporting crowd. He looked indecently cheerful.

'Alice,' said Anthony without hesitation.

'I don't remember a girl called Alice. We're talking about Sophie Wynne's party, right?'

Anthony's smile lost some of its lustre but he bluffed it out. 'It was in one of the bedrooms.'

'I remember seeing you in the garden. You were completely pissed. You crashed out under one of the apple trees.'

'I don't think so.'

'Yes: people had to drag you out of the grass. They turned the hosepipe on you.'

'That wasn't me.'

'And there never was a girl at the party called Alice.'

Most of the boys at the table embraced Julian's version. Anthony tried to dismiss it as the ravings of jealousy ('you'd have to *bribe* someone for the experience') but everyone could tell that he was rattled.

Two days later, Julian Morley was rushed to the sanatorium after being stamped on during a rugby match. The Eversley had been the opposing team. 'It was a nasty ruck,' Anthony said of a vicious game. 'Nobody could tell where he was putting his feet . . .'

I was walking back to the Hereward from buying sweets in the tuck shop. Wasps, most poisonous in their dotage, were doddering about the bins behind the cricket pavilion, and I noticed that someone, wary of getting stung, had dropped a copy of the *Maidstone Downs Mail* on the grass instead of ramming it home. I read the headline –

ROAD PLAN APPROVED
Opponents vow to fight on

– and might have read more but there was dog shit near the paper; so I left it to the groundsmen. The headline slipped from my mind. There were more serious matters brewing.

War was looming in the Gulf, to our general excitement. We did not watch much television – and then the majority appetite prevailed – but Mr Sedley considered that History was happening and we had a duty to witness it. There can rarely have been such audiences for current affairs: even the new boys lined the back wall of the crowded TV room to watch reports of build-ups and bad Scuds and good missiles that would pluck them from the air. There was much eager parroting of talk about ultimatums and high-tech victories, and like a pantomime audience we relished our indignation at the footage of Western hostages. There was a senior pupil at Kingsley (I had never heard of him) who, being Iraqi, was anxious that his father – a hospital consultant – would be interned in the event of a conflict. A disagreement broke out about the justice of such a policy and its supporters, led by the disputatious Proctor, were soundly defeated.

'*You* live somewhere out there, don't you, Jackson?' Proctor was glaring at me.

'I bloody don't,' I said.

'Don't be rude, you gay twat.'

'Leave it, Andy.'

'You've got a fucking attitude problem, Jackson. I only asked you a question.'

'We live in Malaysia.'

'Well, they're all Muslims, aren't they?'

'What's that got to do with it?'

'Don't answer back.'

Proctor shrugged off the tempering hand of his friend and turned to face the television. I sat there, feeling sick, until the adverts came on and I could leave the room without it seeming like an escape.

'It's not about Muslims, is it?'

I was sitting with Anthony in our cold bomb shelter, reading tatty thrillers. I wanted reassurance. Ever since Proctor had uttered those words, a neurotic fear had gripped me that all those I cared about were at risk. I was frightened by what was happening, when everyone around me seemed to find it thrilling and far enough away to be viewed as entertainment. Could a missile cross the Indian Ocean and slam into my parents' house? Would there be riots against Westerners in Kuala Lumpur? I wanted to voice these fears (even though I knew they were foolish), but Anthony viewed the prospect of war with flippant levity.

'I've got a family connection with all this,' he said.

'What do you mean?'

'My Uncle Thomas was involved with the super-gun affair. You remember.'

'Not really.'

'There was this gun they were going to build in Iraq and all sorts of British companies were involved.'

'Your uncle worked for Saddam Hussein?'

'He was never convicted, of course, but there were some sticky moments. Other people were jailed, you know.'

I had visions of a cannon as tall as a building, of tropical gardens exploding in flames. 'Do you think . . . ?'

'What?'

'Do you think my parents are safe?'

'Your parents?'

'Or us here? Isn't he supposed to have chemical weapons?'

Anthony regarded me with an unmistakable air of derision. 'I expect,' he said, 'he'll murder us with a suitcase full of anthrax.' He laughed – a cackle I did not enjoy – at the sight of my anxiety. 'For God's sake, I'm only pulling your leg.' But for the rest of the afternoon he tormented me with prospects of death and destruction.

As deadlines loomed at the UN, I found I was not alone in having reservations about the war. One morning, late in November, Mr Bridge was in such high spirits that he challenged us to write a comic poem continuing two lines by Hilaire Belloc. Someone asked him why he was so cheerful. 'Because,' he replied, rocking on his chair, 'after nearly eleven years, we're free of Maggie Thatcher.'

'Is she dead, sir?'

'No, she isn't dead. She's been deposed, like a mad monarch. Honestly, you boys do live in a bubble.'

To most of the class these words sounded suspect. 'Isn't that a bad thing, sir, what with the war?'

'We're not at war yet, McGrath.'

'But it's inevitable, sir.'

'Who told you that? Who says war is inevitable?'

'Everyone, sir.'

'On the contrary, it's the one thing we should be trying to avoid. Going to war is like using a flamethrower: you never know what's going to catch light. Besides, we were quite happy to be selling weapons to Saddam when he was useful to us.'

'But he's a tyrant, sir.'

'So are half the leaders waiting to liberate Kuwait.'

I remember clearly the sense of disappointment at Mr Bridge's views. He must have sensed it, for he rubbed his hands together and urged us to get on with our poems. After the lesson, as we dispersed to other classrooms, I heard Ollie Radmore whisper 'Queer', as though that settled everything.

I skipped into step with Anthony. 'Do you think Mr Bridge is a pacifist?'

'What difference does that make?'

'I didn't really understand what he was saying.'

'You never do.'

For the next couple of days, Anthony was short with me. The more he brushed me off, impatiently glancing over my shoulder as if expecting better company, the more abjectly I pursued him. In a history lesson I asked him what I had done to offend him. 'I'm going to sit next to Webster,' was his reply, and I watched as he gathered up his books and notebooks.

'Have I done something wrong?' I asked him afterwards.

'For Christ's sake, I'm not your *brother*.'

I had no idea what I had done to provoke his coldness. The few, tepid friendships I had at Hereward House could not console me for the loss of Anthony. Like a beaten dog, I went looking for him at the Eversley, waiting on the steps until someone informed me that he had gone out or was otherwise engaged. 'Are you waiting for your boyfriend?' said a sinister lout clattering down the steps in his rugby boots.

The next day, in English, Anthony was sitting next to Ollie Radmore. 'Oi,' said Ollie, and I realised he was addressing me. 'Blunden's coined a new name for you. *Brown nose*. Instead of Bruno. For being rammed so far up Bridge's arse.'

I looked with undisguised pain at my friend. Mr Bridge swept in, ready to work, and for the rest of the double lesson Anthony avoided my gaze. The next day, however, he came to Hereward House as if nothing had happened. I gave him some of my biscuits and a can of Coke and he sat on Robbie Thwaite's bed.

'Mr Bridge caught me in the English library,' he said.

'What were you doing?'

'Nothing. Looking at books.'

Among the dusty shelves, long neglected by pupils, that lined the walls of the English department foyer were titles that promised superior wanks. Careful investigation had made Anthony perhaps the first boy in a generation to sign out Henry Miller's *Tropic of Cancer* and the faded Penguins of D. H. Lawrence. These we swapped and skimmed: a dirty secret made guiltless by sharing.

'Do you think he sussed you?'

'I don't think so. He called me an endangered species and took me around the shelves pointing out things I'd never heard of, James Joyce and this weird book about a boy living after a nuclear war.' From his sports bag Anthony extracted *A Portrait of the Artist as a Young Man* and *Riddley Walker* by Russell Hoban.

'Are they,' I asked, excited without knowing why, 'the sort of things we're looking for?'

'I can barely understand them,' said Anthony, but despite this we spent ten avid minutes reading. The strangeness and difficulty of the novels intrigued me; I liked the childish music of the beginning of *Portrait*. The other novel seemed more forbidding. Only when I tried reading a paragraph aloud did it start to make sense: a garbled and degraded English embodying the world's ruin. Anthony took the book from me. 'He wants to know what we make of them.'

'*We?* Did you tell him about me?'

'Obviously no one else is bright enough to try.'

'Are they going to be on the syllabus?'

'He says we should read them because we don't have to.'

We shared the books; then Anthony went back for more. Mr Bridge put us on to Mervyn Peake (I would spend a hot Malaysian Christmas lost in the ceremonious labyrinths of Gormenghast) and, sensing Anthony's affinity for Waugh, raised him from *Decline and Fall* to *Scoop* and *A Handful of Dust*. This last seemed to both of us very grown up, and we pictured ourselves as sophisticated readers. For Anthony, each novel provided ammunition; for me, an escape. As for the master who opened those doors, outside of lessons he had little hold on my imagination until a chance encounter on my way to games.

It was almost the end of term: a cold day with the ground hard underfoot as I walked forlornly to rugby. Approaching the dreaded fields, I found myself catching up with Mr Bridge. Or was it the other way round, with him slowing and making a subtle arc to fall into step with me? We exchanged a polite and friendly nod. Then Mr Bridge said:

'You must feel quite at home by now.'

'Yes, sir.'

'You don't have to say that for my benefit. I imagine it can't be easy, travelling halfway round the world.' I must have looked at him strangely, for Mr Bridge nodded into a diffident smile. 'What do you make of this little patch of England?'

'It's very nice.'

'But nothing like the place where you grew up.' We walked under a windbreak of Scots pines. 'I'm not from these parts either . . .'

'Aren't you English, sir?'

'Oh, I'm English – whatever that means. But hills aren't in my blood. I'm from the Fens: flat country out east. I don't suppose you've been there. Well, I've not been to Malaysia. What's it like?'

'Tropical,' was all I could think of saying. Why was I so tongue tied? I wished Anthony were with me. At the same time, I was glad he wasn't.

'Are you happy here?' said Mr Bridge. No one at Kingsley had ever asked me such a simple question. We were close to the playing fields now and, with a customary sense of dread, I recognised the shouts of my housemates.

'I don't know,' said Mr Bridge, as though picking up on a comment. 'I'm beginning rather to like this place. The hills, the wooded valleys. The light's different, too. Where I grew up the sky's the thing but here . . .' He sucked his top lip for a moment. 'They're going to cut a deep scar into those downs there. Do you see where my finger's pointing? Some time next year. It will shave five whole minutes off the commute to Ashford. What do you think about that?'

'I think it's a shame, sir.'

'So do I. Still . . .' He took a deep, hearty breath, like some Victorian greedy for ozone. 'Thanks for the chat.'

I trotted a few yards towards my team and then looked back at Mr Bridge. Among flying balls and shouting boys, in a tracksuit so ill fitting it was evidently borrowed, he looked somehow out of place. He was tall, lean and pigeon chested. In his manners and voice he seemed almost elderly, yet his gait was entirely boyish.

Now

The address was in Mayfair. It was a far cry from my street in Vauxhall with its Portuguese grocers and overheated cafés smelling of fried sardines and tobacco. Instead of litter-strewn tarmac lined with clapped-out Peugeots, the pavements here were barricaded behind Range Rovers and four-by-fours. Through the windows of terraced houses I was invited to admire bookshelves and chandeliers and the ethnic art brought back from exotic holidays. Siamese and Burmese cats squinted at me from their window seats. A Saudi woman shrouded in black returned my gaze. In one house behind a row of palms, three children were receiving supper from a uniformed maid.

The Blundens' flat was on the ground floor of an impressive house at the far end of the street. White muslin curtains protected the living room from prying eyes. I rang the number and waited for the buzz of the electronic lock, but Anthony himself opened the door. Despite the balmy weather, he had on a V-necked sweater and a pair of beige chinos. On his bare feet he wore comfortably battered loafers. 'Hey, thanks for coming,' he said, and wafted me inside. I caught the musky odour of his after-shave. Inside the lobby there was a plush red carpet running up the stairs and a delicious smell of curry from the Blundens' flat. Anthony showed me into their hallway. 'Dipali's just putting the finishing touches to her hair. Can I get you a drink? Martini, gin and tonic? We quite like Kir Royal . . .'

'Whatever you're having.'

'I'm having whatever you're having.' This put me in something of a quandary. What I really wanted was some water: I was painfully thirsty.

'Do you have any fruit juice?' I asked.

'Oh God, you haven't turned Baptist, have you? Or is it Lent or something?'

'Hardly, in August.'

'Well, I'm not much of a God-botherer. *Of course* we've got fruit juice. Just let me pop to the kitchen.' He left the living room where we were standing and called to me from, I presumed, the open mouth of a fridge. 'We've got apple and cranberry, orange juice, sanguinello, some virtuous-looking smoothie . . .'

'Orange is fine,' I said, then added: 'Thanks.'

While Anthony fixed the drinks, I patted my face and dabbed my armpits with a tissue. The living room was sparely furnished, with a sofa and two chairs and a coffee table covered with magazines and books. There was an Indian throw pinned to a wall as well as two Bengali miniatures, one depicting a panther resting by a lily pond, the other courtly beauties disporting themselves in a Mughal garden. There was a fireplace with cobalt-blue tiles and a flourishing yucca in the grate. Above the mantelpiece, a group photograph from an Oxford college had Anthony seated in the front row. He came back in time to see me peering at it. 'My alma mater,' he said. 'Dipali was at Jesus but we never met. Where did you. . . ?'

'Manchester.'

'I suppose it was Fine Arts?'

'Economics.'

'Oh yes, I remember you saying. I'd have imagined you doing something artistic.' He handed me a tall glass of orange concentrate and our fingers touched for an instant. He sat opposite me on the sofa, spreading his legs as if to accommodate swollen balls, and downed most of his gin and tonic in one go. I felt a certain satisfaction to see him nervous. I, on the other hand, felt queasily calm. It was like entering the eye of a storm: at the heart of what shakes you, the vibration ceases.

'Please, sit down,' said Anthony. He looked over his shoulder as if hoping for relief. 'My wife'll be here any minute.'

'She's very nice.'

'Dipali?'

'What does she do?'

'Search me. I mean, obviously, she's a systems analyst, but what that involves exactly . . . I know a thing or two about my own job but that's about as much as I can manage.'

'You work for . . . ?' He gave me the name of a famous legal firm. Until this morning, he said, he had been working with his team to see through a hostile takeover bid.

'Bloody venture capitalists. They're only happy going to bed when there are dozens of other people working for them who have no chance of seeing their own.'

'I don't know how you stand it,' I said blandly, moving to one of the chairs.

'Well, if I stick at it long enough at some point they're bound to make me a partner.'

'And then I'll *never* see you.' Dipali Blunden came into the room wearing a silvery gleaming top and a white silk skirt not unlike a ballerina's tutu which she somehow managed to carry off with style. I shook her hand to disguise the shyness sweeping through me: for there was something knowing about her, something mindful and appraising. 'You're the man who never sleeps,' she said, but there was a smile in her voice that drained all poison from the comment. 'Anthony's told me a lot about you.'

'All of it slanderous,' said Anthony, jumping up from the sofa and enveloping his wife in his arms. 'She knows all about our illicit reading sessions.'

'Oh,' I said.

'Yes, and about Proctor and the cling film. Well, he deserved it, darling.' Dipali gave her husband's wrist a sharp squeeze. 'Uh, Bruno,' he said, changing tack, 'would you like a tour of the flat? That would be good, wouldn't it?'

'The meal will be ready in five minutes,' said Dipali, and as she unwrapped herself from her husband she gave his hip a gentle caress.

Anthony seemed a little less nervous now that reintroductions had been made, and with his familiar assurance he showed me the corridor and the bedroom with its Tibetan throws and the spare room that Dipali used as her home office. I reached out to him as he started to head for the kitchen. He stopped and looked down at his sleeve as if a butterfly had just landed there.

'I don't want to be awkward,' I said, 'but does she know about Mr Bridge?'

'Oh well, of course.'

'She *knows*?'

'About what happened to him? Everybody knows that.'

'But have you told her—?'

'God, Bruno,' he said, brushing past me towards the kitchen door, 'we're not going to talk about that this evening? We haven't seen each other in years.'

'Wait, can't you!'

'This shirt creases.' I let go. 'Look . . .' He ran a hand through his hair. 'It was all so long ago. We're hardly the same people. Besides, do you really remember what happened? I mean *really*?'

Dipali called us from the kitchen. Anthony watched me in silence; then he cracked a smile and, rubbing his hands with culinary glee, opened the door, releasing a jinn of curried steam.

*   *   *

We sat for dinner in the chrome-and-oak elegance of their kitchen, overlooking a communal garden of cherry trees and rowan, and all our talk was scrupulously banal. Dipali and Anthony chatted politics (she was Lib Dem, he was a Cameronite Tory) in a comfortable way, as if discussing plot twists in a soap opera. I chipped in with meagre accounts of ministerial briefings, offering insider knowledge of the Secretary of State's coffee breath and the Deputy Prime Minister's surprising competence in matters of policy. When I began actually to discuss these policies my hosts lost interest, but I blathered on regardless, propelled by a want of other things to say.

Dipali seemed to me very beautiful. Not conventionally (in a few years' time she will be fat like me) but in her manner of speaking and the way her brown fingers folded together, which suggested a frank and sensual nature. She wore too much make-up, perhaps, and this had something to do with a bruised scaliness beneath her eyes. When I spoke she made the effort to listen attentively; but I couldn't fail to notice the frequency with which she glanced at her husband. It was as if she was keeping watch, or following the movement of hands on a clock. Whenever Anthony spoke – interrupting my dreary monologue – she shifted, almost imperceptibly, her whole body in his favour. There was no irritation or anger in her expression: it was one of great tenderness. And yet it did not seem entirely at ease. It was as if, like me, she could not be certain of the words that would escape Anthony's lips.

'So tell us a little about you,' Dipali said when we had finished the curry and Anthony was clearing the table for dessert. 'Do you have a significant other?'

'No, not really.'

'Bruno's waiting for the right *girl*, aren't you, Bruno?'

I looked over my shoulder to where Anthony stood, scooping ice cream from a pot. Was he not afraid of what I might reveal?

Or had he long ago confessed to one who loved and accepted him? I measured in myself my own daring and knew that I could not expose him to his smiling wife. 'Things haven't worked out for me yet,' I said.

'But I'm sure they will. Tell Bruno it's worth the wait, darling.' Anthony had been using my name over and over all evening. He was not so much claiming the privilege of intimacy as asserting authority over me. I resented and resisted it. At the same time, part of me longed to be absorbed by the Blundens: not to feel so gross and clumsy in the ease and comfort of their lives.

'Anthony thinks every person has a counterpart,' said Dipali. 'He won't admit it – he doesn't want to puncture his hard-nosed image – but really he's a romantic. A romantic and a dreamer.'

I managed to grin. 'Every pot has its cover, right?'

Anthony placed a bowl of ice cream in front of me. 'Every bullet has its billet.'

The white wine I had brought was quickly finished and, despite my reluctance, Dipali insisted that we open another. All I could think about, as husband and wife bandied platitudes about celebrity culture and cheap airfares, was how easy life had been for my old friend. Oxford had followed public school; he had drifted by the sound of it into high finance and marriage to a woman who was calm, grounded and in love with his charms while alert to his excesses. Anthony laughed, his cheeks rosy with the wine, and I marvelled at how little he seemed to have changed. He spoke in the same rapid way and his mannerisms, like the steady slow blink of his handsome lashes, were exactly as I remembered them. Dipali rested her face on her hands as he talked about a golf party ('it was work, you understand, we weren't expected to *enjoy* it') at some exclusive resort in the Algarve, and I felt myself succumb to irritation that she should have married him. How could such a man move through the world, causing damage everywhere he went, yet still be so rewarded? Part of me wanted to understand what made their relationship work. Either candour and forgiveness flourished between them or else their love was built on a lie.

'We used to play golf at school,' I said. It was the first time I had mentioned Kingsley since we sat down to eat. Anthony's Algarve story ran out of steam and he reached for the salt cellar. 'Do you remember the golf course on the Downs? We had to share it with old boys and military men but we felt as though we owned it. Well, we were the ones who were paying the fees. Or our parents were.'

'You didn't play golf,' said Anthony.

'That's not the point. You did. I remember you signing up for it. Do you remember signing up for it?'

Anthony fumbled with the salt cellar, covering the holes with his thumb and overturning it above the table.

'Who was the golf teacher again? The one who took putting sessions?'

'I don't remember,' said Anthony.

'Yes, you remember. He taught us English in our second and third years. He taught us for GCSE.'

Dipali Blunden was quiet now and tight lipped. Her right arm slipped under the table. I looked at Anthony with a drunken, sardonic grin, my blood up, thrilled at the danger I was running.

'Would anyone like a coffee?' asked Dipali.

'What was his name again?'

'Mr Bridge,' said Anthony.

'Oh, yeah. Mr Bridge. Did you enjoy playing golf with him?'

Dipali got up, unanswered, and as she cleared away our bowls, Anthony fixed me with an expression of pure hatred.

I lost my resolve. Exhilarating anger changed to fear and I dropped my eyes to the place mat. But I refused to feel remorse. Ever since we had sat down to eat, Anthony had exuded self-assurance. He seemed entirely at ease with himself and monstrously oblivious to the secret that ought to bind us together.

The atmosphere was still charged after my hosts had tidied the table and we retired to the living room with our coffees. Anthony was sullen, expecting me perhaps to apologise, and I sat opposite him with trembling knees and a sick feeling in my stomach. Dipali broached a safe topic by drawing our attention to the Indian miniatures and then gave a précis of her family's history before and after independence. 'You were in India, weren't you, Bruno?'

'India? No.'

'Anthony said you were brought up there.'

'In Malaysia. I grew up in Malaysia.' I looked at him accusingly. 'You know that.'

'Maybe I misheard,' said Dipali.

'I invited you out there. I mean, you nearly came out for the holidays.'

Anthony shrugged. 'I forgot,' he said.

In the silence that followed, Dipali crossed and uncrossed her plump legs. 'My father used to have business in Perak,' she said. 'That's right, isn't it? Perak? I remember him flying out there and coming back with gifts. What's the name of that spiky fruit? Durian. He brought us back some durian saying it was a real delicacy, everyone loved it over there. I almost threw up – it tasted like rotten socks.'

'It's an acquired taste,' I said. 'I'm surprised you didn't have it at home.'

'Home was London,' Anthony replied.

'I rather miss Malaysian fruits,' I said. 'Mangosteen and rambutan . . .'

'Mm,' said Dipali, with a gourmet's relish.

'You clearly make up for the loss, though.'

'*Darling* . . .'

'No, I'm just saying, you're not exactly athletic, are you? I don't think you're the kind of man who bothers much with diets. Or healthy eating. In fact, can I ask, Bruno, just out of interest, how did you manage to get so fat?'

'Anthony!'

'No, no, it's all right,' I said. 'We can't all drift through life's accidents without them leaving a trace.'

'A mound, in your case.'

'Shut up, for God's sake!' Dipali sat erect with fury. The whole room gathered and concentrated in her figure and the shame that had eluded me all evening flooded in at the sight of her distress. 'Bruno, I'm really sorry . . .'

'No, I'm the one who should apologise.' This was Anthony; I could not bring myself to look at him. 'That was out of order. I'm sorry. I've had a bit too much to drink. I don't always know my limits and I get carried away and sometimes say things that I don't . . . that I shouldn't say.' It took genuine resolve to glance at him and I realised that, even though he was ostensibly addressing me, his eyes were turned with a look of almost childish contrition upon his wife.

'Plus I think you're a bit tired,' she said.

'Yes, that's true.'

'He hasn't stopped in a fortnight.'

'I haven't. And then to drink several glasses on top of . . .' He took a deep intake of breath and let it out with a shaky sigh.

'Please,' I said, 'let's not make a big deal out of it.'

'Well, no, but you're my guest. There's really no excuse.'

'Forget about it,' I said. This special pleading was almost embarrassing. I also recognised something in Anthony that I had rarely seen before. *Fear.* He was afraid of me and the shock of it was almost erotic.

I wanted to leave – afraid of this power of mine. I'd been crazy to try to re-establish contact. My first instinct, to keep away, had been the right one all along. 'I think . . .' I said. Dipali had moved closer to her husband and her hand was resting discreetly on his thigh. 'I think I should get going.' They made no attempt to dissuade me. 'Thanks ever so much for a delicious meal.'

'Really, it was nothing.'

'No, it was excellent. Anthony . . .' But I had no idea what I wanted to say. He looked mournful and diminished, his head subtly bowed. Had I wanted a reckoning with *this* creature? Dipali Blunden smoothed the silk of her skirt and gave him a gentle nudge before standing up and seeing me to the door. Her husband followed, sloping like a dog, his hands sunk in his pockets.

'I hope everything goes well at work,' said Dipali, looking about the entrance for a coat or jacket.

'Thank you. And thanks again for the supper. Maybe . . .' But there was no maybe. I held out my hand and Dipali was spared a goodbye kiss. As for her husband, he offered his own without looking at me and I felt his limp, once cherished fingers languish in mine.

They watched my progress from the door, Anthony stooping beside his wife. No sooner had I turned into the street than I felt helplessly alone.

Then

The endurance test of full-school assembly was almost over, along with its teenage smells and the boisterous squabble for chairs that had left me standing, humiliated, at the back of the auditorium. The sports news, delivered by team captains in surly voices, peppered with jargon and, to me, utterly indecipherable allusions to weekend debauches, had been exhausted, and even the prefects standing like heavies at the front of the stage were shifting their weight from leg to leg in reflection of a common desire to get away. It was at this unpropitious moment that the Master invited Mr Bridge to make a 'personal announcement'.

I watched my English teacher unfold a sheet of paper, flick his thinning hair and greet the school. 'This is going to be brief,' he said, 'as I know we all have lessons to get to.' He looked with a smile at the sour face of the Deputy Master. 'We are all very privileged, I think, to live in this beautiful part of England. But maybe we don't always pay attention and it's when we don't pay attention that things of beauty we take for granted get threatened. OK, so why am I standing here today? What the heck am I talking about?' Uncertainly, a few boys tittered. Mr Morris, the Deputy Master, looked at his shoes and frowned.

'Local government, in its wisdom, has decided it wants to build a road through this landscape. I'm talking about Albury

Down. It's visible from the playing fields looking towards Maidstone: that great green dome of chalk. I don't know if any of you have walked there but I do know that you've learned about chalk grassland in your biology lessons and you'll know how rare and fragile a place it is. Well, the roads lobby don't see things that way and they're planning to gouge straight through it.' From my vantage point at the top of the auditorium, I could see the shaggy heads of boys as they fidgeted and whispered. 'Now I don't know about you, but I don't think this is a good idea. We're talking about the mutilation of an irreplaceable landscape. It can't be put back once it's been destroyed. There are arguments to be made for roads but the more you build them, the more they get used, the more you have to build. It's a treadmill of destruction and at some point – if we want to have any country worth living in – we have to get off. So . . .' Mr Bridge searched with his eyes about the sheet of paper. The Master was listening with polite attention but his deputy, Mr Morris, peered over our heads at the clock and ostentatiously checked his wristwatch. I could feel a bristling restlessness about the room.

'So what can we do about it – this act of government vandalism that will last a million years? As far as I can see, though it may not be much of a solution, there's only one course of action open to us and that is to *protest*. To exercise our right and perhaps our duty to make a nuisance of ourselves . . .'

With unsuspected skill, Mr Bridge let his words sink in. I felt the current of attention shift and enjoyed the sight of a perplexed and affronted Mr Morris.

'Now local people from all walks of life have got together to fight this outrage. There's a day of protest scheduled for next Saturday and I propose that – without wishing to get in the way of fixtures and subsequent to the permission of housemasters – we add ourselves to it. We're talking about something that requires restraint, so those of you who want to attend will have to be on your best behaviour. Any mucking about will be severely punished. Isn't that right, Master?'

The Deputy Master was whispering into the Master's ear, a hand cupped over his wristwatch. 'Oh,' said the Master. 'Quite.'

'I'll be putting a notice up in Front Court. Please sign up if you want to get involved. I'm in the English department if anybody wants to ask me further questions . . .'

But Mr Bridge's time was up. At a nod from the Deputy Master, the prefects opened the doors and the boys of Kingsley College, like a migration of savannah beasts and quite as malodorous, jostled out of the auditorium. I rebounded and squirmed until I reached Anthony.

'Well, well,' he said, taking care to walk ahead of me, 'who'd have thought he had it in him?'

'Mr Morris didn't look too happy.'

'*You* wouldn't look happy if you'd been born with a lump of ice up your arse.'

We came out of the theatre into the strengthening sunshine of early May. I wanted Anthony to share my excitement and wondered aloud how Mr Bridge had managed to persuade college to back him. 'There's more to Bridget than meets the eye,' Anthony said, then saw my expression and laughed. 'Oh come on, he *is* a bit of a girl.'

'Don't you want to go, then?'

'On the protest? I don't want people thinking I'm some kind of tree hugger.'

'*I'm* going.'

'Then sign up for it. See if Mr Sedley will let you.'

I did not think much about this throwaway remark until, in the days that followed, it became clear that housemasters disliked the idea of their boys joining the protest. Mr Sedley, for instance, looked on my request with surprise; then insisted on telephoning my parents for their permission. Nobody else in the Hereward volunteered, the cool crowd having quickly decided that the road protest was 'gay'. I did, however, manage to persuade Anthony to put his name down, though at the time Albury Down was little more to me than a name, an abstraction that might help burnish me in the eyes of my teacher.

There were few opportunities to raise the subject in Mr Bridge's lessons. After starting the year prone to digressions, he had wised up to our schemes and now stuck determinedly to his lesson plans. I had another way of getting through to him: another way of making it clear that I was every bit as worthy of his attention as Anthony Blunden.

Kingsley College, as part of its much-vaunted 'grounds improvement' of the 1980s, had thinned several acres of woodland and ploughed up a flower meadow to create a nine-hole golf course. There was also a practice green behind the armoury, to which I presented myself on Wednesday afternoon to learn the finer arts of putting.

Anthony scowled at me. 'What are *you* doing here? You bloody hate golf. Are you just following me or what?'

I blushed and inexpertly gripped my borrowed putter. It was true that, growing up in Kuala Lumpur, golf had seemed a tedious activity, the preserve of middle-aged Chinese executives who never got out of their buggies except to whack a ball or scold me and my friends for trespassing on their business deals. 'A person can change his mind, can't he?' I said, looking across the bent heads of practising boys towards our instructor.

'Hello, Bruno,' said Mr Bridge when he saw me. 'I'm glad you've decided to join us.'

'I'm not much of a player, sir.'

'That's OK: we can't all be born to it like Mr Blunden. Now your grip, if I may . . .'

Mr Bridge reached around me, like someone about to perform

the Heimlich manoeuvre, and took my hands in his. His fingers on my skin felt clammy and foreign. It was my first physical contact with anybody for several weeks.

'You've caught the sun,' said Anthony, looking on, 'you're going red.'

Mr Bridge invited me to putt a bright yellow ball. I missed several times and Anthony scoffed. 'He's not very coordinated, is he, sir?'

'We all have to start somewhere.'

'Are you any good, sir? What's your handicap?'

Mr Bridge laughed. 'Oh, I'm worse than useless on an actual course. I learned everything I know about putting on a mini-golf in the Norfolk Broads.' Several junior boys, overhearing this, sniggered. It was just the kind of candour – a readiness to accept his foolishness – that disarmed me yet weakened Mr Bridge's authority in college. There was something out of place about him: a countercultural strain that played badly with the innate conservatism of schoolboys. Easier to call him 'Bridget' and leave it at that.

He was happy to walk back with us, Anthony and me carrying the golf bags, and at last I had a chance to talk up my commitment to his ideals. Mr Bridge was not entirely forthcoming when I asked how many people had signed up for Saturday. 'We're getting there,' was all he said.

'We're coming,' said Anthony.

'I know. Thank you.'

'How did you manage to persuade the school to give you the go-ahead, sir?'

'An interesting question, Bruno.'

'But you're not going to answer it.'

'Some people can see our point of view,' he said. He must have got the Master's approval to make his announcement (the old man had a touch of the anarchist about him) but few of his colleagues, to judge from their behaviour since, shared Mr Bridge's enthusiasm for protest.

'My housemaster,' said Anthony, 'thinks it's antisocial.'

'What is – building the road or trying to stop it?'

'He says we need the road and environmentalists are just a bunch of dreamers who don't understand economics.'

'Well, the scheme goes against the government's own environmental protection laws. But you'll find as you get older that government is the best place to go in life if you want to be a criminal and get away with it.'

'You can't mean that, sir.'

'Can't I? My wife's a biologist who depends on government funding. She could tell you a thing or two about its priorities.' For the next few minutes we listened, open mouthed, as Mr Bridge expressed opinions wildly at odds with everything we thought we knew about the world. He spoke about corruption, greed and an atmosphere of mendacity in which most human affairs were decided. I decided at once to believe him. When my father used to moan about the director general of the British Council or the gutlessness of his Malaysian colleagues, I had never really paid attention, hearing only the drone of those adult topics that formed the background of family meals. Now, as Mr Bridge abandoned all pretence of complacency to denounce the machinations of the roads lobby, it seemed we were being ushered into a world of sophisticated intrigue: one where all our comforting assumptions about the basic wisdom and benevolence of authority (for all our sartorial grievances against it) came up against a wall of doubt. I knew nothing about the sham democracy of public inquiries. It couldn't be true, could it, that Albury Down's fate had been sealed in a shady backroom at the European Commission?

'That's Europe for you,' said Anthony.

'I read in the newspaper that people are chaining themselves to trees and everything. Is that what we'll be doing?'

'Not exactly, Bruno. We leave that to the hard core. Besides, to be honest, Albury Down was pretty much doomed as soon as the legal process was exhausted.'

Anthony looked bewildered. 'So . . . it's pointless?'

We had come to the gate of Mr Bridge's garden. A woman's straw hat dipped out of sight behind a soft-fruit hedge. 'Yes, Anthony. It is pointless, in the sense that we cannot hope to win.'

'But then . . .'

Mr Bridge smiled, relieving us of the golf bags and hoisting one on each shoulder. 'I'll see you there,' he said.

Anthony soon forgave me for trespassing on his golf lesson. Finding our way to a grassy dell at the back of the school theatre, we lay in a stupor among the tangled roots of a beech tree and he produced from the depths of his pockets a crumpled cigarette. Though no one was around, we were not concealed as in the bomb shelter. He was bored, he said, with our dingy retreat. 'You found it,' I said.

'You can keep it.'

Anthony produced a match and attempted to light it among the roots. 'Bloody safety matches,' he said, and languorously folded his hands behind his head, sucking the unlit cigarette. I began, as so often, to complain about the bullies in my house, Proctor meriting special resentment. Anthony provided the counterpoint of his own grievances. He was beginning to wilt in the macho hothouse of the Eversley. The boys there were no longer perplexed by him: they dared to trust their antipathy and no amount of Blunden bravado could restore him to favour.

'They're all *beastly*,' he said. 'When I'm in their company I feel myself returning to the Stone Age. I suppose I ought to start beating my chest. And, ugh, the *smell*.'

Like all boys our age (though perhaps with more imagination and resolve), he was trying on different personalities. As the mystery that had served him in our first year peeled away, he retreated into a mixture of *Brideshead* snobbery and tousled rebellion. It was an act that bewildered some, alienated many, and permitted him to be cruel, even to me, as if unkind words and aesthetic sneers were part of a game that anyone was welcome to play so long as he had the skill. Why then was I so devotedly his friend? Because I had no choice in the matter, and Anthony knew it.

We had been resting under the beech tree for perhaps an hour when, addled by heat and a neglected thirst, I began to feel my eyelids drooping. Anthony was quiet, the cigarette fallen from his lips, gazing up into the boughs. Its young leaves were latticed in sunlight, fathoms deep, stirring like the waves of the sea. Though I felt tired, a searing pressure in my chest inhibited me from lying beside him. I sat hotly conscious of his body, of Anthony full stretch among the roots, with a sleek, pale sliver of his belly showing between his shirt and trousers. Obliquely I watched the dappled light on his face, the tangled luxuriance of his hair spangled by leaf light. He'd closed his eyes and the lids with their long, dark lashes barely trembled. The tree breathed, the day declined, and I admired as though for the first time the unobtrusive strength of his chin and the band of freckles that extended, in a russet constellation, across his cheeks and nose. His full lips, relaxed, had lost their habitual downward pressure, the almost severe containment of the Blunden overbite. I felt a frightening desire to kiss them and the even more frightening knowledge that nothing was preventing me from doing so save fear of the consequences. I had moved fractionally, allowing gravity to pull me towards that tender sleeping face, when Anthony opened his eyes.

I sat upright, my face burning with confusion at his sideways, ironical grin. Then Anthony was asleep again and I settled away from him against the great smooth trunk of the tree. After another minute or so my friend yawned, stretched like a cat, with feline noises, then sat up, surprised and wide eyed, as though only that instant released from sleep.

'It's there,' I said, pointing to the cigarette that had fallen from his lips. Anthony got to his feet and brushed the dirt from his clothes. He made no allusion to what had just happened; and indeed by the time we had gone our separate ways, back to the boisterous life of school, I had made a dream of the whole experience.

There were twelve of us in the minibus, as well as Mr Bridge in the passenger seat and, to my astonishment, my under-tutor, Mr Houghton, folded up against the steering wheel. We wore our full school uniforms (Mr Bridge had insisted) and held placards – STOP THE DIGGERS, DESTRUCTION IS FOR EVER, SAVE ALBURY DOWN – which had been designed by our only sixth-former, an art school hermit so universally shunned that even First Set boys felt authorised to jeer at him. Half the protesters came from the Lower Sixth – that gilded year – and these did not fit my expectations. They were tolerated eccentrics, ravers and hippies who kept Kingsley supplied with illicit substances. The boy who climbed in last and closed the doors of the minibus was captain of the football eleven and king, therefore, of outsiders in a rugby-playing school.

I sat beside Anthony on the sticky, humpbacked seat and basked in the sense of a lofty common purpose.

Minutes earlier, in the cold shade of the Porter's Lodge, Mr Bridge had briefed us about what to expect. There would be hardcore protesters, he said, of whom we should steer clear. Today marked the legal deadline for their withdrawal from the Down. There would be bailiffs, Mr Bridge warned, and police.

Our task was to make a show for the press and to demonstrate our disapproval of what we could not hope to stop.

As the minibus jogged and warbled, trailing fumes, out of the school grounds, I felt like a prisoner enjoying day release. The journey, which lasted about fifteen minutes, took us through idyllic countryside: a blend of woods and grassland and apple orchards, with genteel hamlets of red brick and flint and, peeping above flowering clusters of lime, the white 'bells' of converted oast houses. Through the joking banter of the older members of the expedition, Mr Bridge attempted to tell us about a painter who had lived near Albury centuries ago and whose house had been demolished when they built the M2. 'It's not like he needed it any more,' muttered Anthony at my shoulder.

The first hint that something was happening was the crump and shudder of helicopter blades. We strained to see the machine hovering above the roadside trees. Then, as we approached the excavation site, with the soft swellings of Albury Down on our left, we began to encounter traffic. Cars and vans had been parked – many of them nosing into hedgerows – on all sides of the country lane, and small groups of people were threading their way between the vehicles. Mr Houghton parked the bus on a grass verge among simmering cars and we got out with our posters. There was a moment's confusion as the men discussed tactics; then Mr Houghton goaded us into some kind of a formation and led us off, Mr Bridge scouting far in front, towards our encounter with the road.

To our dismay, we were not led to where the action was but wheeled across slowly rising ground towards a line of onlookers. These were genteel protesters: the letter writers, committee people and retired lawyers who had fought behind the scenes to prevent the road's construction. Organisers of church fêtes, petition signers and placard makers stood now, some holding banners but most capable only of numbed witness, behind a cordon of police tape and a single placid constable.

'Christ,' muttered the captain of the football eleven.

We were standing on the edge of a quarry. Below us, vaguely triangular in shape and thirty yards across, a large part of the Down had been scooped out already. The great chalk wound festered with police and bailiffs. Ahead of them, where the excavation narrowed into the chalk face, a band of ragged youths had halted the destruction by chaining themselves to heavy machinery and to each other. On either side of the cutting, onlookers had gathered like spectators in an amphitheatre: concerned citizens on one side, police surveillance teams on the other. Would our young faces be registered in some secret service files? Anthony certainly hoped so. Meanwhile the senior boys were looking up and down the cordon for a television crew. When they found one – a burly cameraman and a boom mike operator – they whistled and called for its attention. We were Kingsley boys, England's inheritors, and look, even *we* opposed the road. Eventually a young woman, shielded by a clipboard, made her way to Mr Houghton and promised to come back for footage. Until then, all we could do was stand beside our masters and wait for the action to begin.

'Here,' said Anthony, nudging me with a small pair of binoculars, 'take a closer look.'

At first the world was blurred, with partial eclipses that made me grimace. Then, as I learned how to look through the sights, detail of a cinematic clarity swam into view. The bailiffs, warlike under their safety helmets, with fluorescent jackets glaring, stood poker faced behind sunglasses or lumbered among Land Rovers, hands above their muttering walkie-talkies. Behind them, a phalanx of police officers chatted and sipped coffee from Thermos flasks. The police had come in riot-proofed vans with Perspex shields stacked against the doors. Such precautions hardly seemed necessary, for the protesters were few in number and looked ragged, while the comfortable mums and retired couples that had kept them supplied with cupcakes and sandwiches throughout the days of the stand-off would never dare force their way past the security cordon.

The television crew proved to be local rather than national. Moving round the back of the spectators, they had just begun filming us in our uniforms, and Mr Bridge was negotiating with the young producer to let him have his say, when a great fart rumbled up from the cutting. Contractors, emerging from the ranks of officials, had climbed into the cabins of their arrested bulldozers and were starting up the engines. The activists shouted in alarm, as if drawing attention to themselves and their fragile bodies. At the same time the bailiffs, bolt clippers and fretsaws at the ready, broke the stand-off and advanced in formation.

The police helicopter swooped to watch: there was something hungry, almost lecherous, in the way it hovered.

'Pigs!' shouted someone in the crowd. 'Fascist bastards!'

With a news crew on hand to record every word, we Kingsley boys began to shout. This, in turn, emboldened others to a discord of brays and football yawps. It was an extraordinary scene: conservative, middle-class families howling in support of dreadlocked travellers. Someone in the crowd had brought a whistle. Others thumped, like Dark Age warriors, on their placards. The news crew filmed this alliance of opposites in defence of hallowed ground. As for us, there can be no denying we enjoyed the attention. For all the obscenity of the cutting and the slow, intimidating advance of the bailiffs, there was among the boys an atmosphere of carnival. We were lords of misrule: licensed to be so. Mr Houghton tried to censor some of our language but we could barely hear him through the noise.

The news crew shifted their attention to the scene below. The protesters offered no resistance save their weight and chains, and at first the whole clash seemed oddly quiet, almost peaceful, despite our shouts and the hovering violence of the helicopter. Like disciples or bearers of tribute, the bailiffs knelt before the protesters and began to clip and hack at their chains. Their expressions, clearly discernible through Anthony's binoculars, were stolid and efficient. Some of the eco-warriors were trying to reason with them.

'Is that *it*?' Anthony said in disgust. 'Are they going to give up without a fight?'

'What would be the point?' said Mr Bridge. The smile that followed did not travel to his eyes. 'It would only play into the authorities' hands.'

The bailiffs, neither helped nor hindered, appeared to be making rapid progress, while the bulldozers waited, fuming, to resume their work. With mounting disappointment we watched and shouted: 'Come on, do some bloody resisting!'

Abruptly, as if heeding our instructions, the scene changed. One of the bulldozers, having been cleared of its human cargo, had begun more out of bravado than anything to lumber towards the chalk face. Suddenly there was movement. A cluster of protesters broke away and, bound together like a chain gang, surrounded the moving vehicle. The bailiffs, busy with other individuals, tried to intercept, only to find their previous targets scrambling elsewhere. An almost comical game of cat-and-mouse ensued, with each side playing both roles. No sooner had one lurching, hiccupping machine been liberated, or a path cleared for its passage, than a new clot of resistance formed around it. The bailiffs trotted from one group to another. They began to push and manhandle. Some of the protesters, isolated from their friends, were rugby-tackled to the ground; others, mostly women, were roughly dragged from where they lay and dumped, like rubbish, at the edge of the cutting. The whole campaign was futile; yet there was a kind of splendour to it. Our senior boys shouted, scandalised like football supporters by a foul. Others in the crowd cried out pantomime warnings as one of the bulldozers attempted to edge its way along the side of the cutting and a wiry, dreadlocked girl ran from her central post to cut off its progress.

'Go on, love!' shouted our football captain.

While the drama was playing out below us, the lone constable maintaining the cordon had summoned reinforcements. One of these turned at our cries and ordered us to be silent. 'You must be joking, mate,' said our football captain with patrician vowels. 'We're within our rights.'

'Shut up.'

'I won't shut up.' The red face turned away. 'Do you feel proud of the work you're doing?'

'Leave it,' said Mr Houghton.

'It was the old Nazi excuse, wasn't it? I was only following orders . . .'

The police officer turned to our master. 'Are you responsible for this lot? That twerp is out of order. If you can't control him, I'm taking him in.'

'Yes, Constable,' said Mr Houghton. 'I'm terribly sorry.'

'He's not done anything wrong,' said Mr Bridge.

'All the same, Sam' (it was first names *in extremis*) 'I think we should get going.'

Mr Bridge breathed heavily, indignant, and nodded his head. Mr Houghton was going to get his way. We were preparing to surrender to the inevitable, and some had even begun, shrugging and rolling their eyes, to turn away from the scene below, when a low moan of outrage spread through the crowd. Immediately, we muscled our way back to the cordon.

'What's happening?' said Anthony.

'I don't know. *Look* . . .'

The dreadlocked girl who had sat down in front of the rogue

bulldozer was shrieking as a bailiff attempted to drag her from the ground. She was kicking up chalk dust, squirming against his stranglehold, while her bearded assailant grimaced with pleasure or effort or both.

'Look at them,' said Anthony, jerking his head at the police. 'They're just sitting there.'

The girl gasped; she used all her weight to resist arrest, though this clearly cost her dear and her face reddened as it shrank behind a constricting arm.

'Sam? Sam! What the hell are you doing?'

I stared at Mr Houghton. He was gripping the cordon with both hands as Mr Bridge stumbled and slid down the face of the cutting.

Boys around me began to cheer as they realised what was happening. Mr Bridge staggered, found his footing, and ran to the captured girl's aid.

'Mr Bridge!' roared Houghton. 'Don't be a bloody fool!'

It was too late to stop him. Impulsively, Mr Bridge tugged the bailiff's arm and the astonished man dropped his prize. The news team, having made its way to the lip of the crater, trained its lens on the remonstration.

'Boys, boys, that's enough. Order, all of you! Anderson, you're a prefect: set an example.' Mr Houghton barked in vain. We watched and yelled in jubilation as another bailiff on the edge of battle noticed the dispute and walked over. He moved like a man trying to carry golf balls under his armpits.

'Jesus,' said one of the Lower Sixth, 'look at *him*.'

This second bailiff was huge: a tank of brawn. He jutted with his jaw into the dispute, and Mr Bridge gamely included him.

For a moment, perhaps ten seconds, it looked as if Mr Bridge might get away with it. The first bailiff, deprived of his captive, could only watch as she and others besieged the now stationary bulldozer. His colleague, meanwhile, bent his gleaming head towards Mr Bridge as though trying to hear him. Suddenly, and with peremptory skill, the man grabbed Mr Bridge's arm and hoisted it up his back. Mr Bridge opened his mouth and spun to lessen the pain while the bailiff with his other arm pushed his head forward and made him crumple. In seconds, to our mute surprise and horror, our teacher had gone from upright citizen to grovelling slave.

'Shit,' said Mr Houghton, 'shit, I don't believe it!'

Which of us did? The whole crowd lost its voice as the scene below turned nasty. Finding themselves unable to contain the protesters, the bailiffs had been calling for help on their walkie-talkies; and now the watching police officers were pulling on their helmets. Some ran towards the cutting; others bundled into their armoured vehicles. In a kind of panic Mr Houghton tried to gather us together but we resisted, mesmerised by the plight of Mr Bridge and the sight of police vans as they surged forward, lights blazing, in a cloud of white dust.

The end of the protest came with shocking alacrity. Bailiffs and police dragged protesters to the waiting vans. Young men and women preferred to tear their backs on the ground rather than assist their captors. Others fought back, slapping helmets or flailing with their legs, only to be pounced upon and beaten. I saw a girl being kicked repeatedly in the stomach. A young man with bleached spiky hair was bleeding from the scalp.

'Come on. Back away. Back away all of you.' The police constables guarding us lost their nerve. With back-up from their colleagues who had been filming on the other side of the cutting, they attempted to chivvy several hundred people from the edge of the quarry, extending and flapping their arms like farmers rounding up cattle.

'What about Mr Bridge?' I asked as the crowd began to contract. Mr Houghton was pale and sweating. He breathed like a winded boxer.

'Move *back*,' bellowed a senior officer. 'Come on, you too,' he said, meaning the Kingsley contingent. Looking nauseated and appalled, parents retreated with their children. Elderly couples remonstrated with the police yet backed obediently away.

'Right, boys!' Mr Houghton shouted, impossible to ignore now. 'I want you all to return to the minibus. In good order! There's nothing more to see.'

Plainly this was not true. For a few seconds more we hopped and stood on the tips of our toes to witness the end of Albury Down. Below us, the last protesters were being rounded up and bundled into custody. Mr Bridge was among them.

Like others who had returned in the minibus, no doubt, I became briefly the centre of attention as news spread of Mr Bridge's arrest. Still stunned by what I had witnessed, though guiltily pleased by the notoriety it gave me, I described the events to my housemates.

'He'll be fired,' said one boy excitedly.

'Poor old Bridget: do you think he cried when they put him behind bars?'

I found the nerve to defend him. Mr Bridge seemed heroic to me, his action a lone stand taken for justice. 'At least,' I said, 'he's shown that he's got conviction.'

Andy Proctor guffawed in my face. 'At this rate, he'll have a whole string of them.'

I hated my peers for tittering and decided that I was better informed, that a majority can be mistaken and a minority in the right. Mr Bridge was not respected by the school but I knew his worth, and by association my own. A blush, not of anger but of pride, sent me scurrying from company.

I was still warm with self-approval when my housemaster walked towards me on Main Corridor. 'Shame about the road, isn't it, sir?' I said.

Mr Sedley halted and turned about, his brogues squeaking on the linoleum floor. Whatever it was that trailed behind him – domestic row or financial worry – caught me in its undertow. 'Quite frankly, Jackson, no: I don't believe it is.'

'Sir?'

'You ask me my opinion. Part of growing up is having to accept things you don't like. The whole scheme has been properly assessed. There's been a public inquiry. It is lawful and some would say necessary. And whatever you may think about such things, Jackson, once the legal process has been exhausted you jolly well have to accept it, otherwise there's only anarchy. And Mr Bridge's damsel-rescuing adventure was unseemly and a discredit, frankly, to this college.'

I returned to the room I shared with Thwaite and Toplady (mercifully they were outside playing cricket) and flung myself on my bed. I thought of Mr Bridge cringing on his knees before the bailiff, and imagined the contempt, the Sedleyesque disdain, he would encounter among his colleagues.

Everyone was mistaken. Only I knew that Mr Bridge was admirable. His intervention had changed nothing, but at least he didn't smile at destruction and call it progress.

I considered what I had seen – the desperate passion of the protesters, the sour efficiency of their opponents – and sensed that something more than land was at stake. I understood what was being done to that piece of England, and hated for the first time the unalterable wound that was opening in the Down's belly.

It was too late for Albury. Perhaps the protests had been too small to attract the nation's attention. Two years later, the battle for Twyford Down would see thousands protesting and hundreds arrested as the hungry diggers moved in. But in '93 and '94 I would find myself unable to watch the heroics of the Dongas Tribe and Road Alert. I would have a television, of course, and might even be able to stomach the sight of Twyford raped and mutilated. It would not be ecological sorrow that would prevent my watching. I would have another, altogether more unspeakable reason for turning away.

Now

The habit persists of equating London with rain but the reality is quite different. Our summers now are hot and grimy: grass bleaches, the trees rust and moult, long before autumn the chlorophyll is spent. The season closes not with downpours but the sullen grey of rain-withholding skies. The English are great weather grumblers; but who would have thought we would have to endure so soon these exhausting summer sieges?

September had come and we were between seasons, the days drifting from sun to cloud and back again. The machinery of London ground on, obstinate and hungry, as if all its weight and human matter insulated it from the disorder of the planet. I sat exhausted in my cubicle, attuned to the dull office hum, and looked with resentment at the ever-rising backlog of my work.

Things were scarcely better at home. I had come to hate my flat, its ugliness and lack of character. The framed reproductions of Howard Hodgkin paintings, bought to relieve the monotony of my landlord's magnolia walls, the inherited grime of the bathroom with its loose tiles and brazen spiders, the silverfish-infested toilet with its selection of moisture-swollen paperbacks – all seemed irretrievably shabby. I had not invested in furniture of my own and the rented sofa exhaled a breath of stale crisps and biscuit crumbs. As for the curtains, mere veils of hessian, they were so thin that London's orange glow seeped in at night. I bought one of those face masks you find on long-haul flights and for a time this seemed to help. But my sleep was hindered by noises in the building. That midnight honking of hornbills was my neighbour expectorating. Immediately above me, women danced in clogs, a corpse was dragged across the floor, giants had sex on blocks of sheet metal. I tried listening to Radio 4 and the World Service but sickened of the news bulletins, those hourly doses of the world's pain. I persuaded my GP – a vague, harassed Indian – to write me a prescription for diazepam; but the more I used those heavenly pills, the less effective they became, and I was afraid of falling into a dependency.

'There is a solution,' said Jenny on the phone. 'Find somewhere else to live. Or get earplugs.'

'They give you otitis.'

'I could help you choose new curtains if you like. We could put them up together.'

But I did not want solutions.

'Let's meet,' said Jenny, and I knew (without intending to redeem myself) that I was too caught up in my own troubles to ask about hers. 'I think we need to go on a cheerful bender.'

'How about just dinner?'

'All right.'

We arranged to get together at the end of the week. I swallowed two pills and went to bed. The next day I arrived late at work and received a scolding from my supervisor.

I went to get a consoling coffee and found myself standing behind a senior colleague, one of the diehard road evangelists, who looked down the narrow bridge of his nose and murmured a greeting. I replied and stood back as, with what seemed like deliberate slowness, he selected his morning poison.

I stared at the coarse hairs that stuck out of the tops of his ears. Maybe he felt my eyes on him, for he sighed loudly and said, 'Dear me,' as he turned to the side table with its sachets.

I did not take my place at the dispenser. 'Bill,' I said.

Bill Macready turned. His face was a parody of saintly mildness. 'Bruno,' he replied, and the two syllables of my name were drenched in sarcasm.

'I want to ask you something.'

'So it would seem.'

'You remember Albury Down?'

His face was a blank for a moment. Then memory flooded it. 'Oh, yes,' he said.

'You remember the protests against it?'

'I remember they didn't come to much. Why do you ask? Are we taking a trip down memory lane?'

'I was at school near there. Albury, I mean.'

'Were you indeed?' He stirred his coffee with a plastic spatula. The provocative insincerity of his smile angered me.

'I was wondering,' I said, 'if there had been alternative plans.'

'How do you mean?'

'The cutting was a pretty controversial scheme.'

Macready shifted, almost imperceptibly, in his tight polished shoes. 'Is this of relevance?'

'I mean, you were involved, right? You must have seen all the options available.'

'The Department based its decision on the soundest economic argument.'

'There was going to be a tolled tunnel, wasn't there? Ministers seriously considered it. What happened to the tunnel?'

'We advised against it. In fact it might have worked but the dangers of a delay to the whole project were unacceptable.'

I forced a clot of phlegm down my throat. 'It must have been a relief,' I said, 'when the European Commission cut its deal.'

'Oh, there were celebrations in the Department. We thought

we'd finally routed the antis and the whole roads programme could accelerate. But then you can never underestimate the power of public sentiment.'

'Did you actually go there?'

'What?'

'Did you go to see the road being built? Did you see the damage for yourself?'

Macready looked at me as if I had sprouted horns. 'We leave that sort of thing to contractors,' he said; then, shouldering past me, he added, 'Steady, Bruno. There's no use getting excited about the past.'

I did not get excited. After mouthing curses at Macready's back, I worked at my desk for two hours straight.

I hadn't intended to ask questions about Albury Down. Six years had passed in the Department without my yielding to the temptation. Yet I had moved there in the hope of doing *some* good. In those days, before the Twin Towers fell and the stink of our new century entered everyone's living room, the government seemed on the right track. The triumphant car would recede; hills would not be levelled nor valleys paved over; the word 'sustainability' made itself comfortable in our mouths. Yet somewhere along the line, or in many places, gradually, the aspirations failed. Atavisms reasserted themselves; fuel protests and the gross distractions of war allowed my superiors to roll their good intentions safely and discreetly away. From thinking of myself as a sleeper, embedded in Leviathan and ready to transform it, I came to accept that I was part of a cumbersome animal. Yes, I would say to those few among my friends who challenged me on it, progress is slow, but government catches up with necessity in the end, though it may take years for the pressure to tell, and I was at the forefront of positive changes. Make the polluter pay: wasn't that the whole point of satellite tolling?

Today, as I tasted the sourness left over from my exchange with Bill Macready, I realised that even these last pillars of reasoning could not protect me. I imagined enmity in the faces of my colleagues. I was losing my grip – long tenuous – on the complexities of my brief and lacked the conviction to reassert it.

Overcome by a sense of hollowness, I skulked to the Gents with my briefcase full of chocolates and took up residence in a cubicle.

On a bad day I measure time, I make it manageable, by setting aside food breaks. The prospect of those breaks gets you through your work; but the relief when you get to them is consumed in the process of having them. For even as you eat, a terror builds up inside you of *having eaten*: of being without the comfort of eating. And so the appetite – the guilty, shame-ridden hunger – stokes up again as soon as you're done and you can think of nothing in the meantime except for your next, enslaving fix.

I am not bulimic. I keep the contents of my binges down.

This does not necessarily make them any pleasanter.

I did not blame Anthony for my lapses. As it happened, I had been making great efforts – with some success – to freeze him out of my mind entirely. What, after all, had changed in my life? Was the world any different for my having seen him in his adult form? No. I decided that Anthony was not worth the trouble of a neurotic fixation. Let his wife cope with his disorders: if she could live in a disaster zone, so much the better for both of them. He was not *my* responsibility.

What, then, triggered my bingeing at work? I knew. I knew the answer.

My father had fallen in love.

Books were to blame. They had met at their local reading group. 'We bonded,' my father said, 'over our shared loathing of

Trollope.' A public acquaintance had turned into friendship, with trips to the theatre and Covent Garden and the renewal of subscriptions abandoned when Mum had died. The divorcee fastened on to the widower. Their love was not declamatory or any kind of grand passion; by the sound of it, they had simply reached a tacit understanding no longer to be lonely.

The woman's name was Ann.

'I don't want you to be angry,' my father said, stooping in the garden, deadheading flowers.

'Why should I be angry?'

'It's not like we're going to get married or anything.'

I hacked with my secateurs into the living stalks of his roses.

'Bruno, don't overdo it.'

'It's good to cut them back. Makes them grow vigorously.'

'Bruno . . .'

I dashed to the loo, tossing the secateurs with a clatter into the kitchen sink. My father wisely did not follow. I put the latch on and punched myself in the thigh. I felt furious and bewildered; also, perhaps, a little envious. 'The bastard, the *bastard*,' I whispered, and even as I did so resented the knowledge that I had no right to object. I had known something was up but had not wanted to investigate. His complaints against modern life had diminished. He was spry instead of stiff. He faced the world with a new benignity. I should have been glad for him; but his happiness – this recovery from the mental sclerosis I had pre-dicted for him – seemed almost a betrayal. 'Bruno,' he said gently, knocking on the door.

'What? Christ, I'm nearly finished.'

'Come and talk to me.'

Talk to me? *Talk?* Since when did we do such things? Who was this Ann woman: some kind of Californian? My father did not stay by the door but retreated to the kitchen, and by the time I joined him I had mastered my emotion.

He was sitting at the table in his summer hat. A new teapot, stainless steel instead of the jade-green one Mum had bought at the antiques shop in Hampstead, was complacently steaming beside him. 'I've found this rather good delicatessen,' he said. 'They sell all sorts of things: ginseng and white tea, even mangosteens in syrup. I bought some lapsang . . .'

'I don't want any.'

I sat down but did not look at him. Dad poured himself a cup; his spoon hovered above the rim. 'She's not a gorgon, you know.'

'I credit you with some taste. You did marry Mum.'

'She'd like to meet you.'

I said nothing but set to work on the plate of ginger biscuits. My father sipped his tea. It occurred to me how much I had come to depend on our grief-stained relationship. The fog between us had gathered long before Mum died; she was the conciliator, the light by which we steered, and losing her had meant this loving estrangement. The wound, in other words, had come to *represent* her: she almost lived in our sense of bewilderment. Now that Dad was healing, I felt alone in the dark.

'Ann's a very accomplished painter. Not professional, you understand. I thought . . . given your own interest in painting . . .'

'Dad, I haven't been interested in painting since I was a schoolboy.'

'She does watercolours. I don't mean the sort of wishy-washy stuff you see for sale in doctors' surgeries. They've got vigour and weight.'

'Does she have children?'

'A daughter.'

'How old?'

'Sixteen.'

'Jesus, I can just imagine our Christmas.'

My father stirred more sugar into his tea. I could sense the effort in his throat to speak calmly. 'She's never going to replace your mother.' When I said nothing, he pressed on the table and stood up. For a panicky instant I thought he was leaving; but he walked only as far as the bookshelf in the hallway. I watched over my shoulder as he hooked out a volume and came back with it to the table.

'You remember George Herbert?'

'Wasn't he was one of your colleagues in KL?'

'After a lifetime serving literature, I finally have time to read some. I was a big admirer of the metaphysical poets when I was a student but I'd quite forgotten this.'

With a kind of embarrassed dread I watched him put on the reading glasses that hung on a string about his neck. He had marked his page with a shred of *The Times*.

> 'How fresh, O Lord, how sweet and clean
> Are thy returns! ev'n as the flowers in spring;
>   To which, besides their own demean,
> The late past frosts tributes of pleasure bring.
>   Grief melts away
>   Like snow in May,
>   As if there were no such cold thing.
>
>   'Who would have thought my shrivel'd heart
> Could have recover'd greenness? It was gone
>   Quite underground; as flowers depart
> To see their mother-root, when they have blown . . .'

I had never heard my father read poetry. He was good at it, his deftness and subtlety matched only by one other reader I have known. I thought of Mr Bridge, his meagre frame bent over *The Rattle Bag* as he tried to waken the souls within us, and could not look when my father, his voice cracking, reached the penultimate verse:

'And now in age I bud again,
After so many deaths I live and write;
I once more smell the dew and rain,
And relish versing: O my only light,
It cannot be
That I am he
On whom thy tempests fell at night.'

We were both moved, though too English to show it. My father shambled back to the bookshelf while I secretly, under the tablecloth, pressed my fingernails into my palms. If Dad thought his reading had delivered what he so touchingly sought – my blessing for his fling with this painterly Ann – he was soon disappointed. I was a surly and sarcastic guest for the rest of the afternoon, and we parted without saying another word about the transformation in his life.

'Is that *it*?' Jenny said. 'Is that why you're going off the rails?'

We met on Friday evening at Angel Tube. I had made no effort to disguise my troubles as we sat down for our Turkish meze. 'Thanks for the sympathy,' I said.

'You're not getting any. Just think for a minute how it is for your dad.'

'*He*'s all right. He's come back to life.' What was this hardness in her? Why this scrupulous Jenny? I resented her reasonableness. 'I'm the one who gets left behind.'

'That doesn't make any sense.'

A glass of wine later, I was more philosophical. I acknowledged Jenny's description of my 'cult of grief' over my mother. 'You've got to stop this mythologising. Your father loves you. *I* love you, though you can be a right pain in the arse sometimes. Why can't you look at what you've got? It's as if for you the only people worth loving are those who can't possibly return it.'

I sulked over this and rubbed a wine drop from the edge of my glass.

'I'm not buying this for a minute, Bruno.'

'Buying what?'

'You as a sarcastic bastard.' She would not indulge me and she was right. Ah, but if I let go of my grief, if I stopped poking the scar tissue, it would be like burying Mum all over again. The pain of it made me argumentative; I changed the subject and watched Jenny's expression grow ever more haggard as I talked with poison in my guts about the war in the Gulf and government blather on the environment when I knew for certain that emissions were rising and no one dared tackle the problem.

'The government's decided to commission a new report, yet another one, to look into climate change and transport – as if we didn't already know what needs to be done. Nobody *needs* this report. But it'll allow us to stall on painful reforms; it'll also keep an important but dangerously incompetent civil servant out of trouble . . . and when it's finally released, telling us what we already know, the government will ignore every one of its recommendations.'

'You don't know that for certain.'

'Oh, they'll talk the talk. But it'll be bullshit. You know, I think the most disturbing thing about New Labour is its high-minded mendacity. It proves Goebbels' dictum in reverse: repeat a lie often enough and the liar comes to believe it.'

Jenny tried to interject but I would not let her. I bludgeoned her with facts and statistics. I wanted her to wilt under the heat of my pessimism. But Jenny was tougher than I imagined. She heard me out for twenty minutes, until I felt ashamed at my boorishness and fell silent over flatbread and hummus.

'This has got nothing to do with government,' she said quietly.

'Hasn't it?'

'I know you. This is *personal*. And it's not the business with your dad and his girlfriend.'

'Oh, please, don't use that word.'

'You know what I think?' Jenny leaned forward, her top dipping perilously close to the tzatziki. 'I think you're finding your form again.'

I actually scoffed, sending a flake of pitta into her wineglass. 'You call *this* form?'

'It doesn't feel like it because you're in the middle of a process. You're overeating because it's a *struggle*.'

'What is?'

'Getting back to your true nature.' Jenny smiled with improbable delight. There was a little too much colour in her cheeks and I wondered whether her pupils had widened since her return from the Ladies. 'You're an *idealist*, Bruno. I know you like to think you're very jaded and pragmatic – working for the DfT and everything – but you don't fool anyone. You're the most hopeless romantic I know. And I worry about you because of it.'

'Well, you needn't,' I said, though I knew I was blushing. 'The romance has quite gone out of *this* life.'

'It'll come back if you let it.'

Jenny could see that I was wrong-footed; she pushed her advantage. 'Think about it,' she said. 'Even with the best intentions in the world, when you belong to a major institution you lose the ability to see beyond it. You're surrounded by money and power and action and it's seductive. You confuse yourself with the mission – which seems about the kindest way of putting it for New Labour. It's only by stepping *away* from things that you can recapture a sense of perspective. God, sorry, this all sounds so pretentious. What I mean is . . .' She reached across the table, her bangles quaking. I looked at my fat hand under her stressed, pink fingers. 'You've got to try and get back to first principles.'

121

'What . . .' I swallowed hard. 'What if I can't remember them?' I took back my hand and pretended to have a lash in my eye. Lord, I was a wreck. Mercifully she said no more on the subject; it was left to brew inside me while outwardly we concentrated on other things.

Jenny gave me her news. She had sold a sequence of poems to some tiny review in Missouri; she was trying her hand again at the sonnet form, 'ripe, erotic stuff' about an entirely imaginary lover. Was she having better luck, I enquired, on *that* front? 'None,' she said. 'I've been a hundred per cent celibate since Easter.'

Was celibacy for Jenny a proof of life, as new love was for my father? Travelling home on the last Tube (a gang of girls at the far end of the compartment swung shrieking from the handrails), I thought about all that had been said. If she was right, if I *had* lost sight of too much that was essential, how far back had I to go in search of it?

Then

Two elderly Chinese men sat beside me slurping their dinners. I tried to distract myself from the sound of them sucking their teeth with thoughts of the things I would do in the holidays: a trip to the Batu Caves with Sebastian and his parents, a week or more in the Cameron Highlands when Dad got his leave. I thought, as the lights dimmed and my neighbours relished their old men's snores and our jumbo jet roared above the sweltering plains of Asia, about my friends waiting for me in the living haven of my past. I could not have admitted to myself that it was already a dream.

For the first couple of weeks I relished the return to familiar things. I rearranged my bedroom, consigning to the cellar what I considered to be embarrassing stuff, the film posters and books (*Stig of the Dump*, *Watership Down*) that were too childish for my refined imagination. My father was glad to have me back ('Great to have another man in the house. Someone else for the ladies to henpeck') and he patted my shoulder on his way to the office while Mum talked about the day ahead and Mrs Phang's troublesome relatives and the relentless creep of new housing into the Lake Gardens. Dad made great efforts to get home early and we ate our suppers on the veranda, listening to the sprinklers and Bach's *Well-Tempered Clavier*. My parents asked about

Kingsley and I answered selectively, leaving out the bullying and the boredom and making sure that no one boy dominated my stories. They liked to hear about Robbie Thwaite's witticisms and John Toplady's benevolent dimness. I watched myself carefully and tried out words in my head before I referred to my clever friend, Anthony Blunden. Unusually, Dad had no complaints to make about work. My stories filled the gaps left by his comic diatribes and I spent an entire meal recounting the drama on Albury Down.

'Most encouraging,' Dad said. 'It's good to hear a spirit of dissent lives on in the most conservative places.'

I couldn't tell whether he was being sincere. There was a studied levity about him now that declined to take any topic too seriously. It was there in the way he behaved with Mum: a carefulness not to cause distress or irritation, a loving diligence that warmed me and at the same time set off small spangles of alarm in my stomach. Mum had been given a clean bill of health several times now; yet none of us had banished the bitter taste left over from her 'fright'.

Slowly, the prospect of two months in Kuala Lumpur lost its appeal. For the first time since I had started my English education, I found myself almost wanting to be back there. I lay in bed, feeling the sweat coil about me, and imagined Anthony swimming in the sunbeams of an imagined pool or resting his suntanned arms on the counter of a Mediterranean taverna, his hair tangled and coarse as summer wheat, the freckles spreading on his burnished face. Sometimes these imaginings turned sultrier and more thrilling; but I was careful to imagine anonymous bodies, never daring to fuse Anthony with those languid, boyish limbs.

'You shouldn't be wasting your day in bed,' my mother would admonish me, gently for the most part, when I padded to the orange juice left over in the fridge from breakfast. 'I'm going into town this afternoon: let's make an outing of it. Is there anything at the cinema you would like to see?'

'Not specially.'

'If you don't want to be seen with your boring old mum . . .'

'It's not that,' I said, though it was in part. Going out with a parent was no substitute for the company of friends; but these were lacking suddenly. Like someone returning to a disaster-slipped landscape, a place shaken and spilled out of shape in his absence, I found my old bearings gone. Irshad and his family had moved to Sandakan in Borneo, where offshore oil was taking over from the exhausted timber boom. I found out from Sebastian that Gurmit Lal had fallen in with a gang, abandoning his cricket in favour of hanging out, MTV and buzzing about town on scooters. He had no room in his life for an insipid, un-adventurous English boy, milky pale from his lardy-tardy board-ing school. The loss of Gurmit hurt, registering deep tremors that warned of time passing and undoing everything that mattered. Of course, I still had Sebastian, but we saw each other more for old time's sake than as a result of present affinities. Our interests scarcely collided: his techno music and computers to my poetry and novels. Things had changed between us physically as well. I disliked the way he dressed and the boniness that seemed to be knuckling out of him. He smelled of sweat and olives. He offered to lend me some porn but I bailed out, queasy and embarrassed.

As for Sudeep, the last member of my childhood gang, I longed to see him, hoping for something to happen: a kiss, perhaps, or more, that languorous brown flesh writhing into my fantasies. But Sudeep had put on a growth spurt and was no longer so enticing. A holiday job kept him busy and he never returned my telephone calls, anxious to avoid perhaps the temptations that so enflamed and frustrated me.

Lonely in the Lake Gardens, under louring tropical clouds so heavy that I wanted to burst them with my thoughts, I read *Le*

Grand Meaulnes and *The Catcher in the Rye* and devoted myself to tending the secret grove of my desires. My relationship with my parents was happy; yet I knew that time apart, and the shameful secret of my fantasies, had opened up a no man's land that could not be crossed. When my father announced that we would not be going, after all, to the 'boring old' Cameron Highlands but visiting Thailand instead – and for two weeks instead of a measly five days – the prospect did not delight me. We visited Phuket and Bangkok, and the hot, sweaty trudge between temples with their pointy, gleaming Buddhas was an agony of unassuageable lust and impatience. When we returned, sunburned and weary, to our house in KL, the Siamese imp of longing came too. I could not shake it off: the conviction that life was elsewhere. The weeks dragged on so that I was almost glad when the last days came and I could pack my bags for the long flight back to England.

Half drunk with jet lag, my throat sticky and travel-clagged, I made my way to the Eversley – a Third Setter now, in the middle rank of school – and asked directions to Anthony's room. He was not in; his clothes were heaped on the bed. A photograph of a smiling girl in a tie-dyed shirt stood on the otherwise empty desk.

'Loiterer,' said Anthony in the doorway.

'Just looking for things to steal.'

He brushed past me and sat on the only chair. I wanted to ask about the girl in the photograph. He smelled of aftershave and after-smoke peppermints. 'It's hardly the Ritz,' he said, looking up at the ceiling as if at the roof of a cave. 'How d'you suppose they managed to get puke up *there*?'

'I'm sharing a room with Robbie Thwaite,' I said.

'You should keep your back to the wall, then.'

'How were your holidays?'

'Sordid. We went to this place in Provence where there were all these girls celebrating the end of their A levels. I couldn't believe my luck. I told them I was going to Oxford.'

'We went to Thailand.'

'You've been at the rice bowl, I see.'

I blushed and felt a damp hot flux in my belly. Anthony transferred cigarettes to a hidden compartment cut out of one of his books. His indifference to my presence lasted just long enough for me to become his captive.

'So,' he said at last, and the whole weather of his person altered, 'tell me about Thailand.' He cleared a space on his bed and I sat down to tell him about Bangkok and my father's altercation with a traffic policeman and my encounter with a cobra in the grounds of our hotel. I thirsted for his attention, for the light it cast upon me. When Anthony listened I felt I mattered. He sprinkled the favour of his smile, his laugh, sparingly, like a lord with rival courtiers. I told him about my Malaysian friends and the rebellious transformation of Gurmit Lal. The door to his bedroom was ajar but I ceased to notice the voices of boys, the crosswinds of music and the sullen thump of a rugby ball being tossed about the corridor.

A passing senior leered at us. 'Look at you two queers.'

'Fuck off, Michaels.'

'Oh, very witty, I'm sure.'

I barely had time to turn my head. 'Who was that?' I said.

'That,' said Anthony, 'was a turd. The Eversley is a turd farm. I have to hold my nose every day.'

The spell of his audience was broken. Anthony looked distracted: he had things to do before house inspection. 'You've heard about Bridget, I take it?'

'No. What?'

'The police have dropped charges.'

'Oh,' I said, though at that moment my thoughts were else-where.

'I thought you'd like to know.'

'Good. I'm glad.'

The topic had lost its piquancy with the novelty of the year, its new lodgings and fresh victims. Who cared about Albury Down now? Nick Coulter tried to revive the subject in History but only as a stalling strategy. Mr Wimbush inveighed, obligingly, against radicals and hippies who stood in the way of progress.

'Do you think Bridget's a hippy, sir?'

Mr Wimbush blinked; I could see the injection of wariness in his eyes. 'Who?'

'Mr Bridge, sir.'

'Ah . . . well, I wasn't . . . Now look here, Coulter, I won't have insolence in my classes, do you hear?'

'I'm not being insolent, sir.'

'You are by answering back.'

'I'm not answering back.'

'Shut up.'

Mr Wimbush blocked out Coulter's aggrieved expression simply by shutting his eyes. Irritated with himself, he made us write an impromptu essay on Hitler's rise to power. If it had been me and not Coulter who had brought collective punishment on the class, there would have been hell to pay.

Mr Bridge himself was discreet on the subject. He greeted us under the spiky thatch of a new haircut and launched straight into *Beowulf*. He seemed refreshed by the summer and defiantly cheerful, declaiming in strange and sonorous Old English. It was Anthony who dared to ask the question.

'They got their road,' answered Mr Bridge, 'they had nothing to gain from persecuting me.'

At the end of the lesson, I pretended to search the floor for a fallen ink cartridge. Mr Bridge clacked and shimmied with his wiper across the blackboard. 'I don't suppose it's much of a consolation,' he said over his shoulder, 'to be back in cooler climes?'

I wanted to tell him that he was in the right, for him to know that I was on his side. I took a few steps towards the door, longing to tell him about the books I had read, yet fearing to seem like a try-hard. 'I got through *A Portrait of the Artist*,' I said.

This provoked a startling response.

' "Welcome, O life! I go to encounter for the something time the reality of experience and to forge in the smithy of my soul the uncreated conscience of my race." ' Mr Bridge set down the board wiper in its milling nimbus of dust. There was a touch of the impresario in his nature. 'Did you *enjoy* it?'

'I did.'

'I love the hellfire speech. But of course, never having believed such things, the terror of it is lost on me.' I did not know what he was talking about: the novel had defeated me after Dedalus left Clongowes College. All the same, the slime of the ditch, his blindness, the whole *matter* of the school chapter had made a great impression on me. 'Anything else you got your literary teeth into?'

'I read *Hamlet*.'

'No, seriously?'

'My father has the video with Laurence Olivier. We watched it together.'

'That was a shocking haircut, wasn't it?'

'I like the way the monologues went on in his head.'

'The soliloquies.' Mr Bridge fastened the buckle on his brief-case. 'Yes: he does that in *Henry V* too. O God of battles. A very Christian sentiment. Are you coming?'

I followed him out of the classroom into the corridor; it was gloomy even on a sunny day. The paperbacks on their sagging bookshelves looked grey and uninviting. 'Do you have anything else you'd recommend, sir? I, uh . . . I read the books you gave Anthony.'

Mr Bridge halted by the swinging door. I felt myself violently blushing. My whole body throbbed with imploration. 'Bruno, I'm afraid I have a staff meeting to attend. Can we pick up on this later?'

There was nothing I could do to detain him. The brush-off was politely done. Unwilling to seem strange or infatuated, I turned away as Mr Bridge slipped into the arcanum of the English staffroom.

The card came through internal post. It was handwritten in a florid calligraphic hand:

Anthony Blunden & Bruno Jackson
are cordially invited to the house of
Mr & Mrs Bridge (21 Conquest Lane)
for poetry & biscuits.
Monday 8 p.m. RSVP Mr B.

I stared at it for a minute, sitting on my bed while Robbie, opposite, gasped in his sleep. (The gong had been struck but he always slept through it. Late for breakfast most mornings, he had been taken aside by Matron and warned of the dangers of excessive self-abuse. Anybody else would have curled up with embarrassment but Robbie found it funny enough to share with his friends. He was not, to my knowledge, a lavish wanker but kept such things to a parsimonious minimum.) I looked so hard at the handwriting that my eyes crossed. I banished my suspicion that it might be a fake and began to worry that Anthony would turn the offer down. There was a vein of perversity in him, an obstinate desire to upset expectations, which I was learning to fear. I imagined our forthcoming history lesson with him pretending to know nothing of an invitation. I began to wonder whether it was hopeless; whether clumsy as I was it would be possible for me to attend on my own. And yet here was the invitation! I had been singled out: a poetic soul in so much drabness, receiving at last the attention it deserved. With a sense of special favour, I trundled down to breakfast.

Half the tables were empty and Robbie had finally come down, scruffy and ponderous, when I went to the trays for a third helping. Mr Sedley was standing with the ladle. He was not impressed. 'This is pure gluttony, Bruno.'

'What do you mean, sir? I'm hungry.'

'You *think* you're hungry. It's a question of mind over matter.' I looked at the dripping ladle. Did this mean I was not going to get any more beans? 'I'm sorry to say this, Bruno. You're running to fat – though I don't suppose the phrase is appropriate. I understand you've given up all sports.'

'Yes,' I said, my ears burning.

'You're not an old man of seventy, for heaven's sake. *Mens sana in corpore sano*. Ever heard the saying?'

'I walk a lot, sir.'

'Walking is hardly enough for a boy your age. If it's team sports you take exception to, take up tennis. We have *got* a court: someone might as well use it.'

'There's no net, sir.'

'Then you should have no difficulty.'

I returned to my room in a murderous mood. All I needed now was for Anthony to play silly buggers with me and the crapness of my life would be complete.

In the event, I need not have worried. Anthony was an enthusiast for what he called 'an evening of Bridge'. For all his bravado about not wanting to suck up to masters, he had gone already to the staffroom pigeonholes and left a note confirming his attendance.

'You didn't say anything to me,' I complained.

'I knew you'd say yes.'

Bowed and apologetic, I was a caricature of humility as Mr Bridge welcomed us into his home. Anthony, on the other hand, accepted the hospitality as if it were his due. Walking tall in the kitchen, he barely glanced at the pagoda-like ceramic sculpture with its copper and cobalt glazes, at the blowsy yellow stocks in a vase of marshy water or the woodblock prints of wading shorebirds above the pinewood table: so many tokens of a shared domestic life.

'It's a bit of a mess I'm afraid. My wife's off on one of her expeditions: in pursuit of rare birds in uncomfortable places. I'm left to look after base camp.'

There was no disorder: Mr Bridge wanted to speak well of his wife. Smiling softly, he opened the door to his living room. A kitchen chair and sofa were arranged about a coffee table. Three of the four walls were lined with books and my admiration turned to envy: of the sophistication of adults, of the years it would take to catch up and the money I would need to amass such a collection.

'Do you read in your spare time, by any chance?' said Anthony, sniffing about the shelves.

'Spare time? What's that?'

Mr Bridge stood by the waiting chair but he was in no hurry to get us to sit down. Since it was obvious that he did not mind our snooping, I joined Anthony by the bookshelves. The room had a faintly spiced odour, of cinnamon and nutmeg and cloves, and that wonderful fusty smell of well-thumbed paperbacks. Instead of the dull strip lighting we were accustomed to in our dormitories, table lamps cast rhomboids of soft light across the walls.

There were more bird prints here, and river-rounded pebbles in a wooden bowl on the mantelpiece, and small wooden sculptures in cornices among the shelves: a soapstone Buddha, hardwood demons, something Mayan or Aztec with obsidian teeth, a trumpeting Ganesh made of bronze, a golden plover in painted balsa wood.

'Did you buy these things abroad, sir?' I said, emboldened by Anthony's assurance and Mr Bridge's air of genial benignity.

'I can't pretend to be a Bruce Chatwin. My wife's the globetrotter: it goes with the territory. I, on the other hand, like geriatrics and certain kinds of orchid, do not travel well.'

'How do you know,' said Anthony, almost aggressively, 'if you've never tried?'

His insouciance had vanished. As I felt my inhibitions falling away, Anthony seemed to tense up, and I realised that his earlier manner had been defensive. He was anxious to impress, and this anxiety made him confrontational even with masters.

Mr Bridge took the challenge with good humour. 'I once threw up,' he said, 'over an entire family of Belgians on the ferry to Ostend. Boats and bridges do not get on. As for flying, it puts the fear of God into me. It's not heights that I'm afraid of so much as the ground when you strike it at a hundred and twenty miles an hour.' Anthony was on the verge of scoffing. 'Yes, I know it's irrational, but I'm confined by unreason to this island. Not that I consider it any kind of imprisonment. The world's a prison, if you think about it: just a very big one. And there are rewards in getting to know a small place intimately. We put such value on movement and quantity but it's the *quality* of our experience that matters. One can spend a lifetime travelling without seeing very much. Maybe it's better to choose a local patch of the earth and really get to know it?'

Precocious jetsetters, Anthony and I must have looked doubtful. Mr Bridge excused himself and, while he was gone, Anthony picked up the statuettes on the bookshelves and replaced them with an expression of studied disdain.

Mr Bridge returned with tea and a plate of assorted biscuits. We sat down by the coffee table and while I attended to pouring the milk, Anthony appropriated the custard creams.

'Tell me,' said Mr Bridge, noticing nothing, 'how are things?'

I looked for Anthony to volunteer but he was eating. It was up to me to speak. 'Do you mean in lessons?'

'I mean overall. How's Kingsley treating you?'

'You make it sound like a person,' said Anthony.

'Yes,' said Mr Bridge, 'I suppose I do. When you're a small cog in a big social engine, it helps to humanise it. Many poets adopt the same conceit. Shakespeare, for instance, often draws this analogy between society and the human body. We're all part of one functioning, or malfunctioning, whole. So for instance, I suppose you could say that pupils are like the blood cells pumped about the body of college . . . Which would make us teachers the heart.'

'Sounds revolting,' said Anthony, licking crumbs from his lips.

Mr Bridge produced from his briefcase three library copies of *The Rattle Bag* and placed them, one by one, like rescued bullion, on the table. I racked my brain for something to say.

'Is it true, sir, about General Montague's horse?'

'Good Lord – what a question. Is what true, exactly?'

'That its, uh, privates were buried near the cricket pavilion? It's something we had to learn as fags.'

'Well, you've been here longer than I have, so you'll know as much as me.'

'I suppose it's one of those silly college traditions,' I said, 'like toast queues and exeat slips and the bloody awful Fun Run.' Anthony snorted. 'Have you ever done it, sir?'

'Done what?'

'The Fun Run. I knew it was going to be hell the minute I heard what they called it.'

Mr Bridge laughed, tilting back his head to show a pronounced epiglottis. It was most gratifying. 'Boys are supposed to *enjoy* getting muddy,' he said, 'and half drowning in lakes, and breaking their legs on tree roots. It's all good bracing fun, Bruno – shame on you for your unsporting attitude.'

'I hate sport,' I said.

'Well, it takes all sorts.'

'The way the master always puts his favourites in charge and you have to wait for selection like an idiot and when everyone's been taken they whine: Ooh, sir, not Jackson, sir, he's a total flid, sir.'

Mr Bridge gave a sour expression, between amusement and sympathy. 'Yes,' he said, 'it is crappy. But it was ever thus. I bet, when the Stratford boys got together to kick a bladder around, there were loud complaints about Will Shakespeare and his two left feet.'

Anthony joined in the merriment. 'Isn't it in one of his plays that he talks about football?'

'*Shakespeare* never talks about anything. One of his characters does: King Lear, I think. "Thou base football player." And that was long before the birth of Vinnie Jones.'

We laughed, more for the novelty of the conversation than its content. It was as if Mr Bridge had taken a weight from our shoulders that we only noticed once it was gone. He had brought us to a refuge, a neutral zone where, for a moment at least, it was possible to let down our guard. Anthony took up a comic litany of grumbles and described some of the viler members of Eversley House. I felt unbidden words rising in my belly. They wanted to escape like a belch, I couldn't keep them down. 'My housemaster hates me,' I said.

Anthony stared through the steam of his raised mug. I realised with pleasure that I had surprised him.

'Do you think,' said Mr Bridge, 'that you might have a word with him about it?'

'Hardly, sir. It's Mr Sedley.'

Mr Bridge made a small, involuntary grimace. I felt confident enough, in that entirely un-school-like setting, to say exactly what I thought: that my housemaster had achieved his ambition of becoming a wrong-headed, curmudgeonly old bastard. I explained how he took out his frustrations on his pupils: not through acts of overt cruelty but with carping and belittling displays of disapproval that wore you down. It was not *fair* of him to take it out on me for being (I actually said this) *different* from other boys.

Anthony gathered in his knees, stiffening with embarrassment. When I had finished, Mr Bridge did not refute what I had said, though I expected to be rebuked for having said it. 'It's good to be forthright, Bruno. You should speak how you feel. On the other hand, when we have dealings with people, we don't always know what context their behaviour is coming from. Often it has little to do with us, though we get in the way of whatever precedes our meeting . . .' Mr Bridge saw my incomprehension. 'What I mean is . . . masters are only human. We never know what's going on in other people's lives.'

'Do you know, sir? What's going on in Mr Sedley's life? Because I really think he dislikes me.'

'I'm sure that isn't true. It's not an easy job, you know, looking after fifty boys at a time.'

'I'm hardly the worst of them.' Sympathise with me: oh, be on my side! But I knew that I had gone too far. Teachers, even Mr Bridge, always close ranks in the end; and I had spoiled the tone of our banter.

Anthony sat in silence, turning his teacup about in its saucer.

My elation at being able to speak freely soured to self-reproach. Mr Bridge proposed that we make a start on his selection of poems and handed us photocopies.

'Outlandish as it might seem to some of our Kingsley colleagues,' he said, 'poetry exists for *pleasure*. A good poem is like firewater: a concentrated burst of life, distilled from as few words as possible. I don't want you treating this as a lesson or a test of literary cleverness. Bugger cleverness: I want to know if a poem makes the hairs stand up on the back of your neck. I want to know if it makes you feel: "*Yes*, that's it, exactly, that's how I feel, that's what sunlight is like through mist, that's what it's like to be alone". Or else, if you feel nothing, say so. It's all legitimate. There is no right or wrong response. Just taste the words and see what they do to you.'

He spoke about those rectangles of print on a page as if they were pieces of cake in *Alice in Wonderland*, one bite of which might send us whooshing up to the ceiling or dwindling to the size of mice among the threads of the carpet. I found his excitement thrilling, but Anthony protected himself from contagion behind a carapace of sarcasm. If Mr Bridge failed to notice it – or pretended not to – I could sense it in my friend's glib observations, in the tiny snorts, like breaths gone awry, that greeted every stanza. It was unfair on Mr Bridge, who read well, cleaving to the sense and letting the tone assert itself. We were spared those slow, mournful cadences so beloved of lazy actors on *Poetry Please*. His choices were too earthy for poetical drawling. It was enough to concentrate on the images forming in my head: Ted Hughes' pike and their implacable grinning; the grassy mind of John Clare, watching a field mouse rescue her young and then standing up to survey the world from the height of himself, its 'broad old cesspools' glittering in the sun; then the dirty thrill and unexpected repose of Larkin's 'High Windows'.

Perhaps the seduction of that evening lay as much for me in the *idea* of poetry, of *being* a poet (for at that moment I had no doubt of my vocation), as it did in the poems themselves. Does that diminish the revelation? The hour we spent in Mr Bridge's house whisked me away from myself and the shabby conformity of boarding school. From out of the squalor shone a light that showed me as I wished to be. I was the Bruno my parents had known; I was myself again.

There were two more 'Bridge evenings' (as Anthony called them) that Michaelmas Term, and both renewed the enchantments of the first. Being welcomed into the house was to be ushered into an almost forgotten world of domestic ease, with soft furnishings instead of utilitarian sturdiness, personality instead of sameness. Accordingly, I looked forward to those evenings as other boys looked forward to their weekend exeats. It was like going on leave from some particularly dull and disciplinarian branch of the services: a taste of civilian comforts, a poignant approxima-tion of home life, though the set was not quite up to scratch, lacking the broad teak beams and the house geckos and the avenue of fan palms outside. I loved, all the same, the spicy odours of the kitchen and the cushioned haven of the living room, which lacked only a sleeping cat to be a perfect summation of bookish repose. Mr Bridge was genial, didactic, yet open to our juvenile interpretations and willing to glean what sense lay within them. He introduced us to Seamus Heaney and Sylvia Plath and the sardonic, prickly erudition of Tony Harrison. He perplexed us and made us dream with 'Kubla Khan' and several parts of 'The Waste Land' – the last inspiring me to pen my own verses full of dry bones and rats' feet and hooded figures in rocky places.

For some reason, Anthony and I did not discuss our evenings afterwards. We were disinclined to shared retrospection, and it was as if, cast out into the cold again, we wanted to keep the experience in the warm privacy of our memory. I, for my part, could see what effect Mr Bridge's patronage had on my friend. On our third evening, he shed his defensive posture. Liberated of the compulsion to please or intimidate, he seemed to access reserves of inner calm, attaining a stillness I had never seen before.

Both of us hoped, each time we went there, to see *Mrs* Bridge. The house was filled with the fruits of her wanderings; everywhere we seemed to hear her melody, and her husband spoke about her so frequently and with such affection that she became in our imagination a summation of femininity, combining the sexiness of a film star with the all-forgiving competence of our mothers.

Her absence on the first two occasions was tantalising. On our third visit, it was she who came to the door. 'Come in,' she said, 'before it starts bucketing down. Or has it started already?' With one arm holding on to the porch pillar, she swung out to peer at the rain-swollen clouds. It was night already and cold and she wore trousers and a sweater accordingly; yet Mrs Bridge seemed to inhabit a cool summer's evening, for her face was tanned when ours were pale and the lightness of her movements belonged in cotton rather than wool.

I hoped for introductions but she was too brisk. Politely, warmly even, she made us welcome; but we were in no doubt that we belonged to her husband's work and that her life and its responsibilities lay elsewhere.

She was not classically beautiful but her height and athleticism conferred a gracefulness which in turn gave lustre to her face. I found attractive its neatness, the roundness of her small chin and the supple carnality of her mouth. Her eyes were large and without make-up startlingly blue; though they might captivate in love, they suggested a fierce capacity for close scrutiny. Her thick hair, blonde with threads of a darker seam, was cut short in a practical, tomboyish bob which, together with a deep tan from her expeditions, stirred in me and doubtless in Anthony a chord of erotic deference.

Mrs Bridge seemed oblivious to any effect she might have on us. 'Sam's just stoking the fire,' she said, extending an arm to welcome us inside. Her accent was northern: Lancastrian, I've since discovered. It had a blunt, humorous edge that found no equivalent in the clipped tones of masters or the affected cockney consonants and snobbish vowels of my contemporaries. 'He reckons he's a proper Prometheus and does all kinds of strange things with log pyramids and whatnot. It seems daft when we've got central heating . . .' (this monologue delivered over her shoulder as we passed through the kitchen) '. . . but there you have it, boys will be boys.'

Her husband was just getting up, with a hip-clasping air of achievement, from a roaring hearth when Mrs Bridge waved us into the living room. She did not linger, and I recognised my own obscure feeling of sorrow in Anthony's face when he turned around to see the door closing behind her.

'She's just back from Borneo,' said Mr Bridge, slapping wood dust from his fingers. 'They found a new species of parrot. At least, they think it's a new species – the specimen's now in the hands of experts.' We sat down in our places on the sofa and prepared ourselves for a reading; but Mr Bridge had other ideas. 'Slight change of plan this evening. Since you've sat your mock GCSEs and the holiday atmosphere is all pervasive, I want to play you some music . . .'

The dreadful expectation of a squeaking recital on clarinet or bassoon was allayed when he produced from his briefcase a library copy of a CD. It was Schubert's Quintet in C major, recorded by the Alban Berg Quartet. Anthony let out a groan intended for me only but Mr Bridge caught it. 'Oh, don't be so cloth eared,' he said. 'I'm not going to force the whole thing on you. I just want you to listen to one movement.'

'I already know it,' said Anthony, and this surprised me, for he was not musical. 'My mum plays that kind of thing all day long, mostly to annoy my dad.'

'There's a difference,' said Mr Bridge, 'between hearing and listening.' He got up and slipped the disc into a small player among his books. The CD spun on pause. 'Schubert was scarcely older than me when he died. This quintet was composed in the last year of his life. I want to play you the second movement, the most famous.'

I had not paid attention to the impressive arrangement of speakers in the room. As Mr Bridge stepped away from the shelves, turning off all but one of the lamps in the room, they whispered momentarily. Then the music began.

It was not, perhaps, a true revelation. Such things catch us by surprise and I was too guarded, my sense of the moment too melodramatic, for the music really to pierce me. It was stately, melancholy, consoling: so much I might have said. But the profundity of it passed me by. The Schubert was the ambience, the background to the true music of the scene: the sad rapture of a ragged autumn night, with the rush and patter of rain outside and Mr Bridge in a chair, resting his chin on his hands, gazing out of the window that reflected him in a spectral shimmer. Anthony sprawled beside me on the sofa, a scowl of concentration (or was it boredom?) unsettling his brow, and his brooding, which passed for attention, seemed handsome to me. I believed that it might be profound, that he had access to regions of thought and feeling to which I could only aspire. I longed to know and understand him. I felt that I could be a better friend to him – a true confidant – if only he would let me into the fullness of his life. I had noticed lately how he was often aggrieved against masters or fellow pupils. A special soul collects enemies; it needs the validation of intimate friendship, and that friendship was celebrated in these meetings at Mr Bridge's house. There it was given room and we became an entity: Anthony and Bruno, Bruno and Anthony, our initials the rhyme scheme of a stanza. Our special natures had been identified and were to be nurtured; for Mr Bridge was of the civilisation to which we aspired. In him we had found a mentor, and among the hostility of our peers we could bask in the knowledge of his friendship.

So I surrendered to the seduction of the evening – a space cleared amid the disorder of our appetites and the rigid discipline of our days. The wind snored in the hearth; the light of the flames danced on the bookshelves. My friend breathed beside me. The music passed through a period of tension and fear; it subsided to supreme calm. Mr Bridge listened with folded arms. Anthony closed his eyes. I heard the music for the first time, and understood that I was in love.

Now

It was to be the warmest September on record. People in London were still wearing T-shirts; retail slumped as nobody rushed to change wardrobe. Dad spent much of his time in the garden, marvelling at the non-appearance of autumn. Bees stumbled, half drunk, from flower to flower; the beech hedge, which had shed its foliage in the heatwave, now put on a doomed leaf spurt. 'Weird,' Dad said, his hat tipped at a jaunty angle. Not even the planet could threaten his good spirits. His girlfriend, Ann, was preparing the table for tea.

I had dreaded meeting her, expecting some musty devotee of Glyndebourne, a culture vulture with roosts at the Royal Academy and the Wigmore Hall.

In the event, the woman who had stolen my father's heart was a kind, toothy divorcee, big boned and unlovely, posh in a reticent and down-at-heel fashion. She greeted me with only a hint of nervousness in her eyes. As she blathered, I took in the physical fact of her existence. I could tell at once that it would be difficult to hate her. She seemed anxious to please, as if I had regressed to petulant adolescence, and I wondered whether I really was that difficult to live with.

My father took me by the arm; we never touched, normally. We went inside and sat down for tea and shortbread biscuits.

Ann was looking nervously between us. I felt sorry for her: infiltrating an established world, no matter how unhappy it was, cannot have been easy. I munched biscuits, dunking them in sweet milky tea, watching the slow capillary action. Dad talked about a programme he had heard on the radio, and Ann said that she had heard it, too, and wasn't it one of the marvels of British life, having Radio 4 on day in, day out? The whole conversation was for my benefit. It was as if they were reading lines from a play. I wondered what they talked about when they were alone together.

'Christopher was telling me,' said Ann, 'about your paintings.'

I looked at her, my biscuit dripping. 'My paintings?'

'He says you're very talented.'

This was a revelation on several fronts. I had not painted since I left school, and what I had brought home and was now gathering dust under my bed in Vauxhall he had not liked much, thinking it garish and obscure, pretentious maybe. Was he talking me up because a podgy, gay civil servant is nothing to boast about? Or was he trying to rekindle something long extinct within me? I let my eyes wander to his face but he was gazing diffidently at the table.

'I was a . . . I used to do stuff when I was at school. But, uh, I've not painted anything since.'

Ann's smile congealed: she must have heard the creaking of thin ice. I felt churlish for killing the conversation but, damn it, what was there to say? My dad came to the rescue. 'All I meant,' he said, 'was that you *had* something. I'm sure it's still in you. Maybe at some point you might think of going back to it?'

What was this – a lifestyle ambush? Was Ann going to be our salvation, new life breathed into broken lungs? Dad could play at resurrection as much as it pleased him. Let him read his Herbert and listen to Auntie Beeb but leave me out of it. I felt, or imagined I felt, a reproach in their innocuous words and this made me angry. I wiped my fingers on the seams of my pockets and excused myself from their company.

When I returned from a vacuous sit-out in my father's study, I was no longer the centre of their attention. My father sat with his left leg resting on his right knee, hands folded upon his raised ankle. There was something intent about his posture, and I recognised the delight with which he received and blessed her talk.

Ann saw me first and, despite her smile, I knew how she felt from the unconscious flight of her hand to the chain about her throat. Dad greeted me as if I had just returned from the bush and I took my teacup and sat on the sofa to finish it. I felt shaken: excluded and sorry, envious of the bond that was flowering between them. I wanted to redeem the afternoon and leapt at Ann's suggestion of a walk on Putney Common.

Dad held forth throughout our ramble. It was a grand performance in the old style: a mix of erudition, outrage and literary gossip, and I understood, looking at Ann's unlovely, equine face, the cliché about hanging on to someone's every word. It made me queasy to see such enthusiasm; there was something indecent about it at their age. It was as if both were starting afresh in spite of past, painful experience. I should have been glad to see their affection for each other but it was unsettling. I wondered whether such potential was wasted in me for ever.

It was a balmy afternoon. The common was crowded with families, young and old lovers, loners following their dogs with supermarket plastic bags in their hands. The vegetation looked tired, as if it had been kept up all night, and we looked in sorrow and bewilderment at an avenue of horse chestnuts thoroughly browned, every leaf mined by some insect or other. Ann wondered whether conkers were about to go the way of the elms, and surprised me, who thought her an urban creature, by pointing out the skeletons of saplings in a hedgerow: suckers that had tried again in the nineties only to succumb afresh to the disease. I tried not to see a portent in them: it proved I was not immune to hope.

Ann had something on that evening with her daughter. She had to get home before seven, and I joined my father in his car as he dropped her off.

'It was a pleasure meeting you, Bruno.'

'Likewise,' I said. I stayed in the back seat to spare us the dilemma of farewell: would a handshake do, a kiss on the cheek, or just a reticent nod of the head? We exchanged glances merely, and Dad got out of the car to walk her to her door. As they parted, I was careful to look the other way, into the swash of London traffic.

When Dad returned to the car, he waited for me to say my bit. I searched for kind words. What was so hard about wishing him well? Still, nothing came to my lips, and I was glad when he turned on the stereo and bathed us in the consolation of a Bach cantata.

The truth was, my thoughts were lonely. I was thinking about love, about the talent for love. Was it finite, or differently apportioned for each individual? Could some people do it, like some can draw or play the guitar? I have loved once, and though I was not requited, there was some reward for my efforts. Anthony let me near him. I became essential to him because of his value in my eyes. He never returned my affection, let alone my love; but in the last year of our innocence he became dependent on me and, in all the years since, I cannot pretend to have occupied such a role in another man's life.

Jenny's tough words were haunting me. Back at the office, she emailed me a poem by Rilke, and though it was a heavy-handed tactic ('You must change your life,' says the poet), I managed to appreciate the concern behind it. I had ranted about the prime minister and government inaction on the environment and, beyond that, had seemed to hate life. I had to get back to first principles, she had said, and that meant to the place where the rot had set in.

On Saturday morning I stayed in bed mulling these things over. I got up to make myself some porridge. I took a long shower. At eleven o'clock, just as a mizzle came floating down outside, I telephoned the Blundens.

Dipali answered. I felt my resolution falter but withstood her cheerful hello. 'Hi, it's Bruno Jackson.' She did not immediately respond. 'I'm, um . . . not calling at a bad time, am I?'

'Not at all.' There was no warmth in her voice. I could hear jazz music in the background.

'I'm sorry I never thanked you for dinner.'

'Anthony's out, I'm afraid.'

'Oh. When will he be back?'

'He's gone to his parents. There's a big family do.'

'Are you not invited?' Her silence made my ears burn. 'It's OK, I'll try his mobile . . .'

'He's lost it.'

'What?'

'I mean, it was stolen. Do you want me to take a message?'

I hesitated. I could hear the small plastic sounds of the receiver in her hand. 'It's quite important that I speak to him,' I said.

'I'd rather you didn't.'

'I'm sorry?'

'I'd rather you didn't call.'

My first thought was that their marriage was in crisis (who could stay attached to such a man?) and I felt a thin, ignoble sense of triumph. 'Isn't he coming back?'

'He's gone for the weekend.'

'I don't understand. Have I done something wrong?'

147

I listened to her breathing, the fractional modulations of responses tried out in her head and rejected. 'No,' she said at last, very softly. 'I'm going to hang up now. Please don't call again.'

She hung up. I called again. The phone rang for perhaps a minute before Dipali answered.

'Bruno,' she said, 'I've asked you nicely.'

'You didn't let me leave a message.'

'Oh.' This caught her off guard. I could hear her making an effort to rally. 'What do you want to say?'

'Look, is there no way he can call *me* when he's up to it?'

'I don't think that's going to happen. He's . . . Please, I have to put his interests first.'

'His interests?'

'Please understand . . .'

'How can I possibly threaten his interests?'

'Just leave us alone.'

It was my turn to stumble. There was such a tone of weariness in her voice that I felt suddenly desolate. When the line went dead, I walked to the window and gazed out at the moistening tarmac. People and papers drifted by; a dog pissed punily on a dead rowan. I heard the siren wail of the exposed receiver and returned to fling it at the holster. It missed and slid into the wastepaper basket. I dug it out and, in a fury, rammed it home.

Every time I tried the number again, it was either engaged or rang without answer. I fetched a paperback from my bathroom and sat, notionally reading, while the dial tone sounded in my ear.

What *right* had Anthony to such protection? I would besiege her if necessary. The telephone rang and rang: then nothing. Dipali must have pulled the cord from its socket.

Perhaps if she had spoken to me – even if only to fob me off nicely – I might have lost my intent. But the brush-off made me angry; I spent several minutes stomping about my flat, swearing. It was a simple enough matter to find Anthony's law firm on the Web; his email address would be the same as his colleagues'. Accordingly, I wrote to him.

Anthony,

I'm not threatening you. I don't want to expose you to Dipali or harm your career in any way. But since we met I've been haunted. The past never really leaves us, does it? We are the host through which it lives. I know we have both tried to lock away what happened – but it DID happen, Anthony, and just because it was years ago and we were only boys doesn't make it any less real.

Is there a chance we can talk? Can we find a time and a place? You have my phone number. If you can't bear to meet me, at least write. But don't ignore me. Whatever you do, don't think this, or I, will just disappear.

Bruno

I read the words over and over. I erased the last paragraph and restored it three times. It would have been the easiest thing in the world to shut the window down, to let it die in cyberspace. But I remembered Jenny's words about first principles, and the new life in my father's eyes, and dispatched my cursor to send.

Then

'Doubt wisely,' said Mr Bridge. 'In strange way, to stand right inquiring is not to stray.'

I looked at Anthony and saw my emotion reflected in his face. Our classmates made little or nothing of the words but *we* knew that Mr Bridge was quoting Donne. I remembered the lines he had read to us in a rain-slicked corner of his garden.

> . . . on a huge hill,
> Cragg'd, and steep, Truth stands, and he that will
> Reach her, about must, and about must go.

I felt again the hard music of the lost soul, driven by raging streams 'through mills and rocks and woods', 'consumed in going' even before it reaches the sea.

'It's all right to be uncertain,' said Mr Bridge. 'It's the journey of the thought that counts. Likewise, I want you to stop worrying about *messages*. A book isn't a bottle thrown into the ocean by a shipwrecked author. Nor is a poem a code you're meant to crack. Just engage with what's in front of you and see what it does.'

This guru stuff was too much for Tom McGrath. I had felt him seething and steaming behind me all lesson. 'Sir,' he burst out, 'why can't you just *tell* us?'

'Tell you?'

'What to *write*, sir. We've got our exams next month and I wish we could just concentrate on that.'

'But we are concentrating.'

'*No*, sir. I don't know what I'm supposed to think. I mean . . . I only want to pass the exam.'

'You will. Your essays on Golding have been excellent . . .'

'But the *poems*, sir. Why can't you just tell us what we're supposed to write?'

This threw Mr Bridge. Inspiration he could do – he fancied himself as an inspirer – but as a coach? Tom McGrath was not to be satisfied, and Anthony had no sympathy for him as we trudged down Ashford Hill half an hour later.

'Fucking philistine. I could have strangled him. I could have *puked*. Why can't they stream English like other subjects? We're being kept back by these knuckle-scrapers . . .'

I was struck by how personally he seemed to take it. There was real venom in him, a contempt that could only engender resentment in others. Many boys picked up on it; but only I experienced the full amplitude of Anthony's scorn. In an odd way, I treasured the intimacy. Gone were the days when he used to keep me apart from his college self. Though he was never bullied as I was, he was avoided, and the scorn implicit in such neglect rankled him. More and more, he brooded on real and imagined grievances, railing against master and pupil alike.

'Ollie Radmore's a greasy little arsehole,' he said. This *was* a change of tune. Until the weekend, when Anthony had been volubly ejected from a kickabout on the playing fields, Ollie had been a 'sound bloke' – a sound bloke who called me Brown-Nose Jackson and Borneo Fatson. 'Did you know he keeps a hamster in his tuck box? He probably shoves it up his arse, like that film actor.'

Part of me rebelled against this talk; at the same time I craved it with almost sexual longing. We took a short cut through the copse behind the armoury and, as the ground was muddy, we leapt between hummocks and islands of grass. Anthony landed on a stand of daffodils without even noticing.

'I can't wait to reach the Lower Sixth,' he said as we approached the dining hall. 'No more of that cunt Wimbush breathing down my neck. And I'm giving up Latin: Plater can find some other boy to wank about.'

I blushed. 'Bloody hell . . .'

'You think I don't know? I've seen the way he looks at me. Why else would a grown man want to take boys on a rugby tour? It's to watch them in the shower.'

Mercifully we reached the lunch queue and the obscenities ceased. 'What,' I said, 'are you going to do for A levels?'

Anthony sniffed at the promise of grease wafting from the kitchens. He was, he said, going to stick with English. He intended to read it at university. 'Oxford, if I can get in. My dad was at Christ Church: it's where all the talent goes.'

I said I was hoping to focus on English and art. Anthony dismissed the latter as a waste of time; it didn't come naturally to him, whereas I had a knack for sketching and loved the way a line hatched beneath my pencil. After Mr Bridge's house, there was no place more comforting to me than the art department. I went there in my free time, when the only other boys were fellow devotees, breathing over their projects with the rapt attention of small boys picking at scabs. The art department was tucked away in one of the oldest parts of the college. I loved its broad and sun-smudged windows, the blemished wood of the benches and the tinny music of Mr Fisk's transistor radio. I liked the smell of oil paint and clay slip and the darkroom's latent alchemy.

We barged our way into the serving area, where the real shoving began. I stood close to Anthony and yawped, 'Are you nervous about exams yet?'

'Not yet,' he bellowed, and by and large it was true. In a school hardly famed for academic excellence, we were star pupils. It was not arrogance exactly: intellectual work was the one area of school life over which we felt some measure of control.

Escaping a food riot, we found a corner of table by the water dispensers and hunkered down. The 'chicken Kiev' was battered gristle with garlic bilge at its centre. Chips were pallid wedges of potato fur. I bathed my sliced bread in tomato blood. 'Honestly,' said Anthony, 'I don't know how you can eat that crap.'

'Don't you like it?'

For dessert we had settled for bananas in custard. Anthony wrinkled his nose at it. 'How do they manage to get so many strings? Do you suppose they add them?'

'I'll have it if you don't want it.'

Anthony slid his bowl towards mine and I transferred the contents. 'Honestly,' he said, 'you're a glutton for punishment.'

It may have looked gross, but I got great satisfaction from eating his food. He soon forgot his disgust at my appetite. 'Hey,' he said, 'I called my dad about Malaysia.'

The custard cooled in my mouth. 'You . . . you did?'

'Well, you meant it, didn't you?'

'Of *course*.'

'He says he can't see any reason why I shouldn't go out there with you. He's ready to pay for the flight and everything.'

'That's . . . Jesus, that's wonderful.'

'Yeah, it's pretty cool. I should get a proper invitation, mind you, from your parents.'

'I'll get it.'

'God. Imagine. A whole summer without *any* homework. Of course, you'll have to show me the sights. Mum's terrified I'll step on a snake . . .'

I tried to conceal my mad delight. Anthony would be coming with me! I would have him in *my* house; he would be sleeping in the room next to mine, for a whole month! My heart felt ripe to burst. I wanted to take the hand that dawdled on the table. I forced myself to eat a pudding made suddenly tasteless.

'Come on,' said Anthony. Burly seniors were starting to emerge from the serving corridors. 'Let's get out of here.'

We spent the afternoon in the library, diligently revising. Anthony sat opposite me in a slowly drifting halo of light, his face close to the notepaper and his lips open with a sleeper's steady breath. I could not help studying the sandy down on his cheeks, the tiny creases parallel with his earlobes, the open collar of his shirt where his freckled skin continued out of sight. My mind remained aflutter with the news about the holidays, and I thought how I would have him sitting next to me, his thigh pressing against mine, in the sticky crush of the homeward flight. We would fall asleep together and I could engineer a slump towards him, or else my dozing hand might settle accidentally in his lap. I sat distracted above my schoolbooks and pressed my erection against the underside of the table. It didn't matter if he never found out. I did not *want* him to know if it meant losing his friendship. Enough for me to be near him: enough for him to trust and confide in me and tell me sexy tales of his encounters with girls. What did girls matter to me? They would come and go. I would remain.

It was to be our last Bridge evening of the year. Our mentor had informed us (or warned us) that we would be reading poetry in translation, and I heard for the first time the resonant names of Rilke and Rimbaud and García Lorca. Anthony pretended to groan at the prospect of 'foreign muck' but I could not imagine a better way to end the day.

I was not to make it. Walking back to deposit my books before supper, I found the Hereward in a state of frenzy. Boys stood whispering outside their doors or churned about Main Corridor, the prefects looking wan and shocked, those with less of a stake in the House gurning and barking with laughter.

John Toplady rushed past me. My arm stretched into his velocity and spun him round. 'What's happening? What's going on?'

'What's going on? Where've you *been*?'

'In the library.'

'Mrs Sedley's run off. She's taken everything but the dog.'

'What do you mean?'

'She's left Sedley. For another man.'

Other boys, realising that someone was left who had not yet heard the news, gathered round. I disliked their hungry faces, the avid sheen in their eyes. They were hooked on scandal. Talking it over was like trying to recapture your first, cigarette-induced head rush. With each puff the thrill diminishes; so you keep compulsively at it.

'Barclay says he heard them arguing. He could hear them through the wall.'

'You can hardly blame her, can you, for shagging someone else?'

'What, with all of *us* waiting next door?'

'A woman like that doesn't want boys. She doesn't want *virgins*.'

'You would know, Gilligan.'

'Houghton's called a special assembly. Apparently Sedley won't be there.'

'He's probably had a nervous breakdown.'

'He's probably killed himself.'

I stared at John Toplady. 'What do you mean?' I said. '*When?*'

'This morning. One of the First Setters was in sickbay with Matron when he heard the Sedleys on the drive. He was pleading with her. She got in his car and drove off.'

'No, I mean, when's the assembly?'

'After prep tonight.'

The news of the Sedleys meant almost nothing to me. My dismay was all to do with Mr Bridge. 'I can't go,' I said.

'You *have* to go,' said Andy Proctor with his customary scorn.

'I've got something else on.'

'It's compulsory, you dimwit. Mr Sedley has just lost his wife: don't you think that's more important than your little hobbies?'

'What's it got to do with us?'

Proctor looked to his peers for support. Ordinarily a scourge of authority, he had been transformed by this crisis into its most loyal supporter. 'You really are,' he said, 'the most selfish cunt in England.'

'We *have* to be there,' said one of the prefects more mildly. 'It's not an option.'

I tried to swallow this bitter news and my eyes nearly filled. While the other boys tittered and whooped at news of the Sedleys, I could think only of the evening I was going to lose. And for what? What did I care about the bald old coot? He didn't pretend to like me: it served him right to have lost his wife.

There was no way out. I couldn't even telephone Mr Bridge to apologise for my absence. With minutes to go before the lockdown of prep, I ran through the evening emptiness of college and into the Eversley; but Anthony was not in his room and I had to content myself with leaving a scribbled, self-pitying note on his desk.

I felt bitter all evening. Though I had set aside the time to make sense of chemistry, my attention simmered above the textbook like a heat haze. I was tormented by the image of Anthony alone with Mr Bridge – impressing him with his wit, set free by my absence to shine and dazzle. It was jealousy and I knew it. The gong sounded for our House meeting, and I scowled ungraciously at the back of the assembly room while Mr Houghton talked in hollow tones of a 'personal matter' that was going to detain Mr Sedley 'for an indeterminate period of time'. None of the boys – not even the most sardonic and daring – asked any questions. Like monks informed of a change in abbot, they nodded at the news that Mr Houghton would be taking over the running of the Hereward. As soon as our new housemaster had gone, however, the room filled with excitement. Cut off from the outside world, it must have seemed like revolution. Opinions divided on Mr Sedley's future. It was all over for him: he would never come back. Maybe hot Miss Fuller would become the new deputy? I slid like a cartoon sleuth towards the exit.

Outside, I contemplated the austere plastic clock in the lobby. Even if I ran, I would arrive almost an hour late. Having left a note telling Anthony I could not attend, it seemed impossible to barge in on them: pudgy Bruno, all in a sweat. My friend hated surprises. Perhaps he would resent my intrusion and I would foul up, in the smallest way, the intimacy that was the one precious thing to me in the world.

'Don't worry about missing the session,' Mr Bridge said to me first thing next morning. It was in front of all our peers. They fidgeted and daydreamed and picked their noses regardless. 'We didn't do all that much in the end, did we, Anthony?'

I looked at my friend. He had refused to talk, or even mention my absence, as if I had shown him up instead of liberated him.

'We made a start on *Waiting for Godot* – which will probably be on the A-level syllabus for those of you who decide to stay on the path of sweetness and light.'

It was a dull morning and there was much for us to get through in our revision class. When it was over, and Anthony left in a theatrical huff, I loitered for a word with Mr Bridge.

'I imagine,' he said, 'that things are a bit crazy in the Hereward.'

'Have you heard?'

'Kingsley's a small place. A very miserable business, I must say. Let's hope it doesn't distract everyone from their exams.'

Mr Bridge, as he spoke, looked suitably saddened, but I left the bunker of the department with my spirits soaring. I had not, then, missed a transformative evening! Our haven had undergone no alteration; my love was safe and the harbour of our meetings remained. Crossing the little wood that divided the Hereward from the rest of college, I even found space in my self-obsession to think of Mr Sedley. I remembered Mr Bridge's words: how we never know what's going on in other people's lives. It was the sour, sexual whiff of scandal that had set boys talking; ordinarily we were oblivious to the private reality of our teachers. If they existed at all, it was only to support or thwart us. How strange, then, to realise that we weighed no more in their lives than they did in ours. It was hard to make sense of other people; just as well, perhaps, that some things stay hidden. To feel the whole world's pain would be unbearable.

The atmosphere in the Hereward under Mr Houghton's crisis management was one of barely suppressed hysteria. Mr Sedley lived in the private quarter of the House and no one knew if he was still there, lurking and sobbing behind Victorian brick, or whether he had escaped the grounds completely. Hugo Barclay, who liked to give the impression of special knowledge, spawned a rumour that Mr Sedley had gone off in search of his wife, and I imagined him loping over field and moor, the lank meshes of his comb-over awry, like an escapee from a Gothic asylum. There would be a bloody confrontation, *Taxi Driver*-style, with his well-endowed rival, and Mrs Sedley would fall in love again with her imprisoned husband. Naturally, the school authorities would try to hush things up; but they would never quell the cruel rumours. Reasons surmised for Mrs Sedley's departure included her husband's impotence, his appalling kinkiness and his refusal to give her children, knowing only too well what monsters they turn into.

One subject of speculation was put swiftly to rest. 'Hot' Miss Fuller – the assistant art teacher whose reputation came from her open collars and a readiness to lean, without obvious guile, over boys' handiwork – was not to join us in the Hereward. It was Mr Wimbush, of all people, who was commissioned to serve as Mr Houghton's deputy, and though other boys groaned with thwarted lust, I enjoyed the thought of the old jingoist scowling at his superior over Mr Sedley's whisky.

For those of us doomed to it, the prospect of exams kept our wits ticking over. When my parents telephoned to wish me luck and give me courage, I felt no inclination to snoop about the Sedleys' home for signs of the missing housemaster. Anthony soon got over whatever bug had bitten him (he could not sulk for long, having no other friends to turn to) and we spent the afternoons sweating over our revision notes in the library. It was almost exciting to see an end to lessons and be plunged into the chair-creaking, neck-aching intensity of examinations. Who would have thought that sitting GCSEs could feel so much like a holiday? There was an almost festive atmosphere as we gathered, pencil cases in hand and mascots in our pockets, outside the old gym. I couldn't wait to be finished and back at home (at home!) with Anthony.

The gauntlet of exams was swiftly run. We had a fortnight to go before the end of term, and complete freedom to enjoy the season. I should have asked Anthony, long before, about his tickets, but I thought nothing of taking the plane: such practicalities were always sorted out for me. In a state of blissful complacency, I sauntered with my friend through the oak and beech woods, kicking flints and sucking a grass stem. We were like Huck Finn and Tom Sawyer. 'Just wait till we get to Malaysia! There's this golf course my dad goes to – you're not supposed to walk on it but I sneak in anyway – it's got a big lake with a family of otters and there are monitor lizards and bats and everything . . .'

'Ah,' said Anthony. He looked silently at the burgeoning Downs. 'Listen, about Malaysia.' His grass stem seemed to tickle him. He spat out its juice and picked a fibre from his tongue.

'What?'

'We're going to the Algarve. It's been planned for ages. I'm going to work on my golf swing.'

A cavity opened in my ribcage. The earth seemed to spin away from me. 'I don't believe it.'

'The villa's been booked and everything, there's nothing I can do about it. Christ, you're not *crying*?'

'Of course not.'

'You look like you're going to blub.'

I loped into the trees and Anthony came after at a walking pace, giving me time to snaffle up my tears. I sat on a pile of rotting logs and stared, my hands on my knees, at a miniature landscape of leaves and roots and wandering ants.

'It can't be helped,' he said. 'It's not like it's the end of the world.'

'I don't *care*,' I said bitterly. 'I don't give a shit about the holidays.'

'Could have fooled me.'

'We see each other all term anyway.'

This was not what he wanted to hear. 'You were crying,' he said.

'Fuck off.'

'You're trembling. Look at your knees.'

Desperate for some dignity, revolting against this humiliation, I looked for an excuse. 'It's not what you think . . .'

'Isn't it?'

'It's . . . it's a boy in my house.'

'A boy?' It was Anthony's turn to be troubled. Was I about to make an erotic confession?

'Someone in the Hereward.' I said nothing more, trying to think and make the effort look like emotion.

'Someone in the Hereward *what?*'

'It doesn't matter.'

'Come on, tell me.'

'He's been making my life hell.'

Anthony breathed in this information. 'Who?'

I could not tell because I could not decide.

'Not that bollocks Proctor?'

My eyes darted at the name. It would not be entirely a lie. I hated Andy Proctor with a passion: his sarcasm and constant mockery gave me reason enough to accuse him. 'He threatened to beat me up,' I said. 'He's got nothing better to do now that A levels are finished. He's just waiting to leave and he picks on me for fun.'

'He beat you up?'

'No . . . he threatened to.'

'What did you do to him?'

'Nothing.' The scandalised expression on his face – an expression on the verge of jubilation – made me panic. 'Look, it doesn't matter . . .'

'It fucking does. He threatened to *beat* you?'

'He didn't actually do it . . .'

But Anthony would not give up. He took me at my word and there was no way, suddenly, for me to take my invention back. 'I think we should teach him a lesson,' he said, grim with moral purpose.

'What do you mean?'

'Proctor. We've got to hurt him.'

'No . . .'

'It's not like anyone *likes* him. Why should he get away with this kind of abuse?'

Though it was a grey day and cool, I began to sweat. I was in a trap of my own making. 'You mean a practical joke?'

'Yeah, if you like. But not just a joke: something really disgusting.' Anthony could not be dissuaded. Perhaps he felt guilty about the holidays, the news of his escape to Portugal. I had no time to brood on the matter, for already he had a plan.

'If we get found out,' I said, 'we'll be suspended.'

'Who's going to find out?'

'If Proctor reports it . . .'

'He'll be too embarrassed.'

'Yeah, but he might *suspect*.'

'He'd never think you were capable of it. Relax, Bruno.' Anthony pushed affectionately at my shoulder. 'We're going to get the bastard. We're going to *nail* him.'

'Yeah,' I said weakly.

'It'll be one of our secrets. No one will ever find out.'

The carefree atmosphere that came with the year's end (lessons consisted of videos and – with Mr Bridge – a downland ramble) made it easier to contemplate the shaming of Proctor. I worked up a froth of indignation towards him, recalling his insults and brooding on the injustice of his loathing. I'd done nothing to deserve it. Fat, sharp tongued, a scurrilous bastard, Proctor embodied the unhappiness of my past three years; and soon he would be gone, an ex-Kingsleyite, incapable of retaliation.

Had Anthony 'punished' anyone before? He seemed to relish the challenge; all I had to do was assist him, taking my instructions in a spirit of nervous excitement. I giggled with dread and incredulity at the small brown vial of laxative he somehow acquired. His plan seemed fantastic and farcical; I could not believe we were *really* going to do it. But the days and the breakfasts diminished: there was no time for delay. We chose the last Sunday of term, when chapel would be late and languishing universal. Anthony ran over to the Hereward as the breakfast gong was sounding for the last time, and I sneaked him like a lover into my dorm. It was raining, I remember, and his face was lustrous, his hair dampened into curls, his freckled cheeks flushed with the speed of his run. I would have chickened out had not doing so demanded greater courage than going ahead. Instead, I put the laxative in my pocket, nodded at the crumpled ball of cling film in Anthony's palm, smuggled him to Proctor's door and, checking that Proctor was out, left him to his mission. My own consisted, simply enough, of going to the dining room and dosing my enemy's breakfast.

I had given a lot of thought to this enterprise. It helped that Proctor was a big eater and liked to hold forth at breakfast. I had studied him since we had hatched our plan and duly noted how he would wait until Mr Houghton or now Mr Wimbush had retired from the serving area before going up for a third or fourth helping. Would it be possible to sneak the laxative into Proctor's plate? Not without giving myself away. Could I dose his teacup while his back was turned? Other boys, hirsute and bleary eyed, lingered at the table and one of them might notice. The solution entailed some risk, as it involved sitting close to Proctor and poisoning my *own* tea. This I did behind the hatch of the kitchen. Then I walked to the table.

Creeping up and sitting by his elbow was unpleasant. I braced myself for invective; but Proctor was sluggish, sunk in dreams or nursing a hangover, so that he seemed barely to notice me as I sat down with a single, empty chair between us.

For five or six minutes he did nothing. His teacup (milky, I had noted, with two sugars) steamed unattended beside his plate. I gnawed at a piece of toast that might as well have been polystyrene and watched him out of the corner of my eye. He sipped his tea and for a dreadful instant I feared he might down it in one; but the brew was still too hot for him and he left it to cool. In the serving hatch, a junior boy aired his molars in heavy boredom. The breakfast hall was almost empty. I began to panic, convinced that heat coming off me would give my guilt away. The dosed cup of tea in front of me ran out of steam. It and the plan for revenge were getting cold.

Proctor unleashed a devious and malignant fart. 'Excuse *me*,' he said, and this release of gas seemed to wake him, for he got up, salvaging his plate from the greasy wastes of the table, and walked ponderously towards the kitchens.

No! He was going *away* – and Anthony upstairs might still be on his mission. I found myself rising, knees bent, from the table. But Proctor changed course halfway down the room and bore down on the serving hatch. He regarded the serving boy as a sort of sentient ladle: more eggs, more beans, and make it *snappy*. My muscles tensed as if for a blow, I reached across the exposing plain of the table and swapped Proctor's teacup for my own.

At once I wanted to get away. I knew I should do nothing to rouse his suspicion (but why should he suspect anything?) so forced myself to eat another piece of toast and drink the revolting, sugary brew that had Proctor's germs floating about in it. The price was worth paying if the plan worked and I got away with it.

He lumbered back to the table with his plate heaped and sat down to eat. I watched him surreptitiously and blocked from my mind the sadness of his gorging face. He swallowed a cheekful of scrambled egg and reached for the teacup. My own bowels could have liquefied at the sight of his lips closing about the rim. He took a sip – hesitated with the mixture in his mouth, swallowed – then emptied the cup in one draught.

I took my tray to the kitchens, and it was all I could do to keep from running. I could not bring myself to go back the way I had come and took the long way round to Main Corridor.

Anthony sat, waiting for me, on my bed. 'Well?' we whispered simultaneously.

'Done,' said Anthony.

'Done,' I said, and laughed out loud.

The best place to wait was the locker room at the top of the building; for Andy Proctor had a small flat of his own (the antiquated privilege of those who had won a place at Oxbridge) separated from the junior boys by a thin plyboard partition, and no First Setter would dare challenge us as we waited for sounds of victory. I felt nervous as we sat, with crossed legs, among grass-stained boots and dented cherry-tattooed cricket bats, listening for sounds of Proctor but hearing only the clank and treble of First Setters in their dorms. Several times I had to swipe the perspiration from my brow. Remorse for what we had done mixed with excitement at Anthony's proximity. I was conscious of a mounting urge to crap. Ten or fifteen minutes passed in expectation, until I could bear the wait no longer.

'It's not going to work,' I said.

'*Shush*.' He sat so close to me that I felt his breath on my cheek. 'Do you want revenge or don't you?'

'I don't want to get caught.'

The contempt on his face made me pick at my shoes. Anybody would have thought *he* was the aggrieved party, so intense was his resolve. He had never so much as spoken to Proctor, let alone endured his corrosive scorn. Was it really love for me that had sent him to a stranger's bathroom to stretch cling film under the rim of the toilet bowl? Now that my part of the mission was accomplished, I realised that Anthony had taken by far the greater risk and endured the unpleasantness of his crouching task to atone, perhaps, for deceiving me over the holidays, or else (and this thought occurred to me fully only years later) to see whether he was capable of it – to see how far he could go.

'I'm going down,' I said when I could wait no longer. 'I want to see what's happening.' ·

'Isn't that him now?'

The heavy tread sounded familiar. We strained to listen, two blind men, and I recognised Proctor in the sigh that heaved up the stairwell. He stopped outside his door, shoes scuffing the linoleum, and for an insane instant I was convinced he detected us through the partition. But he was attending to more intimate signals. He sighed a second time and gasped at a salvo of gastric pain. He turned the handle – bundled as it seemed into his rooms – and made a lunge for the toilet.

We heard the lid go up and the tinkle of an unfastened belt. A groan of distress was followed by a cough from the cistern lid as a body leaned against it. What if we had overdone it? What if he shat himself to death? The fanfare from Proctor's bowels almost drowned out his moans of disbelief. Anthony put a hand over his mouth and rocked like a zealot at the Wailing Wall. Next door, there were cries of alarm and despair; I imagined the rising swill, Proctor's breakfast oozing over the rim. 'Oh fuck, oh *fuck*!' we heard him sob. Anthony gripped his nose to suppress a sneeze of laughter. I was too appalled even to grin. There were sounds of movement and the trill of a toilet-roll holder. Then a silence too horrible for words, followed by desperate curses.

I fled the locker room, not caring who might see me, and raced my own terror to the stairway, past Proctor's door – the scene of my crime – and down three steps at a time. Anthony came jolting after, tears of mirth streaking his cheeks.

'What's the matter with you? Why are you running?' he said.

No one was about in Middle Corridor so I continued down the echoing stairs and into the garden, where I walked briskly towards the trees with Anthony panting and laughing at my heels.

'You've got to admit,' he said, 'I'm a genius.'

I slowed down, pained by the beating of my heart. I leaned against the trunk of a pine. 'So you're a genius.'

Anthony stopped beside me but could not keep still. He fidgeted and shook out his fingers and puffed out his cheeks. He turned on his fabulous grin, expecting some return from me; but I could only look at him, empty headed and reaching for breath. 'What . . .' I said, 'do you suppose he'll do?'

'Who cares?'

'You think the cling film worked?'

'Sounded like it.'

'We should never have done it.'

Anthony ignored this comment and, still grinning, began to tug at the bark of the tree. Watching him do it, I felt a calming sense of unreality. Unfamiliar chemicals raced in my blood. Emptiness gave way to elation and, before I knew it, I had begun to laugh. Anthony rallied to me, grinning, with the tip of his tongue between his teeth. We leaned so close that our foreheads almost touched. Only when our eyes met in a cycloptic blur did Anthony sway out of danger's way. My laugh evaporated but he continued defensively to chuckle. I watched him spin, childlike, on a heap of pine needles and look out across the Downs.

'I'd better stay away from the Hereward,' I said.

167

'Why?'

'Well . . . Proctor will be on the warpath.'

'You think so?'

'Once he's got himself . . .'

'Cleaned up?' I wrinkled my nose at the image. Anthony grinned. 'He'll find that difficult,' he said, and unfolded from the depths of his jumper a roll of toilet paper.

Then

I

I returned to England and I had *arrived*. The outward signs were banal enough: the right to wear a college blazer, the licence on warm days to dispense with a tie. It was inwardly that we felt the change. For we had reached the Lower Sixth, that longed-for year of freedom from social and academic dread. Given the advantages of seniority without its burdens, dashing lieutenants to the grizzled captains of the Upper Sixth, we were welcomed, with a solemnity that seemed apposite, by new prefects into the dusty Nissen hut of the Senior School bar. Though I knew I wouldn't be spending much time at the mangy baize of the snooker table, or downing pints of urinous shandy above the stale bog of the carpet, I took pride in my theoretical right to do so.

'Pity we don't have any girls,' said Hugo Barclay, and he contemplated the enormity of this omission. 'Fuck, why *don't* we have girls? Other schools take them at sixth form: Harrow and Marlborough and Wellington . . .'

'Yeah,' said Laurence Nevins, whose qualities hadn't improved since 1989. 'It's a bloody disgrace. What's the point of being sixteen if you can't get laid?'

'Oh, please,' said Robbie Thwaite.

'It's all right for you, there's plenty of *cock* about.'

Robbie did not rise to the bait; he never did. He just smiled the whole thing off, reducing Nevins with a wordless snuffle of contempt. We finished our glasses of bitter and weak cider and, wiping our mouths like labourers with the backs of our hands, made space at the bar for boys from another dormitory.

I was not a drinker at the time. For others, boozing was a major part of boarding-school life; the aching tedium of Sunday afternoons could be relieved only by getting tanked up on vodka or Gordon's gin or (for those with nothing better to steal from their parents) lashings of gruesome Bristol Cream. It was forbidden, of course, but few housemasters wasted time enforcing the law. The whole point of the Senior School bar was to contain and subvert the subversion of drink. Only for those of us who did not booze in secret did it have the opposite effect, introducing us to one of life's few pleasures when we were least conditioned to cope with it. As a result, that early September evening of my last year at Kingsley, I arrived back in my single room in a state of some confusion. I fell asleep on the narrow bed and woke up only as the neon strips on Main Corridor were extinguished for lights-out.

The next day, I had my first ever hangover. It made me less than careful and I obstructed a gang of new boys in Main Corridor. They sensed my woozy condition and, instead of apologising, greeted me with an earful of invective. It was the beginning of my disillusionment. I had looked forward to expressions of awe in the pale, shrewish faces of First Setters as I sauntered past their serried ranks; but seniority did not bring with it all the blessings I'd been conditioned to hope for. If strict discipline had prevailed when *I* was a new boy and had to plod under its yolk, it seemed, now that I stood to benefit from it, to have withered under the headmaster's reforms. The deference of fear that used to make junior boys cower before their elders had evaporated. First Setters refused to yield at the toasters; like rebellious serfs in thrall to a low-born leader, they moved in groups, plundering the bread bins, congesting the corridors and laying siege to the TV room until the lone sixth-former in charge had to surrender the remote. I soon realised, with disbelief, that I was scared of the new intake. Christ, half of them were taller than me: thirteen-year-olds on steroids, Jolly Green Giants in face paint. To hear them talk, to see them swagger, you imagined they had mammoth balls; in voices already broken, they boasted of sexual conquests when most of our prefects were still burdened with virginity.

I was not alone in feeling intimidated. What had been going *on* in the world while we had been confined to barracks? I could see, occasionally, my perplexity on the faces of friends: Robbie Thwaite gaping at some brilliant obscenity, John Toplady trying with limited mental resources to make sense of a witty rejoinder.

I asked Anthony about it when I saw him. He had grown in the holidays – the gawky adolescent becoming a man – yet there was something loping and satirical in his movements. He seemed braced for adversity, cocked like a pistol against insult.

'They don't get sarky with me,' he said. 'They wouldn't dare. But then the Eversley always was a tougher place than the Hereward.'

'Well, I think they're a bunch of toerags. They've got no respect. When *I* was their age . . .'

'When you were their age you were frightened of your own shadow.'

'Oh, thanks.'

'Who cares what they think? They're only vermin. Even their parents probably wouldn't give a shit if they ceased to exist.'

'You're in a cheerful mood.'

'What can I say? I'm back in the asylum.'

'Yeah,' I said. 'Well, I'm here, too.'

Anthony sighed and looked out of the window. He was in a room of his own overlooking Front Court, where the luggage cases of a hundred boys were awaiting removal. Though I was glad to see him again, I felt the chilling breath of his gloom. Had something happened during the holidays? We had not spoken or written to each other: me in my solitude in Kuala Lumpur, him in the sweltering heat of a Portuguese summer. Anthony kept his head turned to the window. I was terrified of exclusion, of exile from his favour, and struggled to think of something positive to say.

'At least,' I managed eventually, 'we've still got our Bridge evenings.'

'You know he's not teaching us any more? I checked. We've got that twat Robinson. He's going to get us through A levels – a bloody rugger bugger.'

This was news to me. I took it in unhappily, though I was determined to stay cheerful. 'Yeah,' I said, 'but that doesn't stop us having our poetry readings.'

'I suppose not.'

'Bridge is hardly going to drop us just because we're no longer in his set.'

This seemed to reassure Anthony. He looked at me with something resembling a smile and the day turned in an instant. I was delighted to see how much Mr Bridge's friendship meant to him. It confirmed me in my own affections.

'I've written a novel,' said Anthony.

'Come again?'

'A novel. I wrote it over the holidays.'

'A whole book?'

'Well, it's pretty short. About twenty thousand words.'

'That's short, is it?'

Anthony shrugged, smirking with pleasure.

'Jesus, you're a dark horse. How did you find time among all the golf and the flirting? I take it you did flirt?'

'No. I just wrote. My dad lent me his computer.'

'What's it about?'

'What?'

'The novel.'

Anthony grinned, a diabolical cherub. 'You'll see . . .'

So I would, I would see. But not yet. Though I begged for a glimpse, just a sniff, of the opus he had somehow managed to produce in a season, Anthony grinned and dangled the prospect in front of me. I was the kitten tormented by a string. I knew (for he had told me) that the novel was autobiographical; it was about the school; and so it contained a numinous promise, a key to understanding my place in his heart.

Another novelty of the year (though only a square like me could have taken so much pleasure in it) was the A-level syllabus. Gone were the mind-numbing perplexities of chemistry and physics, the wincing improvisations of French and Latin. I could concentrate at last on the subjects that interested me. I had chosen English, of course, as well as wonderful art; also, for the tidiness it left in abstract pockets of the world, I had opted for maths with genial, myopic Mr Crawford. It was a heavy workload, but I was not distracted by sport, booze or drama. With no more prospects of double French or mind-crapping woodwork to appal and dismay, I firmly expected my senior years to be a working holiday.

It was disappointing, of course, to lose Mr Bridge for English. We were lumbered instead with Mr Robinson: rugby enthusiast, womaniser (to credit his own insinuations) and all-round 'good bloke' for whom we felt little affection and less admiration. He did not seem to care, as Mr Bridge and others did, about his subject, and would drift readily from Wordsworth to sport, from sport to gossip, from gossip to – 'Stop pissing about, Radmore. Do you think your parents pay thousands of pounds for you to make a prat of yourself?' It was as if two men, the one laddish and familiar, the other almost Victorian in his pomposity and rigour, were waging insoluble war within him. Half the time he was sloppy, the other half his anger, at himself perhaps, found a public outlet. He picked on people; he made nervous boys read aloud and poured scorn on those of us who shunned the playing fields. It's true that, very occasionally, a glimmer of enthusiasm would escape the lazy cloud of his sarcasm; but even at his best, Mr Robinson's teaching of *The Prelude* and Wordsworth's selected poems seemed pedestrian, lacking the fiery opinions we had come to expect of Mr Bridge.

Happily, Anthony and I were still the latter's protégés. On our first meeting of the year, his wife was home from her travels and Mr Bridge was in high spirits. ('There's a man,' whispered Anthony when he left the room to fetch the tea, 'who's getting his oats . . .') He wanted to know all about our holidays and what books we had read. While Anthony boasted of Tolstoy and Dostoevsky, I took in as evidence of a feminine presence the earthenware vase with its hand-picked Michaelmas daisies, a smell of spiced and sophisticated cooking, and the greatest hits of Blondie playing on a stereo in one of the unknown rooms.

'Where's your wife been?' I asked, interrupting talk of Raskolnikov. Anthony looked put out.

'Charlotte? Oh – Borneo again. Something to do with horn-bills, how they need the tallest trees to nest in. I mean the trees that are coming down.'

'I've been to Borneo.'

'We know,' said Anthony.

'I've got a friend who lives in Sandakan. That's a city on the coast.'

'Yes, the name's familiar,' said Mr Bridge. 'Now then . . . *Sailing to Byzantium* . . .'

We spent an hour in the salmon-falls, on the mackerel-crowded seas. Mr Bridge was letting us in on something: the poem that resounded deepest within him. We were looking at our photocopies and it was only on a second reading that Anthony and I realised Mr Bridge was reciting from memory. Faced with our excited bafflement, he tried to explain but the paradox remained opaque to us: that life means flux, that sensual music fades and permanence, if it is attainable, exists only in art's mausoleum.

'A book or work of art is inert, an object on the shelf. It takes a reader, it takes the viewer, to give them substance. My wife will tell you it's the reason she's an environmentalist. Yeats's poem claims to despise what it's really in love with: the 'dying generations' of the natural world. Likewise, some deep ecologists seem to wish the world free of humans. After all, humans are destroying the world. But you can no more have Art without Life than you can have Nature without Man. We need human beings – the human imagination – on this planet in order to make it fully itself. Some *mind* . . . um, it's hard to express, I'm not even sure if I know what I mean . . . Look, if humanity suddenly vanished, life on earth would go on without us. In fact, it would be a damn sight better off. But 'Nature' would no longer exist, because *we* created Nature.'

Mr Bridge was perched on the very edge of his chair, with something wild in his look. He took in our perplexed faces – blinked – and tilted back his head to laugh.

For the rest of the evening we read 'Leda and the Swan' and 'Politics' and 'The Lake Isle of Innisfree'. We ate chocolate-covered malt biscuits and drank sweet, milky tea and Mr Bridge said, with a benevolent smile: 'Do you want to know the pleasure of teaching? When you set aside the hours and the problems with discipline and the slog of marking essays that all regurgitate what you said in the first place . . . it's being able to share your enthusiasms. I can't discover these poems as *you* are discovering them. A first encounter happens only once. But I can see, if I'm lucky, the light come on in your eyes that once came on in mine. Something is added to the store of life. That . . . that's what I value . . . it's what makes it worth it, for me.'

There was nothing to be said. A gust of wind ran through the obscure garden; it tugged at the patio door. Headlights of a car picked out an azalea, a length of privet.

'Sir?' said Anthony.

Mr Bridge threw out his elbows in a yawning stretch. The session was coming to an end on a note that pleased him; but Anthony was trying to tongue something to the front of his mouth.

'Can I bring something?'

'Bring something?'

'Of my own.'

'Something you've read?'

'It's sort of a novel. I wrote it.' A most surprising thing happened: Anthony blushed! I watched him run a hand through his mane. 'Obviously it's just a . . . a first draft, but I think with a bit of work it might get, you know, published?'

Mr Bridge couldn't disguise a quizzical look. 'I'm impressed. When did you write it?'

'Over the holidays.'

No doubt Mr Bridge was curious: Anthony was bright, what if he had talent, too? Flattered by the request – a little burdened, also – he agreed to take possession of the novel. 'Just leave it in my pigeonhole and I'll try to read it – or some of it – before our next meeting.'

'It's not long, sir.'

'That's good. Brevity is the soul of wit, as the man said.'

Anthony was thrilled, like someone promised a first date. He almost skipped in the wind as we headed back into college. All he could talk about was his novel: how daring it was, a great settling of scores. Mr Bridge would have to laugh.

'Isn't that a bit risky?' I said.

'How do you mean?'

'You don't want to offend him.'

'Bridge isn't in it.'

'Yeah, but other teachers . . .'

'It's a *satire*, Bruno: it's not supposed to spare people. Anyway, don't you think this dump deserves it?'

With more reason, I felt, to resent the place than Anthony, I could not share his fury. Kingsley College was just small enough for a boy to have some idea of every master; but I was not outgoing, and after more than three years still had only a hazy notion of the dormitories and their whereabouts within the great brick maze of Main School. Likewise, many teachers were familiar to me only by sight. I didn't know their names and didn't particularly need to, since every one of them was 'sir'. Anthony, on the other hand, knew everybody: boy and master. Perhaps it was innate, or else he was honing skills that would serve him in the future. He didn't seem to try: he simply absorbed the information, clocking people and grading them as harmless or dangerous, fool or foe.

The challenge of preparing the novel kept Anthony out of my way all week. Though he sat beside me in English we were apart in other subjects, Anthony having chosen economics and (to my surprise, given his phobia for all things foreign) French with Monsieur Geissmann. As soon as lessons ended, he spurned my conversation and retreated to his dorm. What was he doing there?

'You know,' he said, 'polishing.'

Could I have a look? No. He was guarded: he wanted Mr Bridge to be the first to read it. Wittingly or unwittingly, he continued to torment me, so that, in the days before he handed it in, I began to dream of the book, imagining something perfect and true, with the full burning amplitude of my love at its core.

On the Friday evening before prep, my fast of Anthony ceased. I came back to my room to find him waiting for me, his shoes crossed on my desk.

'Have you been running?' he said.

'No.' I tried to master my breathing. The truth was that I had ascended the stairs too quickly and found myself, as so often, panting, a fat boy's sweat on my brow.

'I thought you'd like to know, the book's finished.'

'Can I read it now?'

He swung his feet from the desk, a petulant frown on his face. 'Aren't you going to congratulate me?'

'Well, I don't know if it's any good.'

Anthony watched me slyly. 'You *have* been running,' he said.

'Did you hand it in?'

'I'm going to the computer department to print it out.' He was silent, leaning on the ghost of a question until I had to ask it.

'Can I come?'

'What, to the computer department? Why would you want to do that? Looks to me like you could do with a shower.'

The gratifying truth was that he needed an audience. So I followed him to the computer department – past the reptile tank with its basking monsters and the open doors of the design workshop with its solder-iron fumes and screams of tortured wood. We entered the comforting hum and rattle of the computer room and Anthony sat down at a monitor. 'Uh,' he said, like one undressing, 'do you mind?' Grudgingly I turned away while he entered his password, fed the computer his floppy disk and summoned his novel to the screen.

'*Wits' End*,' I read aloud.

'It's like a double meaning. The hero of the novel, Aloysius . . .'

'*Aloysius?*'

'. . . gets driven mad by the stupidity of the teachers and the boys in his school. He's at his wits' end. So what does he do? He kills them off. All the bastards who think they're so clever. And his methods are perfectly suited to their faults. The *wits* come to a sticky ending.'

I read the visible page. Was I expecting to find myself in there, some fictional homage to our friendship? The opening was in dialogue: Aloysius, a precocious dandy hated for his talent, is in full dispute with a foul-breathed history teacher.

'I hope you're not reading,' said Anthony.

'What do you expect me to do?'

'Keep a lookout for Mumford, will you? He doesn't like us printing big documents.'

So I had to stand between the shuddering printer and Mr Mumford's office. As he was not about, I tried to read as much as I could from the spooling and folding-over sheets.

I was never to know the work in its entirety. That illicit scan of the pages was as close as I would get to *Wits' End*. It was enough to get the measure of it.

To a sixteen-year-old it seemed cleverly done, with a coarseness that passed, with its author at least, for savage wit. He could write a crafty sentence; but the characters were lumbering and crude. I recognised his targets: the sadistic, racist Mr Wimble with breath so bad it made women faint, the closet homosexual Mr Platter whom Aloysius discovers masturbating over the annual school photograph, pompous Monsieur Goosestep of the French department, and a Mr Hogget so ancient that 'nobody could remember a time when he hadn't been a teacher – and a crumbling one at that'.

Mr Hogget was the first of Aloysius's victims. A confirmed bachelor, he came back to his flat to find it plastered with pictures of naked girls, and died of a massive coronary. 'The ancient muscle went *kerplunk* in his chest.'

More outrages followed. Here was the school chaplain, a sobbing wimp. 'It was fun for boys to push him over the edge – into a lather of snot and tears. The padre had many pets at home: cats and dogs and mice. Aloysius strongly suspected that his love for these animals went beyond societal norms.'

Mr Mumford stepped into his office, a mug of coffee in his hands. I ducked out of view and knelt before the printer.

The depiction of teachers was lewd and libellous enough. Pupils came out of it even worse. A gross Ollie Radmore had his neck snapped in a rugby tackle. Another boy, plainly meant to be Tom McGrath, was 'monumentally stupid – a kind of genius among morons, the greatest mouth breather of them all . . .'

On and on it went in this vein. My neck ached from the strain of keeping watch and reading. And where was *I* in these dreams of vengeance? Where was loyal Bruno? Not among the doomed caricatures, that was certain. Aloysius was your classic lone avenger. He had no friend or sidekick.

Mr Mumford got up from his chair and, taking his coffee with him, left his office by the far door. In the fictional school, the day of prize-giving was dawning and Aloysius had broken into the armoury.

I went back to find Anthony playing solitaire on the computer.

'Is it done?'

'Almost.'

'Oh, good.' The virtual playing cards cascaded like the pack in *Alice*. 'Mumford hasn't cottoned on?'

'Is he in the book?'

'Old Mumbles? I wouldn't waste my time.'

Once we had gathered up the pages it was almost prep and we parted, Anthony with his 'novel' under his arm, in the wind-blown quad with its lone and half-dead beech tree between the physics labs.

Mr Bridge was accosted outside the staffroom and would confirm only that he had received 'the manuscript'. Anthony wheedled, with a cheekiness he thought charming, but Mr Bridge would not be drawn. Most likely, he got round to reading it only the night before our meeting.

In the weeks and months that followed, Anthony was to work into his mythology of grievance a conviction that Mr Bridge had stored up his response: stringing his young author along the better to enjoy the moment when he let rip. Certainly he gave no inkling of what was to come as we stepped into the musty boot museum of his porch. Our host was less effusive than usual but not disturbingly so, and Anthony grinned as we shuffled to our usual perches in the living room.

Mr Bridge sat down with a sigh, deflating fractionally. Anthony sat in impish expectancy, his hands pressed together between his knees. I looked in vain for a plate of biscuits.

'Well,' said Mr Bridge.

'Don't tell me you didn't laugh.'

His eyes flickered between us. 'I didn't much.' Mr Bridge paused and breathed before delving into the familiar leather briefcase that stood propped against his chair. As he extracted the printed pages, I sensed Anthony tightening beside me.

Mr Bridge laid *Wits' End* flat on his knees, his hands resting upon it.

'It's no mean feat,' he said, 'to write even part of a novel. Someone clever once said the craft of being a writer consists of applying the seat of the pants to the seat of the chair. Day in, day out, even when the sun is shining, you apply yourself, and that's what you've done. It's certainly . . . Making up stories, putting yourself in another person's head . . . it's never been something *I* could do. It's difficult and, um, it takes years to learn. You need to acquire a . . . what my wife calls a habit of empathy.' Mr Bridge hesitated; his hands opened and closed above the typescript. 'That's where, to my mind, I'm afraid you fall down.'

This was not what Anthony had expected. He blinked to understand, like someone hard of hearing.

'I know the book's meant to be satirical. But it seems to me rather crude.'

183

'Crude?'

'In fact cruel. It's a cruel piece of work.'

'It's not *serious*.'

'Well, I think it is. I think it's deadly serious.'

'That's . . . good, then, isn't it?'

Mr Bridge scrunched up his face and opened the typescript. 'I mean, anybody who goes around *killing* people . . . You can write a novel where the main character's a monster – lots of writers do it. The challenge is how we should respond to the eloquent killer or the flamboyant lout. But I have to say, as you get older you come to realise that, despite the Hannibal Lecters and Humbert Humberts of the fictional world, real people who are violent are mostly dull, inadequate or plain deranged. Your Aloysius is not convincing, I'm afraid. I didn't believe in his character, not for one minute.'

I could not bear this. Anthony had frozen: he seemed barely to breathe. 'It's comic,' I said.

'Is it?'

'You're not supposed to be po-faced about it.'

'Is that what I'm being? Anthony?'

It was impossible for me to turn my head and look at my friend. I kept my eyes on Mr Bridge's jacket. He was wearing corduroy over a tieless shirt. There was a speck of gravy or mustard halfway down his chest.

'Anthony, do you expect me to compliment you on these grotesque caricatures?'

'You can do what you like.'

'But do you see why it troubles me? There's skill here. We all know you're as sharp as anything. But it's callous. I mean it's not light hearted – it seems like you really *mean* it.'

A faint squawk preceded a clearing of Anthony's throat. 'You were supposed to laugh,' he said.

'Well, I didn't. It made me wonder if anything I've said, or anything we've read together over the last however many terms, has made the slightest impact on you.'

Anthony's stillness broke. 'I've written a fucking *novel*,' he said. 'How many Kingsley boys have done that?'

My scalp seemed to crawl back on my skull: I wanted to scratch myself bald. 'Sir,' I said, 'don't you think you're missing the point?'

'What is the point, Bruno? That everyone at this school is a pervert or a moron who deserves to be exterminated?'

'It's a *satire*,' I protested, but Anthony said nothing to back me up. I was fighting his corner and he seemed not to know I was there.

'It's supposed . . .' I heard him say, with hospice-carer slowness, '. . . to be extreme. It's supposed . . . to provoke a reaction.'

'Well, now you know mine. There's no ironic distance, Anthony. I mean, it's baffling. Am I supposed to admire what Aloysius does? Am I supposed to root for him?'

'I don't care what you do.'

'It might be interesting, if he had a genuine grievance, to make the reader identify with him – to make us his accomplice, if you like. But that can't possibly happen in this book because it's so incredible. There's no way his casual humiliation can justify such a bloody revenge.'

'So what you're saying, basically, is that you didn't find this book *nice*. It doesn't make you feel all warm and fuzzy about the world. It doesn't make you want to go out and hug someone like they're your friend.'

Mr Bridge uttered a small, bewildered laugh. He seemed lost for an instant, as if he failed to recognise us.

'Well, I'm sorry,' said Anthony, 'if I didn't give you spiritual uplift. I'm sorry if I didn't come up with a cosy little romance to make everyone feel good about themselves.'

'For God's sake, I'm not asking . . .'

'Why should literature be improving? How about *American Psycho*? Can't it be provocative?'

'Of *course* literature can be provocative. But to a *purpose*. Not just some libellous settling of scores. And what . . . what scores do you have to settle with Mr Wimbush? Or Mr Plater? Because you've made no attempt to disguise who you're basing these caricatures on. And they're not even caricatures, because they're absurdly, preposterously wide of the mark. You forget that I know these people as colleagues and friends.'

'They're not very friendly to me.'

'Aren't they? You mean they try to teach you things?'

'No.'

'You mean they believe in things like discipline? They actually know a thing or two that it might be useful for you to hear?'

'No!'

The blood had come back to Anthony's face: his cheeks were crimson, as though he had been hiking up a cold hillside. He was angry and perplexed, shifting from ham to ham on the sofa so that I felt its coils jangle beneath us.

'I'm sorry to sound harsh,' said Mr Bridge. 'But really, I can't let this stand. The boys and masters you take off in this book of yours . . . each and every one of them has a complex reality: as complex as your own. They may not be perfect but they don't deserve this.'

'They're arseholes.'

'Sir,' I said, trying not to panic, trying to keep the air from evaporating, 'there must be good things to say. I mean, it's about more than just characters, surely?'

'What did you say?' Mr Bridge stared at Anthony. He repeated his question in a whisper: 'what did you just say?'

Anthony seemed to shrink into the imperfect cave of his back; his eyes were dark and hooded. 'You heard me,' he said.

'How dare you? How *dare* you sit in judgement on those you don't know? You have no idea what these men and women are like with their partners, with their children. You have no conception how hard they work for your benefit – how devoted they are to the pretty thankless task of trying to improve your minds.'

'My mind doesn't need improving,' said Anthony.

Mr Bridge's mouth opened. He blinked slowly, the breath sighing from his nostrils. I dared to look at Anthony. His expression was something close to a leer.

'I'm sorry,' Mr Bridge said, and sparked a moment's hope that something could be rescued. 'I'm sorry to have to be so frank with you. I certainly didn't want to upset you, Anthony, and I understand that you probably don't mean everything you've just said . . .'

'I thought you might be the one person who gets it.'

'Who gets *what*?'

In a strange way, the quietness that followed was more unsettling than loud disagreement. The skin around Mr Bridge's eyes relented. Even before he spoke, I knew he was not going to take back a word he had said. 'All this stuff, all the pettiness of college life, I know it seems a big deal now but really, it isn't. In less than two years you'll be out of here. And, believe it or not, from the excitement of university life you'll look back on Kingsley College with a kind of tender contempt.'

Anthony sat purse-lipped. 'In other words,' he said, 'I've wasted my time.'

'You haven't . . . No, you haven't.' Mr Bridge licked the inside of a cheek. 'That's not what I'm saying.'

'Can I have it back?'

'Every writer has to start somewhere . . .'

'Can I have it back, sir?'

'I'm trying to make you understand . . .'

'It's my only copy.'

187

Mr Bridge nodded, gathered up the loosened sheaves and handed them back. My bowels felt pummelled and bruised. I could almost smell Anthony's humiliation.

Unwilling to admit defeat, Mr Bridge presented us with library copies of Ted Hughes's *Crow* and struck out for half an hour's desultory reading. Anthony was silent throughout – withstanding the siege. I tried to engage with the poetry and think of something to contribute; but my loyalty was split and a welter of emotions obstructed my hearing. Mr Bridge quacked on resolutely until the college bell struck ten and we could escape.

Anthony couldn't get away fast enough, and Mr Bridge had to scuttle like a crab to reach the front door before him. 'I hope you don't feel too battered by my comments . . .' Anthony was wrestling with his shoes. 'Let's try to meet once more before the end of term. I know you wanted to read some short stories, Bruno. Look up a writer called Saki . . .'

Shod, Anthony righted himself and unlatched the door. I followed him outside, spinning on my heel to thank Mr Bridge. His face was obscure. He raised his hand in farewell and there was something broken in his posture.

'Jesus,' I said, when we were out of hearing.

Anthony butted the air with his head, his mouth an ugly gash. 'I am never,' he said, 'never fucking going back there again.'

I felt shaken but I didn't believe it. He had suffered a blow to his self-esteem; he kept plenty in reserve. We parted at Main Gate and I walked myself calm, taking in the mushroomy air.

It was not that night but the night after that I was notified by a new boy of a phone call from my parents. I took it in Mr Sedley's house, where Mr Houghton lived furtively, like a squatter, installed in a single room at the top of the stairs.

I can still feel, to this day, the plastic heat of the receiver against my ear. I had to grip the banister to keep from falling, I wanted to cry out, 'No, no, *no, NO* . . .' only I could tell my father's voice was on thin ice. They had caught it early, he said, there was a very strong chance it would be stopped. I was not to cry, I was to be strong for her, though surely it was still her job to be strong for *me*. A mixture of self-pity and terror made me sob. I did not care whether Houghton heard me in his bachelor den.

'Bruno, Bruno, listen . . . I know it sounds terrible but many, many people get through this and much worse. What Mummy wants is for you to know the situation. She's promised to speak to you as soon as . . . she will give you a call, I promise. We've not lost her. Do you hear me? We've not lost her, it's a question of trusting the doctors. It's early-stage, Bruno. If you think about it, it's a jolly good thing we had that scare a couple of years ago. It means she noticed immediately.'

'But when . . . but when . . . you say it's early . . .'

'I mean there's a good chance of complete recovery. But listen, before we can think about that, there's some treatment to go through which won't be easy. It's going to be quite tough on Mummy but it's necessary if we're going to knock this thing on the head.'

Like a toddler ambushed by a tantrum, I battled to contain my hiccupping grief. My dad, my dear dad, made his phone creak as he cradled it.

'Hey,' he said, 'the good news is that we'll get to spend Christmas in London. The British Council is paying for us to come over. We'll get the best oncologists . . .'

I didn't know what an oncologist was. I snivelled. 'You're coming to London?'

'We're flying out in a fortnight. You've been asking to have Christmas in England for the last couple of years. Uncle Roger has offered to put us up but, since the Council's paying, we've decided to rent a flat close to the . . . to the hospital. You'll have us around at the beginning of next year, as well. We can see each other on Sundays when you get leave.'

To reassure the two of us, my father repeated his optimistic prognosis. My head throbbed and the pain made me quiet, as if comforted, as we said our goodbyes. I had to wipe my sweat from the earpiece.

The house was silent. If Mr Houghton had heard my distress, he did not come to find me, and I was left to close the door that divided his world from mine.

The world outside went on, as it must. Nothing had shifted in the mild and blustery weather. Boys slouched, their shirts precisely loosened from their trousers, and I paid them no attention on the understanding that they would return the favour.

My legs carried me. There was nowhere else to go.

The Eversley was its usual Hogarthian blend of earthiness and aggression. I picked my way through a raucous game of corridor rugby, past black marketeers and outrageous flirts.

Anthony received me sullenly, leaving me to shut out the worst of the noise. I stood with my back against the door, catching the breath I had not known was missing. Anthony slumped on his bed, a copy of *Maxim* ('all the porn with none of the scorn') sliding to the floor. He looked at me without hostility or affection.

'What are you doing at Christmas?' I said. Anthony shrugged. He looked heavy, despite my being the only overweight person in the room. 'Because I'm going to be in England and I thought . . . you know, we could meet up.'

His only hint of emotion was a fluttering eyelid. 'Why are you going to be in England?'

'My mother's ill,' I said. Anthony looked gormless. 'I thought you'd be pleased.'

'About your mother?'

'About the fact that we can spend time together.'

'What's wrong with her?'

I could not bring the word to my lips. To utter it would have given it too much power. 'She's coming for hospital treatment. We're going to have a flat in London.'

'I'm sorry.'

I found his sympathy embarrassing. I was afraid of crying in front of him and tried to behave like my father, repeating his bromides.

'My aunt had cancer. Aunt Jemima. The poor bitch married to Uncle Thomas.'

'The one who sells . . .?'

'Weapons, yeah. She survived it. They had to carry out a mastectomy but she came through. Have some faith in the doctors.'

'I do, I suppose. But what if . . .?'

'Don't think about what ifs. What ifs can drive you mad.'

Something inside switched. I felt laughter return, like blood to an uncrossed limb. 'You're very wise all of a sudden,' I said.

'I've always been wise,' said Anthony, and he treated me to a gorgeous, sexy grin. I began to blush, and maybe he understood why, for he changed the subject. 'Where are you going to be staying?'

'I don't know. Somewhere in central London, I suppose. We can hang out together.'

'Yeah.' His second smile, at the prospect of jaunts together, was weak. 'But, uh, we get pretty busy with guests and relatives at Christmas. I don't know how much time I'll have free.'

'Maybe,' I said, 'I could come and visit you?'

'Not at my house. My parents don't like visitors.'

Anthony shifted a leg under his duvet. The rebuff was clear, and I took it. The heaviness that had lifted momentarily from him returned and his eyes were dull again.

'Mr Bridge is avoiding us,' he said. 'You know that, don't you?'

'Perhaps he's just busy.'

'If you believe that, you're not paying attention.'

In the days that followed, Anthony's observation seemed to be confirmed. Mr Bridge dodged our questions in the after-lesson flow of pupils; he looked stooped and preoccupied and I wondered whether his wife had gone away on another field trip.

The haven was lost. For the time being at least, Anthony would not think of speaking to him, while Mr Bridge seemed almost embarrassed in our presence. I felt hard done by. Even if he was angry with Anthony, why should *I* be left out in the cold when I had played no part in the hated manuscript? I asked Anthony what he had done with his novel and whether, perhaps, I could read it.

'Impossible. The bastard destroyed it.'

'What do you mean?'

'Ask Bridge,' he said.

No date was set for another meeting; my cubbyhole never sprang a postcard from Mr Bridge. When, finally, I managed to corner him outside the Common Room, he looked sheepish and admitted that there would be no more sessions this term. 'I haven't got time, I'm afraid, what with mocks and so on . . .'

'But they're two weeks away.'

'Bruno,' said Mr Bridge, with undisguised impatience, 'you have no idea.'

'Of what, sir?'

'Of the work involved.'

He turned his back on me and I watched his figure retreat through pools of light and shadow. Disconsolate – unfairly punished – I walked into the squall of a late November night, the smell of burning leaves gathering about me.

II

When Mr Bridge called a halt to our meetings, the winds of dejection swept into our lives. They chilled us all the more for our spending time together over the holidays. What should have been a delight – Christmas in England (with its non-existent snows) in the company of Anthony – turned into a feast of misery; for my friend, when we met in town, railed against the injustice of Mr Bridge's opinion, and I could think of nothing but my mother's chemotherapy.

My father stood outside the door of the bedroom in the flat we were renting. 'How is she?' I asked.

'Asleep. It was quite a dose they gave her. But it's all for the good, you'll see.'

How about him? How about my dad? His face was sallow and blotchy, the skin around his eyes like something kept in a sample jar. We went to the kitchen where – since neither of us knew how to prepare a meal – we ate a baguette with cheddar and pickles. He was never going to complain to me or admit his terrors. Love, for men of his class and generation, means keeping fear from the dining table.

'How about that friend of yours – Alasdair?'

'Anthony.'

'When are we going to meet him?'

My cheeks burned like a spaceship on re-entry. 'What do you mean?'

'Why not invite him here? He could help us set up the Christmas tree . . .'

'I don't think so.'

'Your mother doesn't want us tiptoeing around her as if she were some kind of invalid. I'm sure she'd like to meet your friends. You're not exactly forthcoming with your reports, you know.'

The cheddar became a dry paste at the back of my mouth. I hid my face in a glass of water.

'Your mother was saying, she doesn't think we've seen a single one of your school friends. And you keep going out to meet this Anthony – why not be polite and invite him back for tea?'

'We're not old maids, Dad.'

'You could watch television or . . . or play computer games. You could go to the cinema.'

'We don't *play* computer games,' I said, but he looked tired and I relented. 'OK, I'll ask.'

I had no intention of doing so. It was unthinkable for me to mix my two selves: Bruno the loving son and Bruno the un-requited lover. I feared giving myself away: my mother would notice a light in my eye or else my effort to hide it. She would know whom I loved and what I was, and I could not have survived such a revelation. It was hard enough for me to conceal my everyday lust: a boy in the street, a naked torso in an ad, the lank squirming of pop stars on TV, were enough to set me off. But these were fantasies that could be kept secret: no sane parent lingers outside a teenager's bedroom. If I brought Anthony home, if I let his beauty saunter through my parents' door, it seemed to me that the universe would suffer one of those collapses, an apocalyptic paradox so beloved of science fiction, where everything crumples into chaos.

We met in town, each of us keen for different reasons on anonymous settings. It gave me satisfaction to discover how much better I knew central London than he did. He followed me in Piccadilly; I knew the twists and turns, the bewildering rush of the Underground. We travelled to Camden Market, where he looked disapprovingly at mashed-up ravers and plodding goths. We sauntered about Leicester Square, our toes nipped, alcohol on our breath, taking an age to decide on a film and lapsing into thoughtless observation of shoppers and tourists in their winter coats. Because I was guarded against grief, Anthony did most of the talking.

'You can't say he *destroyed* it,' I said. 'I saw him hand it back to you.'

'Don't be so literal, Bruno. Obviously he didn't physically destroy it. He did something far worse – he made it stink.'

On our third outing, in the slump between Christmas and the New Year, we met at the National Gallery. I had gone there sometimes on previous stays with Uncle Roger, and knew where to find such favourites as Holbein's *Ambassadors*; it took Anthony several irritable minutes to decipher the anamorphic skull. I led him past fathoms of sublime painting to Titian's *Bacchus and Ariadne*. I wanted him to love it as I did but Anthony was hungry and decided to visit the gift shop.

'How's your mother?' he said later, as we tucked into pizzas on St Martin's Lane.

'Not great. I mean, she's a bit sick from the chemotherapy.'

'Life's a bitch, isn't it?'

'I suppose so. Thanks for asking.'

'Hey,' said Anthony, folding a wedge of pizza into his mouth, 'waffa frems for?'

He was kind to me for the rest of the day. His spikiness, that unpredictable side of his nature, was kept in check and we talked about films and politics and literature as though rehearsing for our student life. It was great to feel so grown up. He was funny and clever and made sure our waitress paid us attention.

This was a new tactic for him. The misery of our previous encounters was forgotten, so that, seduced, I failed to sit on the fence when he returned to his theme.

'You know that Bridge is never going to invite us back? He's just like the others – all chummy when it suits him but up goes the drawbridge as soon as you show some independence of thought. Didn't he freeze you out when you went to talk to him? They always say they're so busy, like teaching's really such a big deal, you know? My dad works much harder and he doesn't expect credit for it. That's just what teachers want: our bloody admiration. Well, admiration is earned. You can't just sit in judgement on other people, you can't impose your views like some kind of monarch, and seriously expect affection.'

'He *was* a bit harsh,' I said.

'That's not the word for it. He was out of order.' Though I knew it was childish, I yearned for the hero of old. Mr Bridge had lived up to his name for us; I still admired him, or that more terrible and passionate thing, wanted to, when it was no longer possible. Anthony leaned across the table, his hand straying an inch from mine. 'You don't know what goes on in the minds of people like Bridge. He's jealous of our youth, he's jealous of our class and our money and all the options we still have in front of us. No wonder his wife's never around. Who wants to spend all their time with a loser – a man who can only feel big by making others feel small?'

I changed the subject by asking for the dessert menu. I hated Anthony's interpretation but didn't question it. My thoughts drifted to the flat (my mother wrapped in a quilt on the sofa, the scrapheap of pills on the kitchen table) and I looked in my beer for comfort.

*   *   *

My mother must have smelt the alcohol on my breath as I sat down. She asked me whether I'd had a good time. I nodded and watched her hand settle on mine. The bedroom smelled of eau de cologne and stale farts. The Pléiade edition of Proust lay open on the duvet; a tasselled bookmark I had given her for Christmas had fallen on the floor. Her skin looked so frail that a fingernail might break it.

'What do you want to do for New Year?'

'Um, I thought I'd spend it with you and Dad.'

'You mustn't feel obliged.'

'I don't.'

Her eyes closed with the effort of a smile. 'You're a big chap now. We're very proud of you.'

'You've no reason to be.'

'I know how difficult it was for you to start at boarding school. You were so far away. Aunt Nariza could never understand it and sometimes I wondered if it made sense. For us, I mean. You were always the joy of our household. But you stuck at it and you didn't complain. And here you are, almost grown.'

'I don't feel very grown.'

'No, well, I'll let you into a secret. You never will.'

'How old do you feel?'

Mum feigned affront. 'How old do I *look*?'

'Young.'

'I'm not to blame for my condition. I mean, it's got nothing to do with *me*. Inside, I'm still a girl of twenty.'

She got a little weepy after this. I handed her the box of tissues that was already well within her reach. She clawed and rumpled them against her nose, then snivelled into laughter.

'Sorry, darling. It's the drugs. The *dru-u-ugs* . . .' And she acted out a hippy trip, her face still blotchy and a plug of snot peeping from a nostril. She stopped and honked into a fresh Kleenex. I plumped her pillow for her and kissed her damp, salty cheek.

I found my dad reading the *FT* in the sitting room. A Bach cantata was playing softly on the radio.

For the rest of the evening I followed him about the flat, avid for talk about anything and everything: the news in the world, my Christmas presents (a pile of novels I had been craving and a book on Michelangelo), a conversation I overheard on the Tube, a storyline unfolding in *EastEnders*. I must have been a nuisance but he never showed it. We ate soup and, afterwards, I watched my father pop blisters of foil and arrange her pills on a blue china plate. He attended with an alchemist's precision to the mixing of lemon barley water, then added buttered toast to her evening tray.

The doctors decided to operate. Dad stayed at Mum's side as long as he could, before and after the operation, while I spent the days migrating between hospital chairs, trying and failing to read *Lolita*. The smells of the cancer ward, its whimpering footsteps and unwavering neon, burned into my system. I didn't know how much more intimately, in the years to come, I would have to endure its strained and superficial quiet.

Mum was still in hospital when term started. Dad took a day's leave (she assured us she was on the mend) and drove me in his rented car to Kent.

Mr Sedley was back in charge at the Hereward. His deputy had packed up his bachelor's clobber and returned to whatever den the college gave him. We were sorry to see Mr Houghton go: he had proved a saner, more effective housemaster than we had expected, and now that his predecessor had returned, we braced ourselves for random acts of unkindness.

But Mr Sedley was a chastened man. When, on the third or fourth day of term, our paths crossed in Main Corridor, he looked almost distractedly at my collar and asked after my mother. 'I do hope she's on the mend. Feel free whenever you want to use the telephone. There's no need for you to queue up behind boys who are just trying to chat to their girlfriends.'

I didn't want others to know about my mother. Even Robbie Thwaite, who could be relied upon for sympathy, would have spread the news about. I cultivated a habit of inwardness, becoming even more secretive than before, when I had only my intellect and my appetites to conceal. It helped that I had a companion in whom I could confide – even if he didn't always give the impression of listening.

Anthony found a new place where we could skulk. It was the anteroom to the chapel. Nobody ever came through except the organ scholar, and he ignored us as we stretched our legs on the kneeling pads and breathed on our reflections in the plaques that lined the walls. So many Victorian dead: in the dust of the Punjab, in Kabul, in the war against the Boers. It was hard to connect these old-fashioned names with the boys we shared our lives with.

'We could do with some of that now,' said Anthony, as rugby boots clopped on the road outside. 'Pack off the grunts to war.'

'I take it you haven't sorted out your grievance with the prefects?'

'Don't get sarky.'

'I'm not the one who's dreaming of slaughter.'

Anthony looked at me reproachfully. 'They think I'm a troublemaker just for the hell of it, but my room's *hopeless*. All day long I have to listen to First Setters squealing and farting about next door. The partition's made of cardboard. Honestly, it's the shittiest room.'

'You think they put you in there on purpose?'

'What do I look like – an idiot? They hate me because I won't present them with my greased arsehole. I won't pretend they're not a bunch of wankers.'

'Well, that's not the strongest bargaining position.'

'I'm Oxbridge material. The room they've put me in is threatening my academic performance.'

'You'd get straight As in your sleep,' I said.

This pleased him but he wouldn't show it. '*They* don't have to know that, do they?'

They were all Anthony's enemies: the boys who thwarted or ignored him, the masters who defended a perverse and anti-quated establishment. Beyond the oak door to the chapel, the organ pounced into life. Anthony raised his voice to be heard above it, and I sensed for a moment that something had come loose in him. He lacked the vindication of a discerning adult. Mr Bridge, in withdrawing from us, had taken away more than a pleasant evening of tea and biscuits.

I am not paranoid by nature. Paranoia requires self-impor-tance: it is negative solipsism. After three years at boarding school, on the lowest rung of the social ladder, I could take comfort in the knowledge that I barely existed for the bullies who mocked me. Anthony never understood this; or if he did, he preferred to believe in hatred over indifference, conspiracy over neglect. This was why Mr Bridge's behaviour infuriated him. Anthony had confided in him: he had tried to involve him in a cult of grievance and Mr Bridge had wanted nothing to do with it, had denounced it as puerile and insignificant, the ravings of adolescence. I still believed, in those early weeks of Lent Term, that our self-appointed guru would take us back. But I was mistaken. Mr Bridge had sensed something dangerous in *Wits' End*. He had gone too far in befriending us and now the barriers of age and profession went up.

In the days that followed, I encountered him at several turns: outside the Common Room, in the lunch queue while he was on duty, locking the boot of his car, on the muddy track between the hockey pitch and the school tuck shop. Every time he seemed less sure of himself. I alluded to our meetings and enquired after his wife; I wondered whether he was an admirer of Wordsworth, whom we were studying. Though he was much older and taller than me, I began to feel that I outranked him. It was not a gratifying sensation. I wanted to admire him but he was no longer admirable. There was a hunched and febrile energy pent up inside him. He coughed and raked his hair with long, nervous fingers.

Finally I asked him, right out, when he planned to invite us to his house. 'I don't think it's going to happen this term, Bruno. Really, there are just too many things on. I need a life as well, you know.'

When I reported the conversation, Anthony paced the floor of the chapel trumpeting his vindication while I tried to play angel's advocate. We didn't *know* that this was personal, I said. For all we could tell, Mr Bridge might be behaving this way with everyone. There might be whispers in the staffroom about his state of mind: colleagues fretting, the headmaster informed, a counsellor already turning the ignition key in her Fiat Panda. Anthony sneered and called the idea a load of bollocks. 'The fact remains,' he said, 'that he's treating *you* like shit.'

'I think that's a bit strong.'

'No you don't – that's exactly how you feel. Only you're too nice and well brought up to admit it.'

'He might still change his mind.'

'You don't get it, do you? We were just a hobby for him. He wanted us to look up to him and, when he read my novel, it freaked him out because he realised we weren't a couple of pansies.'

The next day, after double English, I looked at Mr Bridge through the glass door of the staffroom. He was folding his scarf into a noose, like a French intellectual on his way to the café. There was no emotion to be read on his face and I resented its impassive calm. I scuttled away before he emerged and hid my face in the bookshelves.

The cancer treatment ended in early March. I remember the green shoots of daffodils in Hyde Park where we went for a walk, Mum wrapped up as if for a blizzard. She moved slowly, with an elderly person's mistrust of her legs, while Dad gave news from what he called home: how Mr Phang had gone to see relatives in Malacca and Gurmit Lal's father was standing for parliament. It made me ill to see my mother so tired; but she refused to feel sorry for herself and laughed even as she asked to return to the car.

They were keen to get back to Kuala Lumpur: the cold weather gave them aches and pains and Dad was boxing a constant snivel. I agreed that they should go as soon as possible.

I returned on Sunday evening to Kingsley and felt at once the weight of my solitude. I traced the path I could almost imagine that I had made in the tarmac and found Anthony in his room.

The prefects had still not moved him and I could hear the dull thump of little boys running next door. 'All right?' I said.

'Have you seen this?' A sheet of paper jerked in the air and fell at my feet. I picked it up. 'You can kiss the last week of our Easter holidays goodbye. We're going to be freezing our arses off in the Lake District.'

' "English pupils will get a chance to walk in the footsteps of William and Dorothy Wordsworth . . ." '

'Have you seen who's taking us?''

'It sounds OK,' I said.

'It sounds dreadful. They'll have us reading gobbets of *The Prelude* while sitting around a campfire eating marshmallows.'

'Uh, no, it says here we'll be staying at a youth hostel . . .'

'Oh, great. They'd better not put me anywhere near Bridget, I'm telling you. I won't be able to resist thumping him.'

'I don't think that would be wise.'

'But *why*,' Anthony whined, '*why* do we have to go to bloody Cumbria? It's not like we're studying geology – we don't need to walk around the fucking mountains to be able to write about poetry.'

'At least we'll have each other.'

The loading of my remark only occurred to me once it had escaped. Anthony's eyebrows lifted and his nose wrinkled in the beginning of a snarl. But I was not rebuked. He smiled. It was a broad, knowing grin with a huff of laughter behind it, and I was too dazzled and surprised to notice whether it carried into his eyes.

'Yeah,' he said. 'That's true.'

'I mean . . .'

'Us against the world, right? 'Cause we're the only people on this wavelength. No one else even *gets* it.'

I was unsure what he was talking about, but felt so anxious to redeem myself that I agreed with him absolutely. We were the only ones. There was nobody else.

III

Fourteen of us boarded the train at Maidstone under the care of Messrs Bridge and Robinson. Anthony brooded all the way. He barely spoke to me, or anyone for that matter, but sat ostentatiously reading Elias Canetti while shabby south London swallowed us up.

At King's Cross station, our connection was delayed and we sat on our rucksacks in the middle of the concourse.

'I hope that book's racier than it looks,' said Mr Robinson. He peeled it without permission from Anthony's fingers. '*Crowds and Power*. Sounds a bit too intellectual for me.'

'I imagine it would be, sir.'

Mr Robinson's smile collapsed. He flipped the book at Anthony's lap and walked away an enemy.

'What the hell did you say that for?'

'I was agreeing with him.'

'You weren't supposed to.' Anthony shrugged and brushed the book with his sleeve. I felt powerless to distract him in such a mood. It frightened me as well.

Our allotted tickets put me next to Ollie Radmore. He liked the situation even less than I did and, as soon as we were under way, he vaulted over me to take possession of an empty seat. I was left alone to watch as city gave way to fields and woods.

Wordsworth's *Prelude* slumbered in my lap and somewhere in Hertfordshire my attention dissolved.

I awoke half an hour before Kendal, confused and parched, with a latent headache and a nameless sense of desolation. The country about us was hilly and open and lush. I listened to the voices in the compartment and tried to make out what they were saying; Mr Robinson's self-approving bass dominated. Mr Bridge, sitting beside Hugo Barclay three rows ahead of mine, kept his nose in a book.

When we arrived at Kendal, I trudged woozily to the minibus that would take us to Troutbeck. Anthony sat alone at the back with his schemes and daydreams. Mr Bridge was driving, while Mr Robinson wrestled with an Ordnance Survey map and offered fatuous directions.

The landscape made little impression on me that evening; a pang like homesickness occluded the crags and fells. Our bus wound through meadows and woods and all I could think about was Anthony sulking at the rear. Both masters had slighted him. I had not noticed the insults but they were obvious to Anthony.

The minibus pulled up outside the youth hostel and there followed a rowdy disembarkation. Boys ran to stake claims on beds and roommates. I was careful to fall behind Anthony as he sidled into a room where Hugo Barclay and Nick Jones were already portioning out cigarettes. I followed furtively and put my rucksack on the bunk below Hugo's.

We were left pretty much to ourselves at first. There was a TV lounge and most boys ended up there, watching *The Fresh Prince of Bel-Air*. Mr Bridge came in hoping someone might join him for a stroll along Trout Beck. For a minute I was tempted; but Anthony sat behind me with his arms folded, daring a direct appeal that never came.

Mr Bridge departed without a single volunteer. I would have felt sorry for him had not Nick Jones stood up, with all the confidence of his six-foot, rugby-prop frame, and switched on the news. Balkan rooftops smoked to howls of protest and the room broke into factions. Some boys wanted to watch *Top of the Pops*; others thought Sarajevo mattered. Anthony slumped forward and looked across his chest at me. With a start of arousal I understood his intention, and waited a minute after his exit before getting up and following him outside.

We stood in solidarity in the lee of the building, looking up at unknown hills.

'How are you?' said Anthony.

'OK – how about you?'

'I'm OK.'

'Good.'

Anthony looked along the narrow valley. 'Bridget didn't do very well, did he?'

'Do you suppose he's gone on his own?'

'Well, he doesn't want to hang around here. Robinson's stayed behind to keep an eye on us.'

'In case we burn the place down?'

'We're grown-ups now – they trust us.' This surprised me. I scanned his face for evidence of irony but he seemed to mean it.

'Robinson hasn't been too bad,' I said tentatively.

'You didn't hear him on the train.'

'I fell asleep.'

'That's one of your talents. I had to listen to him showing off for the whole journey.'

He did not need to say more: I had the measure of Mr Robinson. He tried to win pupils' hearts, if not their minds, by telling dirty jokes and picking out victims. It was a tactic he practised in lessons, singling out weakness or eccentricity in a boy and subjecting it to heavy sarcasm. He had wit of a bullying kind, and it was a test of character to take it like a man.

'I like what you're wearing,' said Anthony.

'You . . . you do?'

He had a talent for surprising me – for touching a raw nerve. No matter how I tried, I never managed to wear appropriate casuals, flunking on the Gulag chic of torn jeans and baggy shirts, investing in red Converse shoes the very week they fell from favour, opting for tops that proved too garish, or flabby, or inscrutably uncool, for general taste. Everyone felt the pressure of 'mufti'. No one in Kingsley would have dared to call it fashion (the very word screamed of queerness) but the imperative existed all the same. 'I don't know if I've got the turn-ups right,' I said, greedy for more praise. 'Maybe I should change my hairstyle – what do you think? Not that I can do much with this fuzz.'

A look of distaste crossed Anthony's face and I cleared the pleading from my throat.

After sunset, the masters rounded us up and drove us to Windermere for supper. Mr Bridge had booked a room in a pub and we tucked into American-sized portions of scampi and chips. Mr Robinson held forth on sporting matters and sparked a debate as to the likely make-up of the following year's World Cup squad. I sat with Anthony at the far end of the table, while Mr Bridge sat at the other, with his head tipped forward the better to listen to Duncan Fine.

'Have you noticed,' said Anthony, 'where Bridget's sitting?'

'He has to sit somewhere.'

'Yeah: as far away from us as possible.'

I could not work out whether this was true. The seating arrangements had seemed quite random to me. For all I could tell, *we* were responsible for our isolation.

'It's Dove Cottage tomorrow. Can't wait, can you? All those busloads of Japanese tourists wondering what the fuck's going on but taking photographs anyway.'

'Have you been?'

Anthony looked at me as if an ant were crawling on the tip of my nose. 'Why would I *need* to?'

His mood improved when we had eaten, and for once Anthony (who took unusual care of what he ate) joined me in ordering a sticky toffee pudding.

Mr Robinson noticed us the moment his colleague went to pay the bill. 'Hey,' he said, 'you two lovebirds, what are you plotting down there? We haven't heard a squeak from you all evening.'

I blushed, effectively outed, but Anthony retaliated. 'Maybe that's because you haven't said anything worth commenting on.'

There was a lewd and goading 'ooh' from the boys, as if a fight were brewing. Uncertainty gleamed in their faces, and eagerness to be in on the joke. Mr Robinson smiled, his eyelids batting. 'So speaks the college malcontent.'

'That's a very long and impressive word for you, sir.'

'Yes, well, Blunden, I am an English teacher.' He pressed his hands, palms down, against the table. He was not enjoying this exchange.

'*Are* you, sir?' said Anthony.

Mr Robinson blinked, his mouth open. Everyone waited, in mounting discomfort, for the return of Mr Bridge and the security of his bland goodwill.

'You're a sarcastic little toerag,' said Mr Robinson. It burst out of him. His colleague was within hearing, replacing a credit card in his wallet. He said nothing.

On the way back, Anthony was shunned but triumphant. The headlights picked up dodging trees – the scaly reel of a dry-stone wall – a sharp and furtive gash of fox running into darkness. We clambered out of the minibus like troopers. I half expected Mr Robinson to wait in ambush but he had gone off to nurse his wounded pride. Mr Bridge gathered us all together.

'We're getting up good and early tomorrow,' he said. 'Mr Robinson and I will shake you from your beauty sleep at around seven thirty, so if any of you are planning to have a wild night, don't wince and complain to me when I draw back the curtains.'

There were puffs of resignation, a few shrugs and a round of goodnights. Mr Bridge answered his well-wishers by name. He did not address Anthony but then, as I pointed out later, my friend had not said anything either.

It was barely eight o'clock and already the road to Grasmere was clogged with traffic. Ambleside teemed with tourists and ramblers and amorous couples dressed in April as though for St Tropez. Visitors' cars were banked deep against every kerb, and a delivery lorry kept us crawling and fuming for a quarter of an hour.

I didn't mind. The journey calmed my nerves; I enjoyed the branched unveiling of Rydal Water, with its child's fantasy island and the green fells beyond. When we passed the sign for the famous cottage, there were scornful cries, and Mr Robinson explained that we were going to visit Wordsworth's grave.

In Grasmere village, we bundled into a churchyard. The yew trees planted by the poet seemed venerable but Mr Bridge said they were practically still saplings. 'Human generations are brief – a few inches only in the trunk of this tree.'

'Here's the bugger,' exclaimed Mr Robinson.

We gathered, somewhat sheepishly, about the black iron railings that surround the Wordsworth tombs. There was the poet beside his wife Mary, a host of offshoots close by. I waited for something profound to happen. Anthony set off a round of yawns.

'It's plain, isn't it?' said Ollie Radmore.

'Like Churchill's grave,' said Mr Robinson. 'Great deeds don't need fancy masonry.'

'This is a barrel of laughs,' Anthony whispered in my ear.

For the rest of the day, Mr Robinson was a nuisance, deflating serious comment with his 'frank' philistinism. He had it in for Anthony, and made repeated allusions to lonely hermits and shunned leech gatherers, keeping my friend in his insinuating gaze. Mr Bridge paid no attention. He seemed to know his way round the cramped quarters of Dove Cottage, and Mr Robinson wore a supercilious expression when his colleague turned down the offer of an official guide. Several times I had to flatten myself against hallowed walls to give simpering tourists passage. We stood, without awe or reverence, around the poet's chair – home, as Hugo Barclay put it, to the sacred bum.

Mr Bridge surprised everyone with his laughter. 'Wordsworth wasn't a man for desks. He didn't *write*: he composed while walking the fells. You can imagine him speaking his verses aloud, weighing them until they were good. And then crashing back into the overcrowded cottage – Dorothy and Mary cooking, the children at play, Coleridge sunk in his books – and jotting down his harvest of words.' He paused and cast a glance at Mr Robinson. 'The poems we're studying are meant to be heard as much as read. Isn't that right?'

'Whatever you say, old boy.'

Robinson wanted to visit the guest room where Coleridge and De Quincey stayed. 'They were notorious drug addicts. The rock and roll stars of their age . . .'

'Oh, please,' said Anthony, loud enough to be heard.

'*Confessions of an Opium Eater*. It's, uh, pretty trippy stuff, I can tell you. And *Kubla Khan*. That was opium induced. Interrupted by the man from Porlock.'

'Wordsworth,' said Mr Bridge, 'didn't need mental stimulants. He had Nature. He had his fell walks . . .'

'He also had regular bowel movements, which is more than can be said for Coleridge.'

Our visit done, we stumbled blinking into daylight. Anthony's Japanese tourists obligingly lined up to snap the cottage. Mr Bridge was talking to whoever would listen about Wordsworth the early conservationist. 'When the lake road was built in the

1830s, he was against it. And he can't have guessed what it would become with the motor car and mass tourism. The same goes for the train: he campaigned to have it stop at Windermere. And yet he made a lot of money out of selling the Lakes to tourists. He wrote a guidebook. His poems invite us up here: we all want a piece of it. Yet in the very process of loving what's good, we damage or destroy it. The irony isn't lost on anyone, I assure you. It was easy for Wordsworth to be radical in his youth, but much harder in the age of iron and steam . . .'

We ate lunch in the restaurant near the cottage, a phalanx of tour buses obscuring the view. Mr Robinson was in boisterous form, while Mr Bridge buried himself in conversation with Nick Jones and never once looked our way.

In the afternoon we were set loose. Anthony and I wandered off into lush meadows where we sucked straws and smoked, peering every so often over our shoulders. When we reached the main road, we turned back and encountered Hugo Barclay. He told us that Bridget was planning a walk around the lake. I was in favour of going but Anthony preferred to skulk in a pub and I stayed devotedly with him.

When the time came for us to meet up at the minibus, we arrived among the last, stinking of beer and fags and the inadequate camouflage of peppermints. Mr Bridge was at the wheel; he looked tired and impatient and I was sorry that we had not joined him on his tour of Grasmere.

Mr Robinson turned with a creak of leather. 'Have a nice time in the pub, did we?'

Anthony shrugged and attended to his seat belt.

'I'm not saying that we particularly *wanted* your company but it might have been courteous to offer. You know, this is supposed to be a group outing.'

Anthony sat passively while we waited for the stragglers to return from the loo. Mr Robinson would not let go. 'You know,

Blunden, you'd get much more out of life if you put something in. I mean, if you made an effort. Nobody likes a sulker . . .'

Andy Wood and Duncan Fine came on board, sliding the door after them. Mr Bridge turned to his colleague: 'OK,' he said, 'I think that's, uh . . .' He looked over his shoulder at the passengers. 'That's everyone, let's go.'

Half an hour later, having washed my face and hands, I went looking for Anthony and found him sitting under trees on the edge of the hostel grounds. 'What's up?' I said. He shrugged and pursed his lips, his fingers plucking at grass. 'Hey, apparently we're getting pizzas delivered. Hugo told me.' I crossed my legs and plumped down beside him in the damp grass. 'What *is* it?' I asked. 'What's on your mind?'

'Nothing.'

'Are you avoiding me?'

Anthony sighed and licked the inside of his cheek. His fingers in the grass wrenched out blades. 'Have you noticed how he says nothing?'

'What do you mean?'

'That bastard Robinson lays into me in front of everybody and Bridget says nothing. He doesn't even pretend to give a shit. He probably enjoys it.'

'Don't be paranoid,' I said, though I too resented Mr Bridge's neglect. It was unjust and capricious. The sense of abandonment was a kind of grief. 'Robinson does it to everybody. In lessons . . .'

'Well, *not to me*. I won't let him do it to *me*.'

'Answer back, then.'

'Just standing there, letting it happen . . .'

'Who are you talking about?'

'Mr Bridge, you idiot.'

'I thought . . .'

'All that liberal crap he used to throw at us, pretending to be on our side. He doesn't want friends, he wants disciples. Well,

212

we see through him. Robinson's a cunt but it's Mr Bridge who deserves to be punished.'

Anthony's eyes burned into mine: I was excited and frightened and sick to my stomach. 'What are you thinking of?' I said.

'I'm not sure.'

'*Tell* me.'

'I don't know yet, do I?' His expression softened: I thought I saw a shadow of love in it and I took such shelter there that I would have done, at that moment, anything he asked of me. Exhausted, and at the same time watching myself as though in a film, I let my head drop and bow towards him. Anthony got up to leave. I listened to the sound his feet made in the long grass, and opened my eyes on his aggrieved figure as he left me beneath the budding ashes.

The night was far from restful, with boys gossiping and sneaking outside for cigarettes. Ollie Radmore produced a bottle of vodka and a copy of *Penthouse* flitted from bunk to bunk like a visiting nightbird. If the masters heard us, they did not bother to leave their beds. I dozed for a few hours with the blanket pulled over my head.

When we rose the next morning, the lush woods and mountains had vanished. Beyond the ghostly silhouettes of the nearest larches, everything was sunk in mist, as if we were back in the lowlands or on the shore of a creeping void.

'Fuck,' said Hugo. 'We're not going to walk in this, are we?'

Anthony had left the room already. I dressed and made my way to the dining room, where the stink promised runny eggs and fried bread. Mr Bridge was sitting alone drinking coffee and reading. He looked up at my entrance. 'You're down early,' he said.

'Am I?'

'I was about to go up and raise hell. I suppose everyone else is still in bed?'

I sat at the far table and measured in myself a blank feeling, grey and neutral. I felt no desire to know what he was reading and he, in turn, showed little interest in me. He finished his coffee, pushed back the bench with his knee and left me to wait alone for my peers.

I mentioned this to Anthony later as we boarded the minibus to Rydal Mount. 'Why's he so gloomy all the time? He barely said a word to me, like I'm a total stranger.'

'He does it deliberately. We're not worthy of him.'

I put my finger to my lips but there was little danger of us being heard above the expectorations of the engine. I looked to the front of the vehicle. It had been obvious at breakfast from the way they placed a dozen boys between them that Mr Bridge and Mr Robinson could no longer tolerate each other's company. In Ambleside they squabbled over directions. 'I *know* the way,' said Mr Bridge, slapping the road map away from his gearstick. 'I've done this before.'

'After the library you turn left.'

'It comes to the same.'

In life as on the rugby pitch, Mr Robinson was competitive and loath to acknowledge in others skills or knowledge that he himself did not possess. He folded up the map and looked out of the window, a sardonic, obstinate grin on his face. Ambleside in the mist was a grey, muffled place, occupied only by ramblers equipped as though about to scale Everest. To our left, the precipitous flanks of Loughrigg Fell were barely discernible, a numinous, guessable presence. Mr Bridge steered us expertly up a steep lane to our destination.

Rydal Mount looked dull behind its rampart of befogged trees. 'The great man's house,' said Mr Robinson.

'You mean the country seat of the honourable reactionary, Mr William W.'

Mr Robinson kept his rictus. 'Seems to have worked for him, doesn't it?'

We climbed out of the minibus, rucksacks on our shoulders, while Mr Bridge went to make enquiries in the museum. Here, too, we had company. The cars of tourists were parked along the lane and a coachload of German teenagers waited on the driveway. We stood in the warm mist watching them, our heavy boots scraping the damp ground. I could feel the sweat trickling inside my cagoule. Anthony stood apart, tugging at ferns that grew in abundance on the dry-stone walls.

After a minute, Mr Bridge came out of the gift shop shaking his head. The bookings had got mixed up, he said, and there were two school groups ahead of us. Mr Robinson shrugged in a way that made it clear he was quite happy with the situation. 'Let's get our hiking boots on,' he said, jerking his thumb at the misty sky. 'The sun will burn that off. You said yourself, Wordsworth was a walking poet.'

Mr Bridge appeared reluctant to go, but there was nothing else to do with us, and Anthony wasn't the only one showing signs of restlessness. 'If it doesn't start clearing up . . .'

'We'll turn back, don't worry.'

We set ourselves against a steeply inclined concrete path. Several ramblers passed us on their way down, placing their feet sideways against the slope. Mr Robinson hailed them heartily and the boys grumblingly did the same.

The concrete path came to an end. Green space surrounded us, damp-smelling and obscure. We piled through a gate into fields of bracken. Venerable oaks and shaggy ashes loomed like ghosts through the mist. Behind us there was nothing where a valley should have been, and we had to take Mr Bridge's word that he was pointing towards Lake Windermere. As for the fells, we could only sense them above us: their ancient, weather-worn being. 'Better hope it clears,' said Mr Bridge to his colleague. 'These paths can be dangerous in poor visibility.'

'Ah, don't be such a wuss. You know the weather's changeable. By the time we get to Heron Pike we'll have a clear view across the mountains.'

There was no chance to negotiate. Mr Robinson charged ahead, most of the boys keeping up with him, and those of us at the rear had no choice but to follow.

'He seems very confident,' said Hugo Barclay.

'Huh,' said Anthony. 'He wants to race – the view's just an excuse.'

We bowed our heads as if to concentrate on the narrow visible world. The footpath was steep and I was glad to find stones laid down underfoot; but these sweated in the mist and proved slippery. It was all I could do not to fall over: and indeed there was a muffled sound of collapse ahead of us, followed by laughter.

We came level with the main group. Ollie Radmore had slipped and muddied his thigh. He gritted his teeth.

'I think he's still pissed, sir,' said Duncan Fine.

Mr Robinson feigned surprise and disapproval. 'Pissed? How could he be pissed on orange squash?'

Ollie denied the accusation and the mockery worsened. He tried to laugh it off and the group resumed its climb.

'Are you all right?' asked Mr Bridge, for Ollie was limping slightly.

'Fine,' he replied, and quickened his pace to prove it.

We pressed on and caught up with Mr Robinson's group as they queued to climb a ladder stile. Anthony gripped my sleeve to keep me at the rear. Mr Bridge stood behind us, pensive and uneasy. His glasses had steamed up.

'Struggling, sir?' said Anthony, and he pointed by way of explanation to those misted lenses.

'Hm? I really should try again with contact lenses.'

'I wear contacts, sir.'

'Yes?'

'Always have.'

Mr Bridge was not even pretending to listen: he had a distracted air. I climbed the stile and Anthony followed. 'You don't wear lenses,' I whispered. 'What are you talking about?'

'Just making conversation,' said Anthony.

We fell behind again. I was unfit and leaden, panting in the sauna of my cagoule. As for Anthony, he seemed to have trouble with his boots. Twice he stopped to fiddle with laces that looked fine to me while Mr Bridge waited, like a melancholy shepherd, for us to continue. Both my companions were mute, as if the mist had cottoned their brains. It was impossible to tell where we were heading. No strangers clomped past us reassuringly: such ramblers as we had seen at Rydal Mount were not to be found up here. Bad weather had chivvied them to the comforts of a pub or the tat of the gift shop. Only our expedition braved the elements.

It is a strange and unsettling thing, the claustrophobia of open country in fog. A flight of swifts wheeled above us, unseen, like the creaking of some spectral chariot. Voices and laughter from Mr Robinson's group stumbled and echoed down the track. Someone – possibly one of ours – had wrenched a pink tube from about a sapling and flung it across the stones.

'We're going the wrong way,' said Mr Bridge, but Mr Robinson was racing ahead with his acolytes and seemed not to hear. Mr Bridge stopped and muttered: 'This is wrong, all wrong.' He found a level perch in the bracken and tried to make sense of the map. Water was dripping from his hood. Anthony and I watched him turn and turn about and peer into the mist. 'We're on the wrong path,' he said in a tone of revelation. 'We're supposed to be heading north but all we're doing is clinging to the hillside. Just over there,' he said, pointing into nothingness, 'is Rydal Water.'

'How can you tell, sir?'

'Because the topography's all wrong. We wouldn't be climbing this steeply if we were following the right path.'

'Does it matter?'

'I'm not sure. But I don't know the path up here and it doesn't look like the weather's clearing.'

'Maybe . . .' I was panting. 'Maybe we shouldn't go . . . any farther.'

'Well, they've charged ahead of us now and we mustn't split up.' Mr Bridge tutted in frustration and scrutinised the cloud through which his colleague was racing. I put out my hand and fell on my backside into the tickling bracken. 'Come on, Bruno, we've got to catch up.'

'Yeah,' said Anthony, 'where's your sense of adventure?'

'I left it in the minibus.'

Mr Bridge stamped his feet to shake off puzzle pieces of damp mud. 'Since they're ahead of us and determined to make it a kind of steeplechase, we don't have much choice.'

Anthony offered me a hand. I took it gladly and got to my feet. 'Are you OK?'

I smiled and nodded.

Mr Bridge was waiting for us twenty yards or so ahead. He stood in a lion tamer's stance on two large rocks until we had taken the lead; then followed, keeping up the rear.

The landscape ahead was uncertain but we could hear it. Small birds twittered in the bracken. Browsing sheep made obstinate brushing sounds. 'Careful,' said Anthony, seeing my blind, weary feet about to crush a black slug. 'You'll slip.'

'I'm tired,' I said.

'You'll be all right.'

'No, really. I feel sick.'

'It's the mist. Come on . . .' He took my elbow and gave it a friendly, encouraging squeeze. The slow minutes passed and I sank into a kind of trudging torpor. The sightlessness of the mist nauseated me, so that I had to keep my eyes on the footpath. Its rocks were encased in brown mud; their tips emerged obliquely, wet enough to slip on and sufficiently jagged to cut a falling hand or elbow. Here and there on the track I noticed lumps of black-and-white sheep's wool. Mosses growing where they could find space had put forth tiny flowers like tentacles or probes. Doubtless Mr Bridge would have been able to name them but I did not ask. He walked behind us, stolid and silent, and the sound of his arms swishing against his sides made me hate him.

'Do you think we're nearly there?' I said to Anthony.

'I'm not the one with a map.'

If Mr Bridge heard us, he offered no words of encouragement. I began to wonder how far we had fallen behind the rest of the group. Its voices ambled back to us, muffled and incoherent.

The higher we went, the more precipitous our route became. 'Careful, boys,' said Mr Bridge, breaking several minutes' silence. 'It's over the edge here.'

'How can you tell?'

'Well, look.'

'Are there rocks?'

Mr Bridge frowned at Anthony. Like Johnson refuting Bishop Berkeley, he stamped his foot on the stone beneath us. 'What do you call this?'

'I mean, are these cliffs dangerous?'

'This is Nab Scar, if I'm reading the map correctly. Can you see how the mist is a deeper, greyer colour over there? That's open space, with a charming lake at the bottom. So yes, there's a falling away. Which is why we should stick to the path. No clever cross-country, please. And Bruno . . .' Mr Bridge sighed regretfully. 'Do you think you could go a *little* faster?'

'He's going as fast as he can,' said Anthony with sudden anger. Mr Bridge, taken aback, flapped his arms and looked ahead into the blankness.

'They're rushing ahead of us,' I said plaintively.

'Let them,' said Anthony, 'they're idiots.'

Mr Bridge broadened his stride, pacing over rocks that seemed to me a hurdle in my sickness. Wretchedly we followed. I convinced myself that I was all pain, all nausea. The truth, I now suspect, is that some hidden animal sense in me knew already what danger lay ahead. I cursed the mist and Mr Bridge for exposing me to its cloying embrace.

We had conquered another hundred metres, perhaps, and my trance of self-pity was so enthralling that I did not realise until Anthony put an arm about my waist to stop me that we had fallen behind Mr Bridge. 'What is it?' I said. 'What's the matter?'

Anthony did not look at me. His eyes were trained on the rocky slope. 'Let's wait,' he said. 'It won't do him any harm to worry about us.'

'No, Anthony . . .' But he held me pressed against him. I squirmed feebly. 'I want to get on.'

'*Wait.*' His embrace tightened. I lost my will to it. 'Follow me,' he said, and tugged me easily with him off the path.

We cut through bracken and short grass and heather, moving, as I thought, away from the crags. I tugged on Anthony's shoulder to stop him and, looking back, found the path obscured. Breathless again, I gasped unhappily for air, so that Anthony hissed at me to be quiet. We listened. There was nothing at first: the universe had vanished and we stood on a patch of earth in a white void. 'Let's go back,' I whispered.

'Shush.'

He had forgotten us: that was how little we signified. I imagined Mr Bridge catching up with the rest of the group, and a desperate fear of abandonment threatened to overwhelm me. 'Anthony, this is stupid.'

'*Listen.*'

There were faint calls in the mist. From above us on the fells, members of our group were shouting. It was impossible to make out the words; and indeed in that cloaking, cloying mist our bearings were lost – the echoes seemed to fall behind us, then above.

'Bruno! Anthony!'

'Jesus, that's Bridge,' I said, and Anthony let out a snigger. 'He's looking for us.'

'Let him.'

'*Jackson! Where are you, Jackson?*'

Anthony put a hand on my shoulder. Its weight increased the more I wanted to shout back. The vegetation rustled as he leaned ever closer. Both his hands were on me now, his elbows pressing beneath my shoulder blades, as though he meant to hitch a piggyback ride. I could feel his breath, hot and damp, on my neck. His lips were inches from my skin. 'Anthony,' I whispered, 'we've got to go back.'

'In a minute.'

But I couldn't wait. I strode through the heather, as I thought to the path, and shouted, 'We're coming!' Anthony gave me a powerful shove and I nearly fell.

At that moment, Mr Bridge lost his temper. 'For God's sake, Jackson, make a bloody effort!' The voice seemed to surge at me; I looked startled over my shoulder. Other voices – now muffled, now startlingly clear – travelled on the mountain. I wanted to return to the footpath, only realised that I wasn't sure which way to go. We had spun round in the mist. Everything, within that shifting curtain of cloud, looked the same. Some animal came shambling towards my leg and I nearly screamed until I realised that it was Anthony creeping closer.

'Where's the fucking path?' I said.

'Shush.'

Somewhere close by, Mr Bridge was hastening down the track to meet us. I had a sudden conviction that he was not to the left of us, as he should have been, but on our right. I dropped on my knees, afraid to venture farther. 'We're on the wrong side,' I said.

'So?'

'We're close to the edge!'

I clung with my fingers to the wet grass and turned about on all fours to confront the chasm. I had giddy visions of stumbling, of taking the short, hard way home. Anthony crouched low, his shoulders raised like hackles and his eyes intent. 'Wait,' he said.

I was afraid of the drop below us. I disliked our subterfuge, and would have gone alone to meet Mr Bridge had he not given vent, at that instant, to his frustration: 'Come on, Bruno! Keep up, can't you? Don't be such a useless *lump*.'

I looked down and saw my hand in Anthony's. He squeezed my fingers tightly. I nodded, mesmerised by his sympathy, and let him lead us, crawling like infants, to the shelter of an exposed rock.

The hillside fell away behind us. We crouched and hid, alone in the universe.

'We'll give him a scare,' said Anthony, his face so close to mine that I could taste his breath. 'He deserves a scare, don't you think?' And he yelled over me: 'We're here! Over here!'

Mr Bridge came down the path; we heard him clamber down on our right. Only when he was below us did he cry out our names. As the shouts from Mr Bridge continued, adding to the hollering echoes of the group far ahead of us, Anthony shouted again, and the loudness of his voice made me jump.

Other voices crossed and wandered in the mist. Mr Bridge's was loudest. 'Where *are* you?'

'Over here!' Anthony hugged me. I couldn't tell whether it was fear or glee. 'You too,' he whispered.

'We'll get in trouble.'

'Again?' cried Mr Bridge.

'Here!' I shouted, ecstatic with transgression. 'I think I've hurt my ankle!'

Anthony tittered in my ear: I had outdone him. 'It's all twisted, sir! Help! Help!'

We lured him towards us. Our yelps became whimpers; we held our noses as we had once in a locker room in Hereward House.

'Bru-uuno?'

Anthony pressed hard on my shoulder. The voice seemed to sound inside my head. We waited, our eyes fixed on the tiniest details of rock and lichen, for Mr Bridge to speak again. But there came neither call from him nor movement towards our hiding place.

The mist around us was changing; it began to shed as a thin, electric mizzle. I wanted to stand up. I wanted to be found out. But ten seconds passed, then another ten, without any movement. Nobody called our names; nobody flattened the bracken to discover us, arses in the air, pressed against damp stone.

'What's happening?' Sweat was pouring down my ribs. I looked at Anthony's profile until my eyes ached.

A whole minute passed before I found the courage to get up. No Mr Bridge loomed above us, hands on hips. He had not found our hiding place. When it was obvious that nothing was happening, Anthony too straightened.

I can't remember which of us first heard the moans. They became distinct only when we saw them confirmed in each other's faces.

'A cow?' I said, trembling.

Fiercely we listened, heads cocked, and heard the lowing noise again. It sounded tired, almost petulant. There was a bark, half cough, half shout, and before we could think what we were doing we were stumbling along the crags, our knuckles gashed on sharp rock, jarring our knees as we clung to solid ground.

We hunted the gasps of effort. They ceased to be animal and became recognisably those of Mr Bridge. Anthony was ahead of me by a metre or so, his fingers tangled in heather as he clambered. There didn't seem to be a steep precipice, merely a mild falling away; but this was an illusion fostered by the mist.

'Help?'

Anthony was gasping, leaning on a ledge of bare rock, staring at something below. I couldn't look over his shoulder. Nothing in my body worked; my legs were locked tight.

'Jesus Christ,' said Anthony.

Forcing myself to straighten up a couple of inches, I managed to crane my neck past Anthony. I looked down where he was looking. I saw Mr Bridge.

He had already fallen some way and was clinging to a small rock, his face pressed into the moss beneath it. His hands were bloody and I realised that the knuckles were white with effort.

'Hold on,' said Anthony, but the voice crept out of him in a whisper.

I do not know whether Mr Bridge heard us but he never lifted his head. There was a drop from where we crouched of perhaps six feet. Beneath him, the cliff was sheer and sudden.

'Hold on,' croaked Anthony again.

We did not move. It was like watching the end of the world: we were powerless to intervene. The situation seemed at the same time banal and unreal. Our bodies followed their own logic and locked fast.

Mr Bridge made a small, mewling sound. I stared at the top of his head. The pale hair looked almost white, as if the mist had absorbed and transformed it. A bald patch, small and neat as a tonsure, was starting to conquer the crown.

One second he was below us; the next, without a syllable of protest, he was gone.

Now

I

It's a heavy thing to be weary, so weary, before your life has really begun. Even now, once I get to sleep (and that involves much fussing and burrowing in the dark), it's a soldier's crawl through no man's land to surface again. I have no idea what it feels like to wake up refreshed: I emerge rumpled and gloomy, wishing I could stay in bed, unleavened by repose. For years, the graduate years when I began to put on this extraneous flesh, I wondered if I was cursed: whether poor sleep was part of my special punishment, a biological penance for what I had done.

In the immediate aftermath of Mr Bridge's fall, with its police and TV crews, its shocked and pallid delegation of parents and masters, my sleep was dead, not even a brain mist – pure and merciful oblivion. Some boys went home to their families; I had a short telephone conversation with Dad and then returned by train to Kingsley.

The first assembly of term brought the whole school together, listening in freakish stillness to the headmaster's oration. I was not sitting next to Anthony. Neither of us could bear to see the other for dread of what we had done. At the end of that day, after I had taken all I could of avid questions, I had my first nightmare. It was nothing very original: a montage of memories in a loop, soft voices in my head suddenly yelling, the unalterable past dragged into the present.

I do not know whether Anthony was dreaming. My bad nights made me a zombie but he seemed alert as he primed our answers for the police. We had nothing to hide, he said (even the television was calling it an accident), but it was wise to get our story straight. It was common knowledge that the fells could be dangerous in the mist. The coroner's verdict chimed with the general view that Mr Robinson had behaved irresponsibly in splitting up the group, and the school governors, alarmed at insinuations in the press, were quick to secure his resignation.

Anthony accepted the official findings; he swallowed them like a cordial.

I couldn't stand the sight of him. For the rest of that hateful Summer Term, he kept his distance, and I found myself equally shunned by our peers. I did not *smell* right. There was a rotten atmosphere at Kingsley, and I became convinced that I was its epicentre. Sometimes I wanted to choke rather than accept what had happened. I heard rumours that Mrs Bridge had left the country; my throat puffed up every time I walked past the open door of the English department staffroom. My academic work collapsed and Mr Sedley invited me into his office.

He looked bewildered when I announced my wish to leave Kingsley, and for an instant I was the adult in the room, crammed with darkness. Where on earth did I propose to go? I said I would start my year again at a sixth-form college. But surely I realised I was Oxbridge material? Kingsley had the expertise to steer me through the entrance exams. I said I didn't care about exams or Oxbridge, and at the time it was true.

My father liked the idea even less than my housemaster. I sensed Mum in the background, and she must have leant on him to accept my decision, for within a week of my phone call, I was packing my wooden case for the last time.

There was no farewell scene. Hating Anthony and loving him, both impossible emotions, I made no effort to inform him of my departure. On the day my Uncle Roger came to fetch me, only Robbie Thwaite and Mr Sedley stood on the drive to see me off.

There is little advantage in chronicling the decade that followed. I flew back to England in September and started at sixth-form college near Croydon. I was unknown there and adaptable enough to overcome the implications of my accent. I lived with Uncle Roger, in his frequently empty house, where I lost my virginity to an older boy whom surgery as a child to close a harelip had left with a perpetual sneer. I did not love Malcolm and Malcolm could not love anybody who let him fuck them. It was not a catastrophe. I lived; I worked. I abandoned the art module I had so loved in favour of politics and economics. It was a wholly pragmatic decision and I did well enough out of it to gain a place at Manchester.

At university I met Fay Corcoran and darling Jenny, and learned how to make friends with women. (For a time I hoped I might fall in love with one of them but the impulse just never came.) There were moments of excitement and abandon; yet I distrusted happiness. I had no right to it. My former life and the horror of its ending kept me at a remove from others. I binged and seemed to bulk out with my secret. I was not yet twenty and already my life seemed posthumous.

Anthony Blunden faded into memory. I made sure I had no dealings with 'old boys' from Kingsley (Oxford would have been rotten with their braying self-assurance) and attempted to insulate myself from the past. Only my dream life betrayed me. The mist on the fells, the mewling of Mr Bridge as he clung to life, wormed their way into dreams that had nothing, at the outset, to do with them.

If conscience hijacked sleep, it sabotaged love. I had, as a student and then a graduate, several affairs, none of which could survive my secrecy. My partners were plain, yearning, settle-down types who craved affection as much as sex and looked at me with boundless disappointment when I failed to return the gift they so instinctively offered.

In 1999, I joined the civil service, working in the press office of the Ministry of Agriculture before shunting over to Transport. My mother fell ill again. There were cells in her body that refused to die; their appetite was boundless and unappeasable. My parents flew back to England a week before the Twin Towers came down and I got to witness a similarly precipitous collapse. The disease consumed her: it grew and she diminished. Her death made New York and Afghanistan remote misfortunes. *Ours* was the real calamity.

But life has not been uniformly bad. I've had days of beauty and laughter. My friendship with Jenny Gould gives me real, if complicated, pleasure, mixed with the frustration of seeing both of us fail. Yet what of the heart? What of that commodity that sells everything from four-by-fours to throat pastilles? I think I can say that I am safe. This fat, this grossness encasing me, is emotional insulation, cancelling me out of all consideration for love.

My email to Anthony had gone unanswered. After three days logging on to look for a reply, I had resent my original message. I then wrote a second email, along similar lines to the first, though less balanced perhaps, a little more forthright. This too was ignored; so I spent my weekend formulating a *third* email in which I listed my grievances and reminded him in sweating detail about what happened that day on Nab Scar. I got quite drunk before I could send this last, mutually incriminating, message. It bounced back immediately. I stared like an outraged, gouty old squire at the computer screen. I tried sending the email again, and again, with inhuman bumptiousness, the server returned it.

My email address had been blocked.

I was ready to shatter everything. I wanted to bring his life crashing down on his head, even if it meant falling with him. I printed out two copies of my last email and folded them into envelopes. One was addressed to Anthony, care of his workplace; the other would go to Dipali at their flat in Mayfair.

At the last moment, standing before the vacant slot of the postbox, I lost my nerve and tore up the letter to Dipali. Yet it was from *her* that I received a reply, three days later.

It was a very short letter, handwritten, folded into one of those bland, beaches-at-sunset greetings cards one never really looks at. I somehow knew what I would find inside.

Dear Bruno,

My husband does not know that I am writing this. He would not want me to 'interfere' – but I have to ask you to stop trying to contact him. I know about the accident, he has told me everything. I can hardly imagine what it has been like for you to live with the memory for so many years. It must have been a terrible thing to witness and I can understand that bumping into Anthony again brought the whole experience flooding back for you. But there is nothing to be gained from harassing him. Please understand that he's not invulnerable, not the unfeeling monster you seem to imagine.

This is the hardest letter I have ever had to write. Forgive its clumsiness. And please do as I ask – for the health of the man who was once your friend.

Yours respectfully,
Dipali Blunden

Accident? *Accident?* My head throbbed, as with the frightening rush you get – a vice of muscle pain and asphyxia – when you stay too long under water. When the dizziness subsided, I went to the freezer and extracted a tub of ice cream. Then, sitting in my dressing gown amid the grit and fluff of the sofa, I read the letter again.

I could imagine Dipali, the loving companion he had no right to possess, sitting in lamplight at the kitchen table. What was *he* doing meanwhile, the golden boy who earned forgiveness without even asking for it? I ate and swore, and read the letter splayed on my trembling lap. Feeling the drive of obsession, like a drug, I reached for my telephone and dialled Jenny Gould.

Her answer service came on. I listened to the cheery platitudes of her past self and left a snivelling, incoherent message. Could she call me when she got this? I did not expect to sleep: please, please could she phone me back?

I would find out later that she was at her mother's in Cheshire. Jenny always turned her mobile off when she went 'home': regaining the freedom of childhood, before we acquired our electronic daemons. It was just as well, for I was quivering with rage. Would I have confided in her? Had she answered that evening, would I have confessed my crime? For want of the chance to find out, I drank several gins laced with tonic water and doddered out to the street.

I had no clear idea what I wanted: to be mugged, perhaps, or shoved aside by local hoodies. Vauxhall on Friday nights is a launch zone and a place to crash-land in the early hours of the morning. The appetite and frenzy are elsewhere. I followed the scent of money: I joined the migration to pleasure.

When I returned two hours later, I was not alone.

His eyes moved swiftly about the flat – checking, who knows, for signs of sadism or weirdness. The blandness seemed to reassure him. I brought him a can of Coke and watched him drink. He squinted at the ring-pull, his lower lip jutting out against the can. He was scrawny but clean, his face closely shaven.

'You got anything to eat?' he said.

'Are you hungry?'

'I had lunch, like, but that was hours ago.'

I went to the kitchen to make him a sandwich. I was nervous about leaving him unwatched; but if he nicked anything and I came out, with bread on a platter, to hear the front door slamming behind him, it would save me another kind of punishment.

I noticed that my left knee was trembling.

We sat together on the sofa and he devoured the sandwich. He became a little coy when he saw me watching, and tried to eat a slice of tomato with decorum. I noticed the bruised and scabby scurf on his knuckles. 'Can I get you anything else?' I said.

He shook his head. I offered him a Kleenex to wipe his fingers and he was careful to press the tissue ball into the pocket of his jeans. I wondered whether I should put some music on. He stood up abruptly and began to unfasten his belt. I could only sit there, watching, as he pulled off his T-shirt and wriggled out of his jeans and then skipped clumsily to remove his socks. It was perfunctory, no striptease. As for me, ashamed of my bulk (but shame was part of the treatment), I kept my shirt and jumper on. We stood facing each other, he in boxer shorts, me naked from the waist down, and he was obliging enough to stifle any expression. Or was he outside himself, already; had he shut down the moment he undressed?

I turned about and, looking over my shoulder, saw him wince. 'No, please,' he said, 'I couldn't.' For the first time I noticed his Geordie accent. 'I take it. That's what I do.'

I took the lash of his disgust; I accepted it gratefully. I felt no compulsion to fuck him and, without engaging in negotiations, got him on his knees. He was careful to shield his teeth with his lips. I didn't dare run my fingers through his short, gelled hair, so clasped my hands behind my back, like a portly gentleman strolling along a pier.

I came quickly and watched him scamper to the kitchen sink. I pulled on my underpants and followed, backing into a corner beside the fridge. He cupped his hands beneath the tap and swilled. I looked at his small arse, the neat shaft of hair above the cleft, the knots of his backbone visible through his skin. 'Can I go now?' he said.

I went back to the living room to fetch my wallet. He named a sum and I offered him three crisp banknotes. They quivered in my fingers and I snatched them back before he could touch them. 'If I pay you . . .'

'What?'

'I've got more. If I pay you . . .'

His face darkened. 'I told you, I'm not doing that.'

'It's OK. That's not what I'm asking.'

The boy, his eyes shadowed in their sockets, shuffled towards his clothes. I watched him dress and wondered how to continue. 'What's your name?'

'What does it matter?'

'I just want to know . . . I'm Bruno.' I held out the money again, trying not to look sinister. For all I knew, he had a habit to feed. I saw him look at the banknotes.

'Alan,' he said.

He was dressed now: only his jacket lay on the sofa. Breathing hard but trying not to show it, I walked towards him. 'Alan,' I said, 'do you think you could hit me?'

I saw fear seep into him. Had I misread his age? He didn't look so street hardened now.

'It's all right, I'll pay.'

'What are you talking about?'

'It's not such a terrible thing to ask.'

He began to back away, appalled, towards the front door. I went after him.

'Help me, Alan.'

'Shut up, man.'

He was reaching for the latch. He tried the handle, his back to the door, not daring to take his eyes off me. I smiled and showed him the keys on the end of my finger. He gaped at it and I saw anger fire up in his eyes. I goaded him, leaning against him with my gin breath and my bulk. 'Come on . . . Come on, you pussy . . .'

'Get away from me.'

I sniggered, intoxicated with fear, at his attempts to open the door. I tried to grab his elbow – and my head exploded.

I fell back, gripping my jaw, wondering whether it was broken. The pain was astounding: my whole being drowned in it. My free hand reached out, autonomous as a tentacle, to fend him off. Several hard kicks followed to my chest and belly and groin. I curled up like a hedgehog to survive the assault. Alan was keening as he kicked and, looking through the shield of my arms, I saw that he was leaning over me, supporting himself with his arms against the wall.

His fury was quickly spent. He wiped sweat, or tears, from his face and, snivelling, pulled the banknotes and keys out of my hand. The metal rumbled in the lock and slid home and, as I lay in agony, I heard the young man let himself out.

I spent the next day in bed. The day after that, I called a locksmith and kept out of sight until he had finished his work.

Back at work, people looked in shock and embarrassment at my damaged face. I tried to brazen it out, sitting down to work, but Maggie Goss and other busybodies propped their heads above the partition. 'I fell,' I said.

'What, under a bus?'

Julia, my supervisor, got wind of my condition and came to see me. She took in my swollen face and, placing her tartan rump on the edge of my desk, asked whether I was in any kind of trouble. 'None whatsoever,' I replied, ignoring the crack of sullen pain when I smiled.

'You would tell me, wouldn't you?'

She left unconvinced by my assurances, and I realised that I had better keep away from Dad and Jenny for the time being.

Several days passed and the bruises faded to a sour, iodine-stain yellow. The cut on my chin was infected, however, and I decided to take it to my GP.

It was on the Tube on my way home that I encountered an old acquaintance. Had I seen him first I might have been able to shuffle down the compartment, out of sight; but I was too absorbed to notice him until he spoke my name.

'It's Hugo,' he said.

I nodded: so it was.

Hugo Barclay sat forward, grinning. 'I keep bumping into people like this. Who needs Friends Reunited when you've got the London Underground?'

Physically he had not changed so much as amplified, growing into handsome manhood. I answered his polite and predictable questions: where had I gone to university, what did I do now? 'I tried to become a writer,' he volunteered. 'Wrote a crappy thriller while helping out on Dad's farm. Nobody took it. Did me a favour, really.' After several years given over to chasing sheep and publishers, Hugo had reluctantly 'bitten the bullet'. 'Couldn't bear to live with my parents another day. So I went one better, or worse, and went back . . .'

'Back?'

'To Kingsley. I'm teaching history, would you believe? Mostly the Nazis and the First World War. Personally, I always preferred the Napoleonic Wars. Maybe because they were longer ago. Though I suppose not *that* much, for kids born in the nineties.'

Hugo had been present on the fells. My dread that he might mention the Lakes – Mr Bridge – my suspicious disappearance from college – proved unfounded; he was much too English to mention anything unpleasant. Instead he talked about how much the 'old place' had changed.

'It's not as shabby as it used to be. There's a mixture of races, unlike in our day. Whole gangs of Chinese from Hong Kong. And lots of the teachers have changed. The old bachelors are a minority, and all the social events that used to be arranged for them have fizzled out. Most of us – we don't get called masters any more – are married and prefer to live out of the school grounds. Everyone wants to be on call as little as possible. Well, you can understand.' Hugo looked wistful, as if he regretted the passing of the old manly virtues. 'Oh,' he said, 'and there are many more women teachers . . .' I remembered Miss Hartnoll: her staring ears, the scrubbed pinkness of her electrocuted fingers. 'In fact there are girls now, as well as boys.'

'You're joking?' I cast an eye at the name of the station we were passing through. One more stop.

'It's economics, isn't it? With new governors in charge, we can expect to go fully coed within a decade.' The train hurtled in darkness between stations. I could see my reflection in the window above Hugo's head. He was immensely attractive.

'You all right?' he said. I nodded. 'I've got an interesting story to tell you . . .'

'It's my stop next.'

'Oh, is it?' He made up his mind to press on. 'You weren't too happy in the Hereward, were you? Well, neither was I. Sedley was a sour old bastard. And Stoddard . . . you remember Charlie? And Larry Nevins?' All I could do was nod and perspire. 'Well, Larry's fucked up his life, if that makes you feel any better.'

I shrugged: so long ago.

'Yeah, he flunked at Southampton and left without a degree. Last thing I heard, he was parking cars in Norwich.'

Cunning Nevins, ruler of the future? Not so mighty after all. The train was pulling against its momentum; the walls of my station flashed into being.

'And Stoddard has changed. You remember what a bully he used to be? He's a doctor now: a GP somewhere in Sussex. And here's the thing . . . This is you, is it?'

We stood up and shook hands, each holding on to a vertical bar. Hugo's palm felt strong and honest. 'Charlie,' he said, as the door alarm bleated, 'wrote me a letter, a couple of years ago. Quite out of the blue. Asking my forgiveness for the way he treated me.'

'I didn't know he gave you a hard time.'

'He was very unhappy. But he's better now.'

The door alarm sounded again and I rushed through the shrinking aperture. The train departed, and I stood on the platform until the tail-lights of its last compartment had vanished.

I was dozing and a hornet was trapped in a bell jar. It buzzed furiously and inanimate objects cast themselves under my fingertips: lip balm instead of my wristwatch, a hardback in place of my bedside lamp. Not yet fully awake, I thought it was the middle of the night but late afternoon still glowed through the curtains.

The buzzer sounded again and I was up. 'OK, OK – Jesus!'

It was Jenny Gould come to berate me. 'Let me in,' she said, 'don't be an arse.'

'I've got no clothes on.'

'Why won't you answer my calls? I've left about a dozen messages on your phone.'

'It's been off.'

'For five days?'

I buzzed her in and groped to the bathroom for my dressing gown. She must have climbed the stairs in haste, for she was leaning on the doorbell by the time I returned.

'Bloody hell,' she said, 'it's like the grave in here.'

'I was taking a nap.'

'You should open a window, it's twenty-five degrees outside.'

She took in my dressing gown, the dishevelment of my hair and the blemishes on my face. 'What happened to you?'

'Nothing. I fell.'

'You *fell*?' I turned my head to spare her but she managed to survey the damage. 'Where exactly did you fall, Bruno, on someone's fist?' I shrank from her and went to sit on the sofa. She came after me. 'Is this why you've been hiding from us?'

'It's not that bad. Who's us?'

'Your dad called to say you weren't answering the phone. He's been worried . . .'

'Sometimes I really wish people would leave me alone.'

Jenny flounced to the curtains and wrenched them open, making me squirm like some creature of the night. She went into my bedroom, gave a loud cluck of dismay at what she found there, and opened the window. A draught wormed about my naked ankles and I could smell diesel fumes. Jenny crossed the living room, ignoring me on her way to the kitchen, where I heard her crash about, running the tap and filling the kettle and turning on the extractor fan. I sat motionless as I waited for my coffee and a tall, atoning glass of water.

When she came back, Jenny picked up where we'd left off. 'Do you *want* me to leave you alone?'

'Not at all.' She was wearing a denim skirt with a wide leather belt; her summery cotton shirt had long sleeves. 'I'm fine,' I said, 'really, I was only sleeping.'

'How did you hurt yourself?'

'I was mugged.'

'When?'

'It doesn't matter.'

'But look what they did to your face. You must have gone to the police . . .'

'I didn't see their faces – really, there'd be no point. I cancelled my cards.' Jenny could not hide her dismay. She looked at me with such sorrow that I could have thrown my coffee at her. 'Worse things happen to people all the time,' I said, 'it's no big deal.'

'I think it's a very big deal. You were assaulted. They stole from you and . . . my God, Bruno, I'm really shocked.' Jenny pressed her knees together and began to pluck at her throat. 'Do you think . . . ? I mean you could be suffering from post-traumatic stress disorder.'

'That's . . . no . . .' I shook my head impatiently. 'It hasn't affected me that badly. Of course, it was unpleasant . . .'

'Do you think it was . . . ?' Jenny swallowed. 'Maybe it was homophobic?'

I stood up, risking a parting in my dressing gown. I could not take another minute of this. 'Do you mind if I get dressed? I'm feeling a bit skanky.'

This was a mistake on my part: I gave Jenny time to doubt my story. While I showered and yawned and blew water from my lips, she went through my wallet. When I came back, dressed, to the living room, she was primed for a confrontation.

'You cancelled your credit card?' she said.

'Hm? Yes.'

'Your credit card or your debit card?'

'Um – both of them. Why?'

'And your bank sent you replacements?'

'That's usually what happens.'

'Brand-new cards. That were valid three years ago? That expire *next* year?'

Though it was a warm day and I was sweating from my shower, the blood seemed to sink to my feet. 'What are you getting at, Miss Marple?'

'Why are you lying to me?'

'Jesus – don't be melodramatic.'

'This isn't like you, Bruno.'

I snapped: I did not have to put up with this interrogation in my own home. 'What would you know? You take me at my word: how can you be sure I don't make things up all the time? I could be a congenital liar. I could be an entirely different person to the person you think you know.'

'Are you?'

I was breathing heavily, as if I had just climbed a flight of stairs. I sat on the arm of the sofa and hung my head. 'I've got to eat something, I've got low blood sugar.'

'Drink your coffee.'

'It'll be cold.'

I could smell her perfume. Her small breasts were level with my face: I wanted to press against them.

'If you don't want to tell me what happened, I won't push you. But this doesn't come out of the blue, does it? I mean, your life, Bruno . . . your life's a fucking mess.'

I laughed in helpless agreement.

'Whatever it is that's hurting you . . . though you don't want to tell me . . . for God's sake, do something about it.'

'Yeah, like you do such a great job of controlling your obsessions.'

Jenny tugged at her long sleeves. They covered scars that will last a lifetime. 'Because I hurt myself,' she said, 'it doesn't mean you should do the same.'

At Security they were not convinced. A sharp-nosed woman with dyed red hair and crimson nails looked me over while her colleague, a burly escapee from a nightclub doorway, telephoned for clearance. It was a good thing I'd put on my suit.

'You don't have an appointment,' said the bouncer, muffling the receiver.

'No, I know. But it's very important I see him.'

The security guard relayed this in hushed tones. I fought to stay calm under his disapproving stare.

'Please,' I said. 'Is that him? Just let me have a word.'

I was instructed, with a minimum of politeness, to take a seat in the foyer. I waited on the edge of a stylishly uncomfortable chair, reading and rereading headlines in the *FT*. Most of the billion-dollar acronyms meant nothing to me; their smiling chief executives were unknown emperors. I looked across the steel-and-glass cliché of the atrium and wondered which of the lifts would deliver him to me. A door pinged open and a strutting lawyer emerged, clutching her briefcase. A delivery boy in biker's leather and a helmet the colour of processed cheese dodged into the space she had vacated. I looked down at my knees – those barometers of nervous excitement – and found them quaking.

A lift door opened and Anthony was striding towards me in the soft armour of a City suit. I stood up and wiped my hand against my trouser leg. He gave no hint of emotion as he moved, with the briskness of a politician mounting a podium, to head off my attack.

'Thanks for coming to see me,' I said. He ignored the hand I offered him and took me by the elbow. I followed him meekly – swept up in his momentum – to the derisory shelter of a rubber plant's foliage.

'What the fuck are you doing?' His face, close up, was not as calm as it had seemed. Little muscles were flexing and there was a pulse in his tanned jaw.

'Have you ever heard of trigeminal neuralgia?'

'*What?*'

'It's said to be the most intense pain known to man. Tension in the jaw: you want to watch that.'

'Have you come here . . . ? You've come all the way here, to my office, the place where I *work* . . .'

'I know what an office is.'

'. . . to tell me about tension in my fucking jaw?'

'No, that wasn't my express purpose. I've been trying to reach you. You've been avoiding me . . .' Righteousness eroded from his face. For a moment he was my captive. 'Tell me,' I said, 'did you get your wife to write that letter or was it entirely her own initiative?'

Anthony's eyes dipped. 'You're not going to make a scene, are you?'

'You weren't answering my emails.'

'Of *course* I wasn't answering. You don't have a right to barge into people's lives. Jesus Christ, Bruno, get a grip on yourself. It's like being stalked.'

'I want to talk about Mr Bridge.'

He rolled his eyes and sighed as if I were an importunate crank. 'What's the point?' he said.

'There are things I need to understand.'

He looked at his Rolex – uncovering it with a brisk movement of the wrist, like a magician. 'Look, uh . . . can we do this some other day? I've really got a lot on my plate.'

'You'll have me barred some other day. I'm not asking for much – a few minutes of your time.'

It was imperative to get me out of the office: I was polluting it with emotional disorder. We leaned through the revolving doors into warm September sunshine. 'I really don't see,' said Anthony, 'that there's anything to talk about.'

'Only the Lakes.'

'There isn't a single cell in your body that was there on the . . . We're not the same people.'

'But Mr Bridge is still dead.'

'That wasn't our fault. It's not like we pushed him. Listen, Bruno, we were the victims of circumstance. It was an *accident*, but you've obviously built it up into some terrible crime, a dark secret to drag about with you. Maybe it makes you feel important. Well, I'm not interested in tragedy. I don't need it to give me meaning.'

'He was a . . . he was a good man.'

'That's your opinion.' Anthony picked up his pace: I trotted to catch up with him.

'What do you mean?'

'You think he was some kind of inspiration: the teacher we all remember, the one who wakes you up to the world. Can't you see that what he did was irresponsible? He made us feel special, like we were different from everyone else. He gave us power, or at least a sense of it, and when he took it away – for no reason except that he *could* – we were *nowhere*. We didn't belong in school and we didn't belong out of it. So stop idealising Samuel Bridge. He was the same age as we are now and neither of *us* is particularly wise. The truth is we were his power trip. He had us as pets, and when he got tired of us, he dumped us.'

'So we killed him.'

Anthony contemplated me, unruffled on the surface. He shook his head pityingly. 'That's crazy.'

'We killed him.'

'No, we didn't.'

'You know we did.'

'All I know is that you need help. Maybe your life's so empty that you need to make it a soap opera, but some of us are quite happy in the real world, thank you.'

'You just breezed through it, didn't you? You just picked up where you left off, as if nothing had ever happened.' My voice was trapped: I coughed to release it. 'Everything's so easy for people like you.'

'Easy?' Anthony edged towards me. 'Do you think it was easy for me? I had to learn how to get on with people. I had to acquire all kinds of skills I didn't have.'

'Oh, you had them,' I said, 'when you needed them. People like you always do.'

We were coming up to Bunhill Fields, where City workers were munching sandwiches. Anthony grinned, his head moving, as if he had heard all this countless times before. 'Don't pull the class warrior crap on me, Bruno. We come from the same place.'

'I'm not,' I said. 'And we don't.'

'So what do you want me to do? Tear my clothes? Gnash my teeth and wail? Everyone has scars: it's a condition of living. But you have to get on with things. It's a kind of responsibility.'

'What if I can't? What if it isn't possible?'

Anthony sensed an opportunity: a crack in my indignation that he could prise open. He became conciliatory, even kind. 'Don't beat yourself up over this. Consider the guilt you feel as the, uh, fee you have to pay. Well, it's paid. Enough time has passed. You've suffered enough: now get on with life.'

'But what we *did* . . .'

'What did we do, Bruno? We pissed about on a school field trip. We played silly buggers and there was an accident.'

'We tried to scare him.'

'So?'

'We called in the mist as if we were in trouble and he ran to save us. We *knew* we were near the edge . . .'

Anthony shook his head, his chin forward, pursing his lips like a pedantic lawyer. 'There was an official inquiry. It censured the teachers for taking unnecessary risks and it was those risks that led to an accident. We weren't the grown-ups, Bruno. We weren't responsible for safety on that hike.'

'You actually believe it. I don't suppose you even remember what happened, do you? You've replaced that mist, those voices, with the guesswork of people who weren't even there. Because it *suits* you.'

London's traffic wheezed and snarled about us. Anthony was standing, head bowed, with his hands on his hips, breathing like a long-distance runner. It pleased me to see him suffer.

'Look at you,' I said. 'The sweat's pouring off your face.'

'It wasn't that steep.'

'What?'

'It wasn't that steep!' He said this loud enough to turn several heads. 'Bridge should have twisted his ankle, or just fallen on his arse. I mean, it's not like we pushed him off the top of Scafell Pike.'

'I thought you said we never pushed him.'

Anthony's eyes bulged: it was almost comical to watch. 'We *didn't* push him! You know we didn't even bloody touch him.'

'But we made it happen. We led him into known danger and he fell.'

'None of this . . .'

'What?'

'None of this will bring him back now.'

II

Seen from the other side of the loch, the peninsula belonged in a tourist brochure: whitewashed cottages, restored by a new generation of crofters, nestled amid plantations of birch and pine, with modest, artisanal wind turbines dotting the bruise-coloured moors. It looked a perfect antidote to urban living. I said as much to the boatman who offered to ferry me to the peninsula. 'And eco-friendly,' I added, hoping to win him over, for he was huge and suntanned, with the very Bristol burr one expects of a pirate.

'Dunno about that,' he said. 'If we had a road we'd drive, and we only use wind 'cause we're not on the grid.'

I put out my hands to steady myself against the sides of the boat. Heaped about my boots were fuel canisters and crates of tool parts, hessian bags containing food and clothes, the week's postal deliveries in a plastic sack. My ferryman was the postmaster and delivery boy; in his spare time he was also a driftwood sculptor. 'Beachcomber,' he said. 'I like to add to the shapes the sea has made.'

We tacked across choppy waters, in a chill breeze with spots of rain in it, towards the jetty. Autumn was well on the way this far north, though in London people were still sunbathing. The moors had flowered and were fading. I saw, clinging to the rocks of a burn, a few straggly willows whittled by the wind and barely in leaf.

'What brings you out here, then?'

'I'm, uh, visiting one of the natives,' I said.

The ferryman cracked a grizzled smile. 'Make sure he don't cook you.' Like an oarsman he pulled at the handle of the outboard motor and we bobbed against the tide towards the concrete jetty.

There was a tiny settlement on the shore of the loch. This, I surmised, was as close as the peninsula came to a centre: several long huts, like upturned boats, that served as workshops and meeting places, their wide doors facing the pebbled shore.

As soon as the ferryman had secured his boat, I helped him land the provisions. I saw him wave to a white-bearded man on an elderly quad bike that careened along the foreshore and almost crashed into one of the workshops. The bearded biker pulled open the workshop door to reveal other men in jumpers and stained wellingtons drinking tea above the giant cuttlefish bones of a turbine propeller. These men did not greet me; I was there, and since I was, they made it known that I should help them drag a repaired dinghy from the shed.

We heaved and groaned companionably and, beneath the barnacled hull, I caught the unmistakable smell of ganja blended with sawdust and sea wrack.

'Nice one,' said the ferryman once the dinghy had been lowered. I returned wheezing to my rucksack and, attempting to swing it with crossed arms on to my back, nearly threw myself among the dumped gear, boat parts and plastic containers that littered the beach. I righted myself and unfolded a map of the region. The white-haired man with the quad bike asked whether I needed help, and I asked him how to find the cottage.

'I'm going halfway there myself,' he said, and he was no more Scottish than the ferryman: a proper cockney. 'It's quite a trek. I'll give you a lift as far as the track if you like.'

I thanked him and clung to his waist as we bucked and rumbled into the hills. 'You a friend?' he shouted over his shoulder.

'Sort of,' I replied.

We rose above the loch and soon found ourselves among young trees. The man explained something of the area's history: how the crofters had abandoned it for the foundries and ship-yards of Glasgow, how the Ministry of Defence had used its empty wastes for target practice before returning them to the laird. The local estate kept much of the land bleak with the grazing of sheep but here, on the promontory of a peninsula so remote and inaccessible that residents spoke of a mainland, the new settlers had fenced areas off and planted trees: birch and alders, a few Scots pines, rusting larch and fruiting rowan.

'She doesn't get many visitors,' the man said out of the blue. 'We all like it remote: getting away from all *that*. Still, she's the farthest from everything.'

The quad bike slowed to a halt at a crossroads and I reluctantly dismounted. The white-bearded man gave me a nod. 'Give her my best, will ya?'

I said I would but he sped off before I could ask his name.

I knew from my emailed instructions that I should head east; as there was only one track, I had no reason to fear getting lost. All the same, the emptiness came as a shock and my ears thrummed with desolation at the absence of human noise. Slowly they acclimatised and brought home the twittering of birds and the wind's low music. The broad loch glistened in the midday sun. Gannets hung above the water: I recognised the dark tips of their white wings and the sharp elegance of their yellow heads. Other birds I didn't recognise were resting on the pebbly shore, their carrot-orange bills buried in black-and-white feathers.

She would be waiting for me. I tried to imagine her cottage isolated on the moor and hoped that walking would give me courage.

The ground about was boggy, with sphagnum moss and knotty heather and swaths of fading grasses. Even on the track the going was so damp that I had to step between rill-crossed rocks, my great boots obscuring blooms of yellow and brown and pink lichens.

Within ten minutes I came level with an abandoned hut where the track turned inland. It was a small building with a corrugated-iron roof and an odd assortment of peeling timbers. I could not imagine it withstanding a gale; yet to judge by the trees that were planted as a windbreak, it must have stood for years. I wondered what had driven its makers to leave. Was it the climate or the grinding reality of the self-sufficient dream? I walked towards the hut and couldn't resist peering in at the window. There was a single bare bed and a couple of chairs set about a table made from a whisky keg and a sheet of plyboard. A cereal packet stood open on the table with a bowl and a spoon at the ready. Paperbacks were jumbled on every surface and a work table at the far end of the room was heaped with tools and wood shavings. It was as if the hut had only just been vacated, or its owner would return any minute from cutting logs in the wind-stunted wood. I tried the door but, finding it unlocked, shut it hastily and pressed on through the upland bog.

Charlotte Bridge's instructions were precise to the particular. I found the standing stone whose Neolithic origins she doubted, and then followed the remains of a sheep enclosure until I heard the ghostly moan of a wind turbine. A brake of firs surrounded a smoking chimney and I could make out tarred walls and a sloping turf roof. Any thoughts of escape were quickly extinguished, for she had seen me from her vegetable patch and was waiting at the gate.

I remembered that she was tall. She looked stockier than all those years ago, though it was muscle rather than fat. Her lips were still full and more beautiful now for the drying up of the skin that surrounded them. She wore no make-up and her hair was cut short, as it had been fourteen years ago, though it looked as dry as summer straw and meshes of white thrust up from her crown. Her eyes were calm and smiling. I felt villainous as I took her hand.

'Thanks for the invitation,' I said.

'Not at all. It's not often I get to talk about Sam. And I know he was important to you.'

A worm shivered in my guts. She asked about my crossing and I described the man who had given me a lift on his quad bike.

'Old Pete,' she said. 'He thinks I should be married. A smallholding's too much for a little lady. Come on, I'll show you round.'

I followed her about the enclosed garden with its rain-bruised flowers and a woodshed and tiny streams overhung by turf banks. She wanted to show me the good she had created. There were fruiting shrubs, a decorative pagoda made from copper sheeting and river-smoothed pebbles, young rowans peeping out of plastic growing sheaths. She talked about the difficulties of making plants grow this far north: how slowly they rooted and ramified. We passed through a spinney and came to the poly-tunnels with their tilled beds of black earth. Beyond, fields of coarse grass spread down to the sea. What did she grow under the plastic? Kale and spinach, lettuce and leeks and spring onions. Some herbs also: thyme and parsley and chives. It was not enough to keep her going, and none of it was for sale or barter. But it gave her pleasure and kept her occupied in the long months away from the field.

'I understand,' I said, 'that you're an ornithologist. I mean specialised. It must get pretty desolate out on a rock in the middle of the Atlantic.'

She had told me, in the letter that contained her invitation, the name of the island but I had forgotten it: a nature reserve high above the rocky crest of Ulster where she spent weeks every summer watching seabirds and recording their fortunes. 'Yes,' she said, and there was something cagey in her reply. 'I've lost the habit of receiving guests: you must want to sit down. Would you like some lunch?'

She led me back through the spinney and the ornamental garden to her cottage. Lunch was waiting for us in the kitchen. The interior of the cottage was close and warm, the walls lined with books and pictures. It was comfortable but rough: designed for living and not for show, with strips of insulation peeping from gaps in the plyboard panels. A tea towel was laid out on an ancient stove that looked like the engine of a model steam train. In an alcove between quilt-draped sofas, an electric heater glowed orange. I rubbed my hands and sat at the table as Charlotte Bridge served tea. Her back was turned to a wide sink behind which a large window overlooked the sea.

'This smells lovely,' I said, taking off my windcheater.

'I hope you like Scotch eggs.'

'I *love* Scotch eggs. Oh, and I've got those things you wanted in my rucksack.' It was the least I could do. Wrapped in a Sainsbury's bag, the myrrh and frankincense of island exiles: Marmite and HobNobs and rashers of bacon. Mrs Bridge took them with coos of thanks; half embraced or cradled them and stowed them in various cupboards.

'Sam had a yen for English stodge,' she said. 'I tried my best, as a farty liberal, to turn him on to guacamole and hummus but he wouldn't be converted. Marmite? I hated it until he educated me. And HobNobs? They're up there with the Sistine Chapel as justifications for humanity.'

'It's funny,' I said. 'As a pupil you never think of your teachers in that light.'

'How d'you mean?'

'Well, ordinary. As ordinary people.'

'I had a right pain of a maths teacher – Miss Holroyd. She used to terrify me. I thought the only reason she was put on earth was to make my life a misery.'

She sat down and shook out her napkin. I wondered how many of the things on the table were her own produce and resolved not to scoff them all.

'Where, ah, where did you first meet?' I asked.

'At university. We were friends at first and I always think that improved our chances.'

I could not think how to steer the conversation. It was unthinkable to talk about his death; and how to come clean about my part in it? All the way up to Scotland and in the hired car through Wester Ross, I had tried to imagine a scenario but fell back on the hope that a time would come and my courage would not fail. Charlotte Bridge had no idea what she was welcoming under her roof. Her trusting kindness deflected my resolve: it left no scope for vandalism, though I would have to smash my way into her life. I was an ill wind. I ate her food because it stopped my mouth and gave me a pretext for being there. Meanwhile she talked about her husband as a young man: the earnest nineteen-year-old with whom she had fallen in love.

'I was pretty innocent about the world: I assumed it was basically good, like my parents. I suppose you could say I'd had it harder than him: we were poorer, that's for sure. But Sam was the one with a hunger for change. He was educated at a minor public school near Ely. He was sort of embarrassed about it and I couldn't see why, though I'd been through state school. I suppose he had a talent for self-reproach. There was something unreasonable about the way he took the blame for the world. I'm less impressed by that now than I was then.'

For all that, Samuel's idealism had not been a pose: he was too ready to play the fool. There was something childish in him that brought out the mothering impulse. Lots of girls wanted to sleep with him, she said, but he didn't seem to realise it. He was a kind of innocent: religious in every sense but the theological.

'He graduated before me. Maggie Thatcher had wrestled back the Falklands and everyone was going loopy. Sam thought he might become a journalist, and talked a lot about the *Belgrano*, all those lads burned up in HMS *Sheffield*.'

'Did you dissuade him?'

'No, he got real. Didn't fancy the hack work: chasing stories for the *Swindon Herald* or whatever. While I graduated, he trained as a teacher. He was determined to go to an inner city comprehensive but he found, to his dismay, that he couldn't hack it. The pupils hated him for his accent. He had difficulty imposing any kind of discipline and he suffered the trauma of rescuing a boy who had overdosed in the toilets.'

Her husband had stuck it out for several years until his health began to suffer. Then, in humiliating submission to the class system, he applied for a post at Kingsley College. 'Always the square peg,' Charlotte said, smiling. 'Sam was a lefty in a very conservative establishment. I don't think any of his colleagues were openly hostile towards him and there was no unpleasantness. But he definitely felt isolated, especially after his arrest on Albury Down. I think people saw in his behaviour a tacit reproach of the way they lived. Sam didn't mean it that way; but the reproach was there, in the openness of his nature . . .' Charlotte looked at me and smiled. 'Of course,' she said, 'I'm somewhat biased.'

'No.' I recognised the portrait absolutely. 'That's what all the boys thought in private.'

She inclined her head. 'Publicly, though, it wasn't cool to like Bridget. Oh, don't worry: it's a poor teacher who doesn't know his nickname. I think he always felt it could have been worse. And he prided himself on not being too macho.'

For the rest of lunch, it was her turn to ask questions. I told her about my Malaysian childhood, the difficulties of coming to England. I avoided the subject of Kingsley as much as possible, and her curiosity about my father's work and our forays into the jungle (she knew the forest parks of Terengganu) allowed me to steer clear of danger. When we had finished, she got up to clear the plates. I offered to help but she insisted that I remain seated. I looked about the room and recognised the bird prints and the wooden bowl brimming with puny apples. The bronze statuette of Ganesh was propping up a phalanx of field guides; the Buddha was a paperweight on a disorderly, beaten-copper table. There were no photographs that I could see; it was just as well, perhaps. The sight of him would have made me quake.

'I wanted to ask you,' I said when she returned with coffee, 'about the poetry meetings.'

'I remember. You were with Anthony Blunden.' There was weight in the way she spoke his name. I felt pressure in my throat and moulded my hands about the coffee cup.

'It was a relief coming to your house,' I said. 'I liked the atmosphere, it was homely. There's so little comfort in boarding school. Getting a whiff of privacy was like refreshing yourself with oxygen.'

She looked at me, moved, and her eyelids fluttered. 'We discussed the idea of inviting boys over. I wasn't sure it was wise to show favouritism. But Sam wanted to connect. Perhaps loneliness played a part: I was away for half the year, and though he loved books and music and could spend hours in his own company, I don't think he liked being alone.'

'You wrote that first invitation,' I said. 'I recognised the handwriting when your letter came.'

Charlotte smiled vaguely. 'I don't remember doing that. But Sam's writing was cramped, almost unreadable. He'd have made a good doctor. You know, the two of you were his only . . .' She stopped, lost for a word. 'I was going to say protégés. But that sounds a bit ridiculous, doesn't it?' She paused again and a shadow crossed her face. 'I'm not sure, sometimes, if there wasn't something less admirable in it. Like he wanted to be loved, to have a following.'

'Surely that's there in most teachers?'

'He was right, in a way: cramming isn't teaching . . .' A breath passed through her; she looked at me as if I had just materialised. 'He saw a kindred spirit in you,' she said.

'In *me*?'

'You weren't assuming. You had no cruelty.' She must have registered my discomfort, for she set to stirring her coffee. 'I don't know why I remember these things – it was so long ago.'

Our conversation dipped after this. She had taken me at face value: who can be afraid of so much flesh? At some point in the visit she would ask about the Lakes and my fate would be in my hands. Words alone could insulate me from the words I ought to speak. 'How long,' I said, 'how many years have you been living out here?'

'I came up after Sam died. Well, not immediately after – I spent six months first with the Antarctic Survey. If it had been possible to study on Mars, I'd have gone. It was like I wanted to freeze my grief. You know? Put it into cryogenic storage, to defrost at some special point in the future when such things could be dealt with. But in the end, when I wasn't freezing on ships, I was shut up in a data lab with nothing but charts and computers and the thought of Sam so cold, so far away . . .' Charlotte Bridge looked at me, meaning to summon my gaze; but I couldn't lift my eyes from clots of polish on the table. 'I felt like a refugee,' she continued, 'as if a soldier had come to my door and given me five minutes to pack and I had to leave for ever, the life I had known was dismantled *for ever*, in a matter of moments, and I could never go home again.'

I felt sick; the smell of woodsmoke was no longer comforting but seemed to clog up my stomach. The opportunity I had hoped would present itself – a moment of grace when somehow it would be possible to speak – seemed more remote than ever. Sensing my discomfiture, Charlotte went to the sink and began rinsing our mugs. We were silent for perhaps a minute. I made a scuffle on the carpet to protect the privacy of her thoughts.

'Do you, uh, do you ever get seals?'

'I was watching one this morning wrestling a load of kelp. They can be very playful.'

'It must be wonderful to have all this wildlife around you.'

'Yes . . . Yes, it is.'

Awkwardness descended. To escape it, she suggested we go for a walk along the bay. We dressed for wet weather ('wait five minutes in Scotland and it changes') and left the warmth of the cottage.

The beach was a stretch of unsteady, creaking pebbles: pink and grey and strewn with seaweed. Tangles of fishing nets, plastic caps and bottles, a discarded boot straight from God's properties cupboard, were all the signs of human existence. Across the bay the islands were dun, and the sun no longer shone. A chill wind nuzzled at my throat and searched out the gaps in my cladding.

'Not used to the cold?' Charlotte said. She wore tattered wool garments under the waistcoat of a Barbour. There was nothing of the country Sloane about her. I liked her northern manners, her indifference to fashion. Then it occurred to me that she was poor.

'You can't see it from here,' she said, 'but just beyond that point there's Gruinard Island. It was closed off to people for years. The MoD stockpiled anthrax and all manner of chemical and biological weapons there. It was the most toxic piece of earth in the British Isles. The real home of WMDs.'

'Is it still out of bounds?'

'Oh, they cleaned it up – at vast cost. But you have to ask yourself, what were they thinking in the first place?'

257

We trudged among drifts of loose rock, wobbly and uncertain. Charlotte pointed to a dot in the water. There was a beak and the glint of an eye. 'Black-throated diver,' she said as the bird disappeared. 'Haven't seen one of them in a while.'

The sea was calm. I looked for heads breaking the surface: sleek cowls and dark eyes watching as we crossed the shore. Nothing showed. I remembered why I was there, and it was like darkness falling.

'Do you know your birds, Bruno?'

'Not really. I mean, I can tell a robin and a blackbird. I certainly wouldn't know anything I see out here.'

'Ah. That's just it: what the eye can't see, the heart won't grieve over.' This came close to panicking me until I realised that she was alluding to something else. I'd been right to imagine something gnawing at her; it was a trauma more recent than her husband's death. 'Did I explain, in my letter, what it is I do?' She looked at the sky and seemed to assess it, then turned about and led us back to the cottage.

'I work for the RSPB,' she said. 'Every summer, out on my remote island. It's an astounding place: a great rock of seabirds. Gannets and guillemots, puffins and razorbills. The *noise* they make you wouldn't believe. It's like Hong Kong for birds: all high-rise dwellings, with every inch of space inhabited . . .' She hesitated and tiny wrinkles creased her brow. 'At least, that's how it *should* be. It's how it was when I started and all I had to do was compile the data. At the beginning it was easy, you know, helping to map breeding patterns, *eavesdropping* on life that cares nothing for us and just gets on with the business of breeding and feeding and dying.' Charlotte Bridge put out her arms to balance on the rocks. 'Then last summer everything changed. The birds failed to breed. Whole broods starved to death and all I could do was sit there and watch. The usual summer banks of sand eel and whitebait just failed to materialise. For weeks I watched as parents took off and returned with nothing in their beaks, or else a single sand eel when there should have been several.'

'I suppose the problem's overfishing?'

'Yes,' she said with a shrug that said the opposite. 'More likely the population has shifted because of climate change.'

'What, already?'

'That's what we thought. Of course, there have always been fluctuations in sea temperatures but those were gradual shifts, giving species the chance to migrate and adapt. But more and more it looks like the damage we're doing is going to affect things in spasms: like a storm surge that sweeps over an island and never retreats, leaving it wiped off the map.'

She turned to face me and I felt the pressure of her gaze. There was something unflinching in it, a kernel of hardness. But I had not come this far to be comforted. 'I couldn't tell you the number of times I've had to explain my work to people who just can't see the point of it. Well, here's one for you. The sea heats up in the North Atlantic and creates a famine for our seabirds. The same process takes place in the Caribbean and a great American city disappears.'

'It's scary stuff.'

'We're grown-ups, Bruno. We have to look at serious things.'

There was nothing to be said as we clambered through bog and wet grasses to the cottage door. She had not locked it: there was no crime on the peninsula. I sat down, dog tired, while she popped to the loo. When she returned, she made an effort to brighten the mood. She smiled and abandoned herself to the sofa opposite mine. I noticed that her jeans were covered in patches.

'So, Bruno, tell me . . .'

Something snarled up my throat. Was she about to turn interrogator? I felt my fingers clench; I crossed my legs; but she only asked about the work I did. I had been cagey in my emails. I wanted to give little away: little that was not necessary. I talked about the Department and she sat up smartly. 'Oh, so you work for the Creature?'

'I used to. I gave in my notice a month ago. I packed up my things and left last week.'

'Really?' She contemplated me silently. 'May I ask why?'

'I realised I didn't believe in it.'

'And yet it exists. Maybe you could have made a difference from the inside?'

'My God, the *government* used to believe that. I'm starting to think that's how power works. It absorbs you until you can no longer distinguish yourself from it. And then you serve it absolutely.'

Charlotte nodded laconically. 'The rot's at the heart of things,' she said. 'It's there in the language of economics. This obsession with "growth" and "consumption". The only thing that grows unstoppably in nature is a cancer cell. And consumption is an old word for tuberculosis.'

Charlotte Bridge was not good at sitting still. She got up and went to make tea, depositing an iron kettle on the hotplate of the stove. 'I believe there's a battle within us,' she said, 'between a life force and a destructive impulse. You have to choose which one you serve and that takes effort, it takes vigilance. After all, it's the life force that makes people love their children and work to support them. Yet the work done, if it's for an arms dealer or a tobacco company, serves the destructive impulse.' She stopped as though listening to an echo of her voice. 'I suppose that must sound like a load of balls.'

'Not at all.'

'Sam was on the side of life.' While the water boiled, she came back to an earlier theme. 'Look at the nature programmes on television. Do you ever watch them? They're all about competition and violence: the deadliest this, the hungriest that.

One could just as easily document the interdependence of things, the amazing instances of symbiosis and cooperation in nature. If there is a future for us, that's where it lies. But it won't *sell*, will it?'

When the kettle was ready, she filled a teapot and removed a fruitcake from its coat of foil. She invited me to the table. I sat there, dumb and sorrowful.

'You're about thirty, aren't you?'

'Thirty-one.'

She nodded and I knew what she was thinking. Her grief was the surface of a deep lake. 'When he went to Kingsley,' she said, 'Sam found it a barren place. The teachers weren't to blame: they had a whole load of assumptions against them. Most of the boys came from power and they were in training for more of it. Sam thought he could change that. Broaden horizons. We were young, idealistic, and more than a bit pompous. You two were his first – and in the end his only – project.'

'What,' I said, 'what do you think he saw in us?'

'Self-absorption. The usual adolescent guff. He meant to distract you from what he saw as petty and temporary grievances. Make you focus on real things like the world and politics. No wonder he got so angry when he read your friend's revolting little fantasy. It made him realise how little progress he had made. I think, afterwards, he sensed that he'd gone too far in befriending you. Your friend, I mean – did you know his father was a major donor to the college?'

'No. No, I didn't know that.'

'When he saw how badly Anthony responded to criticism, Sam took my advice and re-established some distance. There's nothing more conservative than a public schoolboy. I'm only sorry that you got caught up in it, but you were inseparable from that other . . .'

So I had imagined nothing. He had indeed frozen us out:

finding excuses for not talking, sidling away from us during break-time migrations.

'It wasn't a happy time for Sam. I think it was a combination of things: he didn't really like the school, and then . . . he wanted us to start a family.' Charlotte was still, her arms folded across her chest, listening to the distant muted sea. 'He tended to withdraw when things weren't working out for him.'

I pondered all this, and pondered my next move. The afternoon was drawing to a close and I had not confessed. The words welled up inside me; I felt them pressing against my ribs but could no more let them out than cough up my own lungs. All the resolve that had enabled me to track her down online and by letter, that had brought me to this obscure peninsula on the edge of Europe, all would come to nothing; for it would put me in danger to confess, and I could not bear to imagine the effect my revelations would have on my hostess. She had no idea what I had taken from her; she had made welcome under her roof a thief who had stolen half her life. So I sat drinking tea at her kitchen table, taking perverse comfort in the contemplation of my shame. To an innocent witness, trudging across the waterlogged moor, it would have seemed a cosy set-up. The walls about us were lined with books; a beaded curtain of condensation had formed on the large window overlooking the sea, testifying to the warmth within. I looked beyond the moisture at the ancient humps of hills, and the only sounds were the quiet snoring of the stove and the faraway breath of wind and waves. Then the aircraft came: a gathering sonic rip that made me duck, scalp tingling, as two Tornado jets tore up our patch of sky.

'They're off their usual route,' said Charlotte, peering laconically at the ceiling. 'A little diversion to say *boo* to the hippies.'

'Jesus,' I said, 'they frightened the life out of me.'

'You get used to it.'

The sky, torn asunder, healed over the wound. Silence returned and we sat imprisoned in our heads.

'What became of your friend?'

'Anthony?'

'You didn't stay in touch?'

I swallowed the truth. 'No, I'm afraid not.'

For a moment I wondered what she would say. Had she even the ghost of a suspicion?

'Your friend was clever,' she said, 'but that was all. Sam used to tell me that something was lacking in him. He was all surface. But you, Bruno, were a different matter. Sam said you never recognised it in yourself . . .'

My throat was parched. 'Recognised what?'

'Imagination.' She smiled and this gave her face a supple resolution. 'It's more valuable than cleverness, though for me it *defines* intelligence. Sam and I were alike in that, though our professions differed. We valued imagination. With it we can still save the world. Without it, I don't fancy our chances. Are you OK?'

'Of course.' I tried to clear my throat and it unravelled into a dry, irresolute cough. I knew my face was sweating. I must have looked shifty, like a secret incontinent. 'I'm sorry,' I said.

'Would you like some water?'

'There's something I haven't told you. Something you need to know about Anthony and your husband and what happened that morning.'

Words have the power of the gorgon. Already Charlotte had turned to stone.

'The coroner,' I said, 'was not in full possession of the facts.'

'What do you mean?'

Absurd as it was, I looked to her for encouragement. Her eyes were black water, a vortex behind them. 'I've been carrying this around all these years. Mrs Bridge . . .' I looked into her face. She gasped like a gilled thing caught in a net. 'Your husband . . .'

263

My hesitation saved me. It worked some mechanism in her: the blood rushed to her head and made her fierce. 'Do you *know* what happened? You called for help: you and that boy . . .'

'He was alive. He was alive when we saw him.'

'Alive?'

'He'd managed to catch a hold. He was clinging on to this rock above the drop.'

What I said was true; yet even as I spoke, I felt a lid shutting. The relief was like a morphine rush, my body flooded with its opiates. I was not going to say it: I had found an exit and would survive my own conscience.

'You *saw* him? Before . . .?' Her eyes were horror stricken; worse, there was hope at the back of them. 'Did he say anything?'

I shook my head.

'Did he see you?'

'It all lasted a few seconds. We couldn't reach him. Even if we could have, there was no time . . .' Her eyes flooded but that was not the worst of it. Where she saw solidarity, there was only deception. 'I couldn't bear it, Mrs Bridge. I thought somehow . . . we should have done something. I felt ashamed, I didn't want anyone to know.'

'Did he cry out?'

'What?'

'When he fell? Did he know he was going to die?'

'I don't think so. He can't have had more than a few seconds . . .'

Charlotte wept quietly for a minute. When she forced a smile, a web of saliva spread between her lips. She produced a handkerchief from her sleeve and blew her nose with a loud, cartoonish blast. 'Thank you,' she said. 'That can't have been easy for you to say.'

I shook my head regretfully. I was slime.

'I'm going to ask you the same questions over and over, I'm afraid. He fell quickly, didn't he?'

The question was absurd, especially from a scientist. Gravity does no favours. 'Yes,' I said.

'The coroner said he was unlucky. If he'd fallen differently, if he hadn't struck his head . . .'

'We should have told the police.'

There was a little danger here: should have told them what? That we were reckless, that we wanted to give him a fright, a nasty contusion? But Charlotte was not suspicious. 'What difference would it have made?' she said, and I clammed up for good.

Exhausted, we sat like gluttons bloated half to death. Outside, the clouds had built up, dark on dark, into a great Atlantic bruise.

She invited me to stay the night. One of the sofas could be unfolded into a camp bed: I'd have all of Sam's books to keep me company. In the morning she would walk me to the jetty; her boat was there and she could take me across.

I said it was impossible. I had a bed and breakfast booked in Ullapool: I would have to be on the road first thing in the morning. Charlotte looked surprised and wounded. There was no way I could stay under her roof. The very sight of her repulsed me. Her entreaties continued, and with each approach I retrenched. It was to prove my big mistake. Had I stayed, accepting her hospitality; had I submitted myself to her questioning and applied the balm of sympathy to her reopened wounds, then she might have let the whole thing lie. But I was not thinking straight. Immediate, animal need returned me to my windcheater. I gratefully and apologetically refused her offer of a farewell snack: if I hurried, I said, I might still be able to cadge a lift off someone at the workshop.

Charlotte would not hear of it. Though alarm bells must have been ringing inside her – as small, perhaps, as pins and needles – she remained the consummate hostess. Since I insisted on making tracks, the least I could do was accept her company.

'What do you mean?'

'To the jetty,' she said. Her face was still pummelled; it looked all out of joint. But she smiled at her enemy. 'You came over with Danny but you won't get a lift back so easily: not without a bottle of something for the fare. I'll take you in my boat.'

And so I left the home of the widow I had made; left in her company, taunted by her goodness. We walked across the boggy moor, past the abandoned hut with its unlocked door, through the growing woods. At the jetty, all the locals had gone home and there would have been no one to help me off the rock. Charlotte pushed her dinghy into the water and we clambered on board. I was grateful for the spluttering of the outboard motor: it made conversation impossible.

I fixed my eye on the 'mainland', and retreated into a kind of daze until we reached it. The business of disembarkation absorbed me at the jetty. I thrust out my arm to leave no alternative to a handshake, and Charlotte could not disguise her perplexity. I thanked her for lunch and the boat ride, and surrendered to the luxury of a sigh as I shouldered my rucksack.

I waved to her until the boat was a third of the way across the loch; then she set her face to home and I prepared for the long drive back to Inverness.

III

I was in my pyjamas when he called, the *Guardian* jobs supplement lying unread on the kitchen table. I knew at once that I would never open it. Like a fugitive half longing for the irresponsibility of capture, I slumped to my knees.

'Are you still there?'

'I'm here,' I said.

He was speaking to me from a phone box and I was shocked to hear tears raking his voice. They wanted to ask him questions. They wanted to talk about Mr Bridge. 'You went to see her, didn't you? You went to see her and you *told* her.'

'No. I meant to but I didn't. I couldn't do it. I failed.'

'Listen, if the police are even *thinking* of reopening the case then she must have got something out of you.'

I wetted my lips. 'I didn't incriminate us, if that's what you're worried about.'

'Jesus . . .'

'I said we saw Mr Bridge fall. He was alive at first but we couldn't reach him.'

'What was the *point*? Why bring all that up again?'

'It never went under.'

The calm I felt was unshakeable. People who drown are supposed to feel that way after their last trip to the surface.

'Listen, *listen*,' he said, 'the police seem to think there might be something worth investigating. You planted a seed of doubt in that woman's mind and now . . . What the *fuck* do we do if they reopen the case?'

'You believe your conscience is clear. If the police come asking, tell them the truth. You've got nothing to fear.'

'Except *you*,' he said. 'I've got everything to fear from you, haven't I?'

I laughed, untouchable. 'What's that supposed to mean?'

'You just can't leave me alone, can you? You've had it in for me ever since we met, and when I wouldn't play along with your delusions . . .'

'Do you think this is all about you?'

'Isn't it? You're infatuated, Bruno. You're an obsessive – you need help.'

'Goodbye, Anthony.'

I put down the receiver, pulled the cord from its socket and went to the bathroom. I took off my pyjamas and looked at my body in the mirror. It was strange how little I felt attached to it. A spirit, looking through balls of watery flesh, it was hard to care for what I saw.

If you look at your reflection long enough, you can feel the bonds of self dissolve. It's like holding your breath too long: the mind trembles. You have to hold your nerve, for every atom in your brain is shouting at you to look away and make yourself whole again. But hold on. Outstare yourself and see where it leads you. I have never stuck it out but I came close that morning. I watched my reflection until it seemed to liquefy; and I realised that what mattered was not in the mirror.

I had, as Anthony said, planted the seed of doubt. Did it germinate in Charlotte as she crossed the loch and trudged homeward across the moor? Or did it pierce her sleep, a waking jolt in the darkness? She had taken me on trust but the pollution leached out. I was up to my neck in it: sooner or later, the smell was bound to carry.

Still, it was odd that they had contacted Anthony first. I spent the afternoon in Hyde Park, where autumn had finally arrived, thinking about my father and Ann. I was sorry for what was about to hit them. For myself I felt no sorrow. Fear, yes; it would be painful. But there was nothing I could do to stop it.

That evening, coming back with leaves in my hair, I found my answerphone beeping. I erased Anthony's message on the first syllable. I knew that he would want to liaise with me. Disgusting as it would be for him, he had to get our stories straight.

I unplugged the telephone again. Let him keep calling. People like Anthony have antiperspirant in their veins: it would do him good to sweat for a while.

I took a double dose of diazepam and slept until ten.

In the morning I found the letter sticking like a dead tongue from the door. It spent an hour or more unopened in the kitchen; then I swooped on it, shredding the envelope.

The language was formal and designed to inspire confidence; only a guilty conscience need quail at it. Did I recall the tragedy on Nab Scar? New information had come to light which required looking into. Since I had been present at the scene, the police would appreciate my assistance in their enquiries. I read the name of the detective and his request that I make myself available. Obediently, and without a quiver of trepidation, I reconnected to the outside world. Within minutes, the telephone blurted and I answered.

'What the hell's been going on? I've been trying to call you for hours.'

'Yeah,' I said. 'Sorry about that. I think there's been something wrong with the line.'

'Can you talk now?'

'Of course.'

'Have you heard from the police?'

'I got a letter. Do you know, I think it's the same one they sent you. All they did was change the name and address at the top. I call that a bit half-arsed, don't you?'

'And you've spoken to them?'

'To who?'

'The *police*.'

'Not yet.'

'Look, uh . . . I'm sorry about the way I spoke to you the other day. I was freaked out, that's all. Could we, uh . . . Could we meet in town?'

'This weekend?' I was taunting him: patting him about with my claws withheld. 'I could manage Saturday.'

'No, no, it's got to be tonight.'

I looked at the greasy cartons, discarded clothes and yellowing newspapers of my den. 'I'm not sure: I'm very busy with work for the moment.'

'*Please.*'

I put him out of his misery and let him choose the venue, expecting somewhere expensive. He chose a crowded gastropub in Soho. It was a perplexing choice but I offered no objections. After we hung up, I toyed with the idea of going back to bed; but that would have meant a tussle with bedclothes, butting hopelessly at the locked door of sleep. I picked up the still-warm receiver and dialled the detective's number. I heard his nasal, Estuary-stained accent but declined to leave a message. On the second attempt, I said that I would be free the next day and they could call on me at any time.

I sat on the cramped and howling Tube, unable to ignore the headlines of newspapers and unable to bear what they told me. Things were scarcely better on the streets, with people milling about Charing Cross Road hemmed in by taxis and rickshaws and bloated SUVs. I hurried, head bowed, into Soho. Not for the first time, I marvelled at the punters sitting with their drinks in the unseasonable warmth: how they managed to ignore the press around them, the stink of diesel and the panic of police sirens. A man could erode with distress, groaning and collapsing in front of their tables, and make no inroads on their self-involvement.

Anthony was waiting for me, his hair tangled and greasy. It pleased me to see him awry and unsettled. A packet of cigarettes – Marlboro reds, not the milder, compromising gold – gaped on the table beside him. We did not shake hands.

'I've taken a hell of a risk, coming here,' he said.

'You mean Dipali doesn't know?'

'I mean they may be following me. They may be keeping *tabs*. Don't look all innocent, I know you're behind this. You and your bloody hair-shirt masochism.'

If only I had taken up Fay's offer, in Manchester all those years ago, to learn how to play poker. All my nerves gathered in my hands: like foraging mammals, they snuffled about the sugar sachets. 'I told you,' I said, 'I haven't put you in any danger.'

'It was dead and buried, it was ancient fucking history until you showed up. Risking our future – and for *what*?' He looked at me as if everything was suddenly clear. 'You know what you are? You're pathological. You've got a pathological obsession.'

I looked at the man who had been my friend. His desperate expression made me laugh: I couldn't help it. Anthony leaned into a feral whisper. 'Don't smile at me, you *cunt*. I've got the fucking police on my back. If Dipali finds out . . .'

'You keep saying there's nothing to keep secret.'

'I don't mean there's nothing . . . We both know . . . The point is no one would understand the *context*. No one would see it was an accident.'

'Was it?'

Anthony leaned across the table. 'We wanted to frighten him,' he said. 'We didn't mean for him to *die*.'

'So you want me to lie again?'

Anthony passed a febrile hand over his face. Points of sweat pimpled his brow and, by the look of it, he had not shaved in a couple of days. 'We didn't lie to the coroner,' he said. 'We just withheld information that would have confused things.'

'You should go into politics.'

'Nothing happened today, did it? After my phone call?

'Like what?' I asked.

Anthony sucked air through his nostrils, his eyes dull and heavy lidded. It looked like torpor or the beginning of a stroke. 'I want you to tell me,' he said, 'what you plan to say to the police.'

'I haven't decided yet.'

Anthony's face drained of blood. His chair scraped against the floor as he lurched across the table and pinioned my wrists. I jerked back in alarm but his grip was too strong. 'It's my fucking *life*, Bruno. My career, my reputation: everything at risk because you want to be a bloody saint.'

I felt him press with the nails of his thumbs into my tendons. I was incredulous, breathless with pain.

'What's to be gained from it? Tell me how you hope to profit because really, I can't understand. I can't understand why you went to that woman, why you chose to take such a risk.'

He was desperate, his hair rank with sweat and cigarette smoke. 'Since you couldn't understand,' I said, 'there's no point my telling you.' I had to fight not to cry out with pain. Saliva foamed like acid in my mouth. Even in the agony and humiliation of his grip, I realised how much we looked like lovers. Anthony held my wrists, his elbows resting on the table, the whole of his being concentrated on me. Who, gazing towards us, could have surmised the nature of our passion? The pressure of Anthony's thumbs as they burrowed into my tendons sent galvanic pain up my arms, through nerves and sinews, all the way to my heart. I was homesick and drowning. 'Anthony,' I said. My fingers were curling up, obscenely coloured, like the palps of a corpse. 'Anthony, that really hurts.'

Though hatred and fear had taken hold of him, digging their nails into my flesh, somehow the information got through. The current of pain was cut off, leaving nausea purling in my stomach. Anthony let go of my wrists, and I could see shame – a learned emotion in him, not something innate – spreading like a bruise across his face. He sat back, repulsed, and gazed down at his lap as though he had spilled something there. 'I'm sorry,' he said. 'I shouldn't have done that.'

I showed him my stigmata. 'I've got crescent moons on my wrists.'

'I said I was sorry.'

I got up to leave and he managed to prevent himself from seizing my arm. But the look of scolded innocence in his face made me stop. 'Wait a minute,' he said. 'There's more to this than you understand.'

'I'm tired . . .'

'He touched me, Bruno. You didn't know that, did you? Sit down and let me get you a drink, for God's sake.'

I stared at him. I wanted my eyes to make him wilt. 'That's a fucking lie.'

'I've never told anyone. Not even Dipali.'

'When? *Where?* We were always with him together.'

'I know you don't want to believe it. I couldn't believe it myself and managed to talk myself out of remembering.'

'He wouldn't have done that. You're lying.'

'I wasn't raped. But he made a pass at me when I was alone with him in the English library. He put his hand on my shoulder. He touched my neck and started . . . I thought I was mistaken, I couldn't believe it. You always say you value the truth, so here it is. Samuel Bridge was a paedophile. Why else do you think

273

he took the two biggest weirdos in school under his wing? All that music and bloody poetry – it was to seduce us.'

I hoped, if I looked at him hard enough, that his façade might crumble. Did he believe this shit? Or was it just a tactic to weaken my resolve? 'So he put a hand on your shoulder,' I said. 'That doesn't exactly make him Bluebeard.'

'Don't you think it was odd, the way he used to invite boys to his house while his wife was away?'

'You *met* her. She was there.'

'Some of the time. The fact remains: Mr Bridge was a lecher. And he was a coward. Because he couldn't play with our dicks, he played with our heads. He made us feel special and then he took that grace away. It was a mind-fuck: the only kind men like him can ever hope for.'

Something, at that moment, came loose in my passion for Anthony Blunden. I realised that what remained of love had animated me to this point. For weeks I had been pursuing him, determined to make him confront the truth: that we had destroyed an innocent life. With what fervour had I longed to see him break down: to become, in a sense, my partner, so that I was less alone. Now that compulsion lifted. My feelings for him changed as profoundly and irrevocably as my voice changed when it broke. Calmly, and with pity in my expression that must have enraged him, I said: 'He was a good man.'

'Was he?'

'He was a good man. A bit of a fool, but he was good. And he died because of us.'

Frith Street was churning with people: filmgoers, lovers, pub-crawling Aussies infatuated with their noise, girls on a hen night wrapped in pink boas staggering like moorhens on spangled heels. I tried to melt among them, hoping for camouflage, and listened for pounding footsteps behind me. I braced myself for a hand on my shoulder, a sudden dazzling blow. But Anthony did not chase after me. I turned left on Old Compton Street and began to breathe easily. I had got away from him and could face what was to follow as I always had: alone.

I offered no resistance when they came for me, but followed the cold case squad to their lair. Did I need a lawyer present? There was no need for that, just yet. They were sensing their way ahead, lifting stones with a diffident boot. Apart from a neurotic urge to piss (my bladder was in fact an aching void), I felt comfortable enough in the mirror-backed interrogation room. The coffee in front of me was an affront to taste but we were all in it together: DI Sexton, a middle-aged Londoner with chewed fingernails and a small chunk missing from the tip of his earlobe, DI Conley, a pasty blonde Geordie in her late and charmless thirties, and Bruno Jackson, retired civil servant. DI Sexton did most of the talking, while his colleague looked half asleep. My only reference for the situation was television; sometimes I wondered whether it wasn't the same for them.

'There's a discrepancy that bothers us,' said DI Sexton. 'In 1993 you told the coroner that you did not see your teacher fall. Yet you told his widow, Charlotte Bridge, that you did. Why have you changed your story?'

I said nothing but turned the polystyrene cup between my fingers.

'It must have been a terrible thing to witness – at any age, but especially with your whole life in front of you.' The inspector's nose was so long that the strip lights gave him a Hitler moustache. He was no fascist for all that and no fool. I liked him, really. He was mild and amiable, with sadness tucked up in his pale blue eyes: a softly spoken angel of mercy. 'It can't have been easy, talking about it in a public inquiry. You just wanted to bury the whole thing, didn't you? You wanted it to go away. Knowing that you were the last people to see Samuel Bridge alive.'

'And the first to see him dead,' said DI Conley. The effect was startling, like a waxwork coming to life. We went to see your friend, Anthony Blunden, this morning. He spoke at some length.'

'He's not my friend.'

'But you've been in touch. You've been on speaking terms, as it were.' DI Sexton chewed his lower lip. 'Mr Blunden claims you've been harassing him and his wife. Trying to intimidate them.'

'I don't know where he gets that idea.'

'We have phone records and emails. He says you've been pursuing him obsessively since the summer.'

'That's not quite true.'

'Would you describe yourself as an obsessive person, Mr Jackson?'

'Not particularly.'

'But you are somebody who forms very strong emotional attachments?'

DI Conley came straight out with it. 'As a schoolboy you developed an infatuation with your English teacher. There's nothing especially unusual in that. You were unhappy, far from your parents. You were bullied. He was kind to you.'

'I wasn't infatuated with him.'

'Weren't you?' said DI Sexton, rummaging in his nostrils with a silk handkerchief. 'You convinced yourself that he returned your feelings. After all, he'd let you into his house, he spent his free time in your company . . .'

'But he rejected you. You'd built up this elaborate fantasy and when it was no longer possible to ignore the fact there was nothing in it, your emotions changed. They turned vengeful.'

'*My* emotions?'

'You wanted to punish him in some way. You wanted to make him feel the pain you felt . . .'

'Did Anthony tell you this?'

'Of course, your friend didn't share your feelings. Until one day Samuel Bridge made a mistake. He said something disparaging about your friend's writing. It wasn't much but it gave you a wedge to work with – a wound to prod until your friend became your ally.

'At first you didn't know what you would do. You only knew you wanted to get back at him. There was no premeditation – it was opportunistic, wasn't it? When you found yourself on the hillside . . .'

I shook my head, trying to keep the dark bird of unconsciousness from alighting on my shoulder. DI Conley held a plastic water bottle inches beyond my reach. 'It's only Anthony's version of events,' she said. 'We don't take it as gospel.'

'That's why you're here. To give us your account of Samuel Bridge's death.'

'He fell,' I said.

'You engineered it, didn't you? You lured him to the edge of the rocks.'

'No.'

'It was misty, your voices carried. You pretended to be in some kind of distress. He put himself at risk to protect you. Has that ever occurred to you? Has it ever occurred to you that he put your lives above his own? Oh, I'm not saying you wanted to kill him. You'd probably have been satisfied with a broken leg, a dislocated shoulder. A fright and a fracture. But you wanted to punish him. It was your idea and your execution. Your friend tried to talk you out of it: he sensed how badly it could go wrong. But you wouldn't be dissuaded.'

Anthony had done it. In his attempt to save himself, he had unwittingly saved me. I lacked a hiding place for my tears. They came with the autonomy of sweat: I was barely aware of them before my interrogators. DI Sexton sat back and watched, while his colleague gave me the bottle of water.

'Why did you go to see Charlotte Bridge?' she asked. 'She told us you were a kind person. You are kind, aren't you, Bruno? You've been carrying this horror, this darkness, inside you all these years. And when you bumped into your old friend, it all came flooding back. It was like no time had passed at all.

'So you went to see his widow. You went to make a clean breast of it.

'But you couldn't go through with it. Because you couldn't hurt her, could you? Despite all the guilt you were carrying . . .'

Sitting at that sterile table, under the scrutiny of the mirror gods and their closed-circuit cameras, I was able to make my decision. I almost laughed at it. Snot peeped out of my nostrils; tears oozed in salty gouts from the folds of my chin. DI Conley stretched across the table and insinuated a paper tissue into my fingers.

'Now's your chance,' she said softly, 'to start to live again.'

When he was banged up for fraud, the chairman of Guinness, Ernest Saunders, reckoned he could hack prison. After all, he'd had the training at school. The same, I like to think, applies to me. Instead of the morning gong on Main Corridor there is the wake-up siren. The squalid threat of the shower block is familiar, as are the smells of prison food, the hunkering menace of the dining hall and the rapid scoffing of pestilential grub. But this is an open prison: I'm not in some Shawshankian hellhole. The clientele is made up of fraudsters, petty crooks, lunatic drivers and this overgrown schoolboy. There is a decent library and a gym of sorts, where I drag myself to work out, despite the derision of fellow inmates. I have been here only three months: in the one, almost token, year remaining of my sentence, I intend to whittle myself down to size.

I sleep well. I barely dream. I wake up ready for another day, safe in the knowledge that all its boredom and fear will be rounded in oblivion, a dose of unbeing.

Anthony, thank goodness, is not in here with me. There was no forensic evidence, nothing but our word to resolve the mystery. I let his stand. I pleaded guilty to reckless manslaughter and was convicted on the strength of his false statement and my concurrence with it. I'm not sure that he can have believed his luck. Certainly he'll never understand it. I could see no point in bringing him down with me. Either justice grows from the gut or it cannot take root.

My father has taken the whole thing as badly as I had feared. I must seem a stranger to him, the victim of some body snatch, and this pains me more than anything. I wrote him a long letter (it took me a week to finish) trying to explain my choice and why it was fitting. Without expecting him to understand, I asked for his forgiveness. Ann has come to visit me several times and extended his goodwill. He is not ready, just yet, to see me in person.

Jenny, on the other hand, comes every week. She remains my truest friend, though she makes no secret of the fact that she thinks I'm an idiot. She has been calling on my father: keeping the flame of paternal love alive in his breast. No doubt he has shown her my letter.

'Anyone would think you *wanted* him to frame you. You couldn't make amends on your own and you knew what Anthony was capable of. You needed him to make this happen.'

'It's not that simple.'

'You shouldn't be in here. *That's* pretty simple. Why do you want to protect him?' Jenny pressed against the back of her chair, her eyes brimming with tears.

'Please,' I said, 'I can't bear that.'

'It's out of all proportion.'

'Who's to say?'

'What about your dad? What about *me*? What am I going to do with my best friend in fucking prison?' Her voice cracked. I wanted to hold her; I wanted to kiss her hand.

'It isn't death,' I said. 'I'm still here for you.'

'Bruno, if you're guilty of anything, so is your friend.'

'I can't take responsibility for Anthony.'

Jenny looked at me in bewilderment and wonder. 'You're a stubborn, weird bastard, do you know that?'

'Yes, I suppose I am.'

Obdurate weirdness thrives in prison. There is an awful lot of time for it to gestate in the mind. Stuffed with grievance or anger, you could think yourself into madness. But if you use the time well, you can work your way to clarity.

Looking back on that heatwave summer, I can see that I was ripe for change. Like a fruit on a branch, I could not pluck myself. Do I have Anthony to thank for my deliverance? He would have been quite content – by his own, dim lights – to continue as he was. Why then, in God's name, did he telephone me after Fay Corcoran's party? Could it be that he felt as shaken as I was by our meeting? Dipali knew nothing about what happened that day in the Lakes. To smooth over the mental disturbance, to convince the world – and, in so doing, himself – that nothing *had* happened, he felt compelled to invite me to dinner. It was, as the cliché goes, a high-risk strategy. I might have blurted everything in front of his wife, his tamer and, I imagine, unwitting collaborator in the glamorous lie that is Anthony Blunden. But if the dinner could pass without incident – a masticating conspiracy of small talk – then he could rebury what my presence at the party had exhumed, and all would be as before.

Yet Anthony is no freer than me, for none of us can escape from the prison of consequences. I imagine his mounting dread as the axis of need shifted and I began to pester *him*. Like most fantasists, he must work hard to remain suspended on his branch. What am I to make of his Soho allegations? Were they lies meant to disqualify Mr Bridge from justice? Or was Anthony telling me an untruth of which he had long ago convinced himself? As formerly at Kingsley, my credulity was the foundation of his delusions. If I believed him, he was safe; my doubt, on the other hand, threatened him unbearably.

Dipali, in more recent years, has served the same function.

Anthony believed the coroner's verdict: what reason did she have to doubt his innocence? And yet, one month into my incarceration, Fay Corcoran wrote to tell me that Dipali had left her husband. The last thing I heard, she is seeking a divorce. I cannot work out whether I am sorry to have occasioned such a disaster.

On the subject of disasters, last night a storm ripped through Britain. Even in here you could not miss what was happening. The whole prison creaked like a galleon at sea; the wind played xylophone on the roof tiles, it picked up bins and tossed them across the yard. This morning's papers are full of destruction: fifteen killed and millions of trees uprooted. Is this – and more of this, and ever worse – what it takes for us to change? The stratosphere itself is clogged with our mistakes: the whole world locked into disarray.

Yet what can I do for the world? I am sorry for it, and for all of us, but I have my own work to attend to. Already the mist is clearing. I am no longer bent over myself. From my window I can see only the fenced moor of the exercise yard, yet my view extends to the horizon.